To Eilken,

Sorry about the spelling!

Nice meeting + talking to you at Hendon July 16th 2000

best wishes

Barry Cuham

THE GREAT ILLUSION

a novel by

B.I. GRAHAM

Inspired by a true story

MINERVA PRESS
WASHINGTON LONDON MONTREUX

THE GREAT ILLUSION

ISBN 1 85863 814 3

First Published 1996 by
MINERVA PRESS
195 Knightsbridge,
London SW7 1RE

2nd Impression 1997

Printed in Great Britain for Minerva Press

THE GREAT ILLUSION

To Arthur Frewin
Not just for all your kindness and help,
but for all the encouragement you have given me,
which I so badly needed.

On ne meurt qu'une fois, et
c'est pour si longtemps.

One dies only once, and it's for
such a long time!

Molière
Le Dépit Amoureux (1656) v.iii

Whilst I have made every effort to ensure that the background to this book is as authentic as possible – the action takes place against the backcloth of the 1942 summer offensive – I should like to stress that any resemblance between characters in this book and those who actually served on 7 Squadron at this time is either fortuitous or involuntary.

I am indebted to the following members of 7 Squadron for background information: Reg Brook, Arthur Frewin, John Hankin, Pat Kinsella, Laurie Salter, Ted Walker, Fred Wills DFM and Norman Winch DFC.

PART ONE

CHAPTER ONE

1

The 1000 Plan was Commander in Chief Bert Harris's brainchild, a massive strike into the German heartland. The year was 1942. April was nearly at an end but not the war; defeats, failures and setbacks had made that seem endless. God knew, morale needed a boost, the country a victory and Harris, with other commands clamouring for resources, needed conclusive proof of the power and efficacy of the bomber force under his command.

Portal, Chief of Air Staff, dry as a nut, wasn't slow to point out that there was no military magic in the figure but readily agreed that it would have a potential effect on popular imagination. He gave Harris his unqualified support, as did the PM, whose sense of drama and theatre matched the C-in-C's own. The operation was baptised Operation Millennium.

With political support assured, Harris turned to practical details. Saundby, his aide, pointed out, with due deference, that although theoretically within the bounds of possibility, the raising of such a huge armada would mean risking not only the Command's entire front-line strength, but its reserve strength as well. The consequences of failure were unthinkable.

To ensure success, a full moon was necessary, as was a good visual fix. Suitable targets were soon whittled down to Hamburg and Cologne. The next full moon was to be at the end of May. Harris knew that time and the tide of war waited for no man. Another month would see the opportunity vanish. Operation Millennium would have to take place within the next full-moon period. Harris and Saundby had only weeks and days.

The problem was essentially logistical. Saundby moved heaven and earth, or got his group commanders to. As the days ticked inexorably by, the numbers of available aircraft increased, but when Coastal Command's promise of two hundred aircraft didn't materialise, the operation was in serious jeopardy. The C-in-C, however, was not a man to flinch. Indeed, there was no going back. Harris brought down his fist on his desk.

"We redouble our efforts!" he boomed, in a voice like thunder.

The weather proved to be as fickle as the Admiralty. On 27th May the moon was full but the weather inclement. It was the same story on 28th and 29th. The postponements were annoying but gave valuable breathing space. By Saturday 30th May, a force of 1046 bombers had been mustered.

In the ops room at Bomber Command HQ, the C-in-C sat at his desk flanked by his brass. The Met. man spoke. He might have been a soothsayer, or a prophet sent from the Gods of war. His news was only partially good. A belt of cloud over Northern Europe ruled out Hamburg, but further south there was a fair chance of the weather clearing up around midnight.

Harris had no choice. The die was cast. There was silence except for the ticking of the clock. The Brass waited with bated breath. The C-in-C lit a cigarette. At last his forefinger came down on the map and pushed hard, bending the joint. He turned to Saundby.

"Thousand Plan tonight. Cologne."

Briefing on the squadrons would be at six that evening.

2

It was five to six when Flight Sergeant Arthur Johnson brushed past the armed guard at the entrance to the briefing room at Oakington. The place was already packed: maximum effort. Arthur stood, back against the wall, trying to pinpoint his own crew from amongst the backs of the sea of unfamiliar heads.

Ernie and Elton, captain and navigator, were in the front row, heads bowed, seemingly in deep conversation. Tony, the flight engineer, and Billy, the rear gunner, were sitting just in front of him. Tony sat like a well-behaved pupil awaiting the arrival of his teacher. Billy, squat and fair-haired, was sitting in a semi-aggressive crouch. Robin, the front gunner, was standing next to Arthur. Like Arthur, he had been a gunner on Defiants and had arrived at the station ten days previously from the Heavy Conversion Unit at Waterbeach. That night the squadron's Stirlings had flown to Mannheim and the two of them had been on stand-down. Tonight would be their first operational flight since transfer.

The buzz of conversation had gradually risen, along with the warmth in the room it seemed, to a low roar. For some, tonight's raid would be their first op of any kind. They talked with the nervous excitement of those for whom a moment of truth draws nigh. Arthur, too, although an experienced air gunner having served with both Coastal and Fighter Commands, felt more than a twinge of apprehension at what lay before him. Again he looked out over the assembled air crew. The faces around him were pink and shiny. He was one of the older men in the room, most of whom were in their late teens or early twenties. If he survived another seven weeks, he would celebrate his twenty-sixth birthday. It was something he didn't care to think much about. Casualties were heavy on Bomber Command. The odds he would live that long were no more than even.

The noise of voices suddenly died away. The Wing Commander had entered. He was tall, thin and upright with lank, dark hair well-trimmed about the ears.

"Gentlemen, the Station Commander."

There was a noise of chairs scraping on the linoleum floor. The Group Captain made his entrance down the centre aisle, followed by other senior officers collectively responsible for the briefing.

The Groupie was in his late forties, but his greying temples and stoutness were offset by a schoolboy swagger and a bluff geniality which might, and did, sweep aside most obstacles. He had an abrupt manner, never mincing words, firing questions, answers, commands and bold statements about the weather and the state of the world with finality and machine-gun rapidity. He turned and faced the assembly.

"Sit down, everybody. You may smoke."

He waited a few seconds while cigarettes were lit then suddenly became more grave. The fun was over and the serious business of the day was about to begin. He moved a pace backwards to the roller blind which ran the length of the wall.

The tension which had left Arthur's body under the effects of nicotine was now replaced by anticipation. Everyone at Oakington had known there was something up, not least the Erks who had been working more hours than God had made during the past week to get every machine airworthy. There were also those nineteen Wimpeys which had arrived from RAF Pershore, some of which didn't look capable of clearing the peri-fence. Who could possibly want them? There were rumours and counter rumours – a big raid in the offing – it had to be. Now all would be made known. The Groupie tugged at the cord and the blind rose with a squeak to reveal a map of Europe.

A ribbon of red tape stretched from a point in Cambridgeshire, across the North Sea and Holland into Germany, with a turning point on the Rhine. Another red ribbon ran parallel to and south of the first one. The map was disfigured by ugly blotches of red around the Rhine Delta. The rising columns of smoke emphasised the stillness in the room. The Groupie started to speak. Every eye was on him.

"Actium, Lepanto, Waterloo, Gettysburg, the Marne: battles that changed the fate of the world. The men who fought in them made history. Tonight, you are going to make history by taking part in the biggest air raid in the history of the world. Tonight, this squadron will be part of a force of one thousand bombers, twice as large as any previous bomber force. The target, Gentlemen, is Cologne. Tonight, a major German industrial centre is to be annihilated."

He scanned his audience through the rising fog. The men in front of him made cramped spasmodic movements. Heads turned, and there were sighs and low whistles. Final confirmation. It all figured. The Groupie continued as if they all had a train to catch.

"The tactics are as follows: we concentrate the attacking force over the target in the shortest possible time thereby saturating defences. Bombers will attack in three waves. The first wave will be a target-marking force using incendiaries – taking advantage of the combustible energy within the target itself. The second wave, of which you will be part, will have an area of flame in the centre of the city in which to put their high explosives. The third wave – 'the Heavies' – will level to the ground anything that's still standing. Now I should like to make one thing clear at the outset. Everything points to an unprecedented concentration of aircraft over the target. To cut down the risk of collision, heights have been staggered. When you've dropped your load, get out and get home. I want to see you all back here tomorrow morning."

Arthur saw Elton nod in vigorous assent. Approval was general. The Groupie sat down.

The Navigation Leader rose. He had already briefed in great detail captains and navigators but outlined the route for the sake of the others. Elton followed each word looking continuously from his map to the chart nodding in agreement with his leader's words.

"From here," he said, his hand on the tape, "it's a straight run in. You cross the Dutch coast south of Rotterdam with pinpoints at Eindhoven and Munchen Gladbach. You are recommended to pick out the Rhine north of the target and follow it in to Cologne. After bombing, you are to steer south-south-west for twenty minutes to Euskirchen, then turn for home on a track parallel to your outward track. You shouldn't have much difficulty in locating the target. If we are to believe the Met., cloud should disperse in the Cologne area around midnight."

The Bombing Leader was next.

"The Gee-equipped aircraft of the first wave will aim at a point in the centre of the town: the Neumarkt. They'll have the target to themselves for fifteen minutes. The second wave will bomb at points one mile north or one mile south of this point in order," he passed his hand over his forelock and altered the tone of his voice to denote a quote, "to spread the area of devastation. You'll be bombing south of the aiming point."

Elton nodded again, although less vigorously than when the Navigation Leader was speaking.

"This point is south of the Rhine which," he dropped his voice, perhaps alluding to the unreliability of weather reporting, "you should be able to see tonight."

The Intelligence Officer stood up. He wore thick, horn-rimmed glasses and had short black curly hair. Judging by the state of his collar, he hadn't changed his shirt for at least a month. He was cold, disciplined and unemotional. He always read from his notes in a monotone.

"You'll bomb at 14,000 feet. Stick to your height. To reduce the risk of mid-air collisions, bombing heights have been staggered."

He droned on, outlining the geography of the city, the two main bridges over the Rhine, and the location of the industrial suburbs, the marshalling yards in the north-west. Cologne's defences were heavy but straightforward, organised in concentric rings.

Other officers continued the briefing. There was an exhortation from Flight Lieutenant Mike Smith, the Gunnery Officer, not to shoot blindly at twin-engined aircraft as there would be many twin-engined jobs up that night - "and I don't want any of you trigger-happy lot shooting the hell out of some poor bugger from an OTU..." A number of bods had just come from OTUs and shooting down a kite from an OTU proved a source of amusement to some.

Amidst the laughter and guffawing, Billy shouted, "Give 'em 'ell, Mike!" punching the air with a low raking uppercut.

The Signals Leader gave details of wireless frequencies, and the Met. Officer an outline of the weather situation. Over the North Sea they would find themselves flying over a blanket of dense cloud, but cloud over the target should have dispersed around midnight. Visibility would deteriorate over base during the night.

The last man to speak was the Wing Commander. He held a sheet of paper in his hand.

"I've been instructed by the C-in-C to give you this message."

The Wing Commander unfolded the paper in his hand. The hush was deafening. The only movement was the coiling blue smoke from the cigarettes. He started to read.

"The force of which you form a part tonight is at least twice the size and has more than four times the carrying capacity of the largest air force ever before concentrated on one objective.

"You have the opportunity, therefore, to strike a blow at the Enemy which will resound not only through Germany, but throughout the world.

"In your hands lie the means of destroying a major part of the resource by which the Enemy's war effort is maintained. It depends, however, on each individual air crew whether full concentration is achieved.

"Press home your attack to your precise objective with the utmost determination and resolution in the foreknowledge that if you individually succeed, the most shattering blow will be delivered against the vitals of the Enemy."

Wing Commander Truex lowered the paper and cast his eye from left to right over the attentive assembly.

"Let him have it right on the chin."

As Truex folded the paper, the spell woven by the C-in-C's rhetoric was suddenly broken. The assembly rose as one with the partisanship of a crowd at a football match. Apprehension and fear dissolved in a deafening roar.

Truex held up a hand as the tumult subsided and added a few words of his own. He reiterated earlier points about heights, the bomber stream and the saturation formula. He mentioned the German radar system, the Kammhuber Line and the credibility of the Allied cause, which that night would depend on each one of them. He would be seeing them all later on, but took the opportunity of wishing them all a good trip.

Wing Commander Truex smiled and the men in front of him smiled back. For many air crew, this was the best part of the whole show: the smile and the good wishes from their Wing Commander.

3

The buzz of conversation in the crowded briefing room slowly dissipated in the warm breeze of early evening as crews filed out into the sunshine. The men moved off down the main road of the 'drome, Arthur walking with Robin. They passed the central heating building and the solid fuel store. There was little talking. Security was at a maximum. Phones had been cut off from a central control five minutes before briefing and now nobody was allowed to leave camp. The blue serge figures walked with the gravity of those entrusted with a confidence, but under the surface, excitement and tension was high. When they got to the Sergeants' mess, Arthur stopped. His bike was outside. He said: "Be seeing you, Rob, I'm going for a ride... out to the pans."

Robin said something about high tea at nine, but Arthur was on his way, pedalling hard back the way he had come in the direction of the peri-track.

When Arthur came to the pans, armourers were completing the arduous task of bombing up. He crossed a deserted pan, passing under the oblique shadow of an enormous Stirling. At the edge of the pan Arthur dismounted and looked around. On the next pan a serpentine of bomb-trolleys had snaked its way under the belly of the Stirling. Armourers were steering a bomb into the belly of the aircraft. A faint clanking sound reached his ears but no one saw him. He lifted up his bike and padded through the coarse grass to the peri-fence like a schoolboy breaking bounds. The hole was ridiculously large. He moved through it with ease. Seconds later, Arthur was pedalling hard again. There was a bit less than two hours before high tea. He would have just over an hour with Eve which wasn't much, but was worth the effort with the future so uncertain.

Arthur sped by small detached houses of stone with doors and window frames painted in bright colours and roses climbing up their walls; greenhouses tucked away in odd corners, barns, cow-sheds, fields where dairy cattle had resumed grazing after a rude interruption. Through gaps in the hedgerows he glimpsed wheat and barley already at knee height. There were orchards too where the trees stood smartly to attention as though ready for inspection, and large fields where immaculate lines of strawberry plants seemed to converge into a uniform green mass in the distance. This was East Anglia: a rural paradise sprinkled with tarmac strips, hangars and complexes of service buildings: aircraft carriers at anchor in a sea of green. The rhythm of the seasons contrasted with the urgency of an industrial war machine and Bomber Command's strategy was indeed urgent. It could be summed up in two words: press on. There were only oblique references to military targets. For the past three months, cities and towns had been the targets; and this was no passing phase. From now on, each night weather permitting, scores of bombers would fly according to a predetermined route in a bomber stream to targets in Germany.

Tony and Billy had given Arthur plenty of info, especially Tony. 7 Squadron at Oakington was equipped with the Short Stirling. They were massive aircraft, the biggest Arthur had ever seen, and had had their fair share of teething troubles: wonky undercarts, exactor throttles with a will of their own and an alarming tendency to overshoot the runway. Tony himself, had been involved in two overshoots, one of which had been at Waterbeach. The Stirling had swung violently on landing. The undercarriage, unable to cope with the terrific sideload, had collapsed. Over thirty tons of aircraft had slewed over the tarmac, screaming and grinding on a buckled tangle of metal girders, careered through the peri-fence and come to rest on the main Cambridge-Ely road. As Tony and his comrades were extricating themselves dizzily from the wreckage, a vehicle was forced to stop. Fate ordained that it should be a lorry packed with Italian prisoners of war. Only the mid upper gunner was oblivious to their howls of derisive laughter. He lay on the grass in a dead faint.

The Stirling's stalky undercarriage, Tony said, was prone to collapse. They were strong in a vertical plane but couldn't take shearing.

Billy asked once why the hell they'd built them like that. It was so that the high undercarriage allowed the aircraft to land in the right attitude: with the nose high to give the Stirling a lower stalling speed, otherwise the tendency would have been for more overshoots than actually occurred. Billy said that it was idiotic letting a flying boat manufacturer build kites for dry land.

"Those Sunderlands have got the whole fucking ocean to land on."

Tony's contention was that many of the Stirling's teething troubles stemmed from the fact that Shorts hadn't been allowed to build the aircraft as they had wished. Amongst other things, the wingspan had been cut by some twenty feet – some nonsense about hangar doors –

resulting in a low operational ceiling. This was by far, Tony considered, the Stirling's most serious shortcoming.

If Tony's evaluation of situations was factual and objective, then Billy's was coloured by his own emotions and it was Billy's comments which sprang most readily to Arthur's mind. He said the Stirlings looked like jackdaws and you could sit on your arse and slide down to where he was in the rear turret. Billy had come to the squadron in February and had flown 13 ops. On one occasion, his skipper, Ernie Watson, after a rush of blood to the head, had attacked a searchlight belt and had found himself the prey of four night fighters. Billy had shot down three of them, so he claimed, but was only credited with one and a possible. The award of a DFM and subsequent promotion to flight sergeant did little to smooth over his ill feeling about being doubted and during his more morose moments - Billy was a moody man - he could be seen in the billets, or mooching around the ante room as if harbouring some secret grievance. His initiation into squadron life had come the day of his arrival. He had been given a shovel and directed to the main runway where all aircrew, without exception, had been clearing away snow. His thirteen operations were deemed as nothing compared to that icy cold day in February; a fact he never tired of telling new arrivals (most of whom, Billy claimed, didn't know arse from elbow) whenever they voiced a complaint.

Arthur's last thought as the road widened and the first cottages on the outskirts of Stowe appeared was of Billy's jackdaws. Here, Arthur couldn't agree. On the dispersal pans they looked like lofty birds of prey. It was tragic that with so much to recommend them: armour plating everywhere, magnificent turrets, room to move around, that the Stirlings should have such a pathetic operational ceiling. Some got up to 18,000 or 19,000 feet, but that was rare. 14,000 feet was the rule. Height meant safety and 14,000 feet was neither high enough nor safe enough. The Stirling was a bird of prey whose wings the Air Ministry had clipped because of those confounded hangar doors. It was a depressing thought, and as houses and shops appeared on each side of the road shutting out the evening sunshine, Arthur had to make an effort to push it into the back of his mind. He had arrived in the village of Stowe, not far from the Ouse. It was here he had found digs for Eve and it was here he lived when the exigencies of service permitted.

4

Stowe was an interesting village if only for the fact that its form was so strange. Houses and cottages lay in furtive clusters on both sides of the road from Oakington as if trespassing on the edges of the fields. In one place the village disappeared altogether – the village green was on one side of the road – only to reappear further on down to form the main street: post office, general stores, haberdasher's, greengrocer's, butcher's, the pub and various other houses whose polished brass doorsteps were only inches from the pavement. The position of the church and vast walled churchyard – there were seats along the wall and a bus-stop on the corner – caused the main street to veer sharply left at a right angle. It eventually snaked its way back to the village green, so Arthur had been told. He had never followed the road further than to the right turn opposite the village hall where fifty yards down the road the house where Eve was staying was situated; quaint and detached with a large, gnarled apple tree in the front garden.

It had been simple good fortune that they had found a place like this. The previous Sunday, Eve had been up in Cambridge for the day and by chance they had entered a Church Army canteen. It was early and a middle-aged lady was battling with the tea urns. She gladly accepted Arthur's offer of help and the three of them found themselves in conversation. It wasn't long before the subject of him, Eve and the war came up – the sort of subject it was impossible to avoid for long. It was the first time that Arthur had felt like the miscreant schoolboy, but Mrs Badesby knew about the rule forbidding wives to live within forty miles of a Bomber Command base and her attitude – 'I'm British, I don't give a tinkers,' – Arthur found refreshing.

Mrs Badesby made her offer immediately, they inspected the house that same afternoon when she came off duty – there's no time like the present – and everything proved satisfactory. The only problem was distance – the house was two miles from the station – which Arthur pointed out was a fair walk especially if he were pushed for time.

"We have a bicycle! – just the ticket," she bellowed in hearty triumph.

Payment? Wouldn't hear of it! Only too glad to have somebody in the house. The house was quite large, they could have the run of it. She was a widow, her husband one of the glorious dead: Great War. She was away often: two daughters, grandchildren, war effort, so much to do. The matter was settled there and then, before the search had started in earnest.

Arthur opened the gate and wheeled his bike up the path. The lawn all around the apple tree was covered in petals and there were small, hard fruits on the tree, but these were things he didn't notice. He just saw a small face at the front window and before he had leant his bike against the wall, the front door was open. Eve skipped to meet him.

"Arthur! Darling!" She threw her arms round his neck and they kissed. When their lips parted, Arthur continued to hold her tightly, lifting her gently so her feet left the ground. They went inside the house.

Eve made them both a cup of tea. It took her just long enough for Arthur, sitting on the settee, to question the wisdom of his coming home. They had said goodbye once that day already. It was at times like these that he questioned the wisdom of everything he had ever done since the outbreak of war. Had he done the right thing in marrying her? In many ways, she was having a worse time than he was. And if he died, what then? What would become of her? He would be able to do nothing to help her; not that he could now. He was powerless. Survival tonight would probably mean only a stay of execution. It would go on and on until the finish: either a completed tour of thirty operations, which seemed unlikely; or, which was more likely, he'd be shot down. If he was lucky, he would bale out and spend the rest of the war languishing behind barbed wire. If he was unlucky... Nothingness didn't bear thinking about. Eve came to him with tea and a slice of cake. At first they ate in silence, then Arthur said, "War tonight."

"I know. I guessed. How long have you got?"

"High tea at nine. An hour, not that. Cake's nice. Delicious."

"It's made with real eggs. Mum's. I brought quite a lot for Mrs Badesby. She was overjoyed."

"Where is she?"

"At the village hall. Something about evacuees. She'll be home soon."

They finished eating, then Arthur took Eve in his arms and held her tightly.

"I don't know what I feel like," he said. "Excited and nervous. I suppose this is what I joined up for, although things were different then. I don't fancy bombing civilians either, but I guess there's no other way. Jerry hasn't thought twice about bombing London. I just hope that there aren't too many innocent lives lost – including mine; although I don't suppose mine comes under that heading."

Eve's little body tensed. She took Arthur's head in her hands and kissed him hard, as if purging him from some mortal sin. Arthur responded and suddenly he was glad he had come home. Here was someone who loved him, who cared and, if the worst happened, here was someone who would remember him for ever. He was no longer alone. He prayed to God that Eve wouldn't be either. They rose from the settee.

"I have to be going, darling."

"I'm glad you came, Arthur. Every second's been wonderful."

They went out together, Eve as far as the gate, Arthur to a battlefield, both to a night of terror. The sun was slipping surreptitiously behind the ridge of the village-hall roof, the shadows had lengthened and the air was just a little chill.

"God bless you, darling. I'll pray all the time."

There was a hint of fear and desperation in the little voice. They kissed again, a long lingering embrace which would last until Arthur's return or until the end of the world, then quickly he was away. He turned once to wave and almost toppled over before rounding the corner. Eve turned, went back into the house and closed the door. The tea things were on the table. Arthur's cup, saucer and plate lay just where he had left them. Loath to touch anything, she sat down on the chair opposite, and started to pray.

CHAPTER TWO

1

At high tea, Arthur sat with Robin, Tony and Billy. Between well-masticated mouthfuls they discussed the pyrotechnic merits of thermite and methane-petrol mixture. Afterwards, Arthur smoked a cigarette on the steps of the mess. Exhaling clouds of smoke, he thought of Eve and their chances of a life together after the war. It had already lasted nearly three years. Who would have thought that all this would happen when he mustered three days before war was declared? It was getting so that you couldn't remember what peacetime was like.

Around him, the protective cloak of darkness was enveloping the station, transforming the greens of the trees and the reds of the brick buildings to cavernous uniformity. Arthur swallowed and tried to lick the roof of his mouth. There would be thousands of air crew up tonight. For some, perhaps for him, this darkness would prevail for all eternity.

A group of sergeants piled out of the mess. Arthur watched them go down the road towards the hangars. When another group emerged, he stubbed out his cigarette and followed them down the road, inhaling the cool air. The scent of newly-mown grass mingled with the rising damp as the earth grew colder.

Down by the 'drome, Arthur's gaze swept the airfield. The silent, brooding silhouettes of the nineteen Stirlings were discernible in the gathering gloom. Beyond the pans was the village of Oakington: a church, a pub, a row of houses strung out along a country road. The people in those houses would be getting ready for bed; warmth and security. Arthur swallowed again. He had the uneasy feeling that he was the wrong man in the wrong place. Again he looked over the airfield. The Stirlings were melting into the darkness. In under an hour, these predatory monsters would come alive. An hour; that wasn't long. With sudden urgency, Arthur turned in the direction of the locker-room.

The locker-room was already almost full. Blokes were pushing, shoving, shouting, whistling. Some were stoic and silent. It was the tension. Billy was cursing in front of his locker. Arthur heard the word parachute and Billy, already padded like an armadillo, lumbered through to the parachute section. Arthur went to his locker.

The airman next to him was staring into his, an unlit cigarette in his mouth. He was a small man, a gunner like Arthur. His dark hair was laced with grey. He turned and fixed Arthur with wild staring eyes.

"Would you light it for me, matey?"

"Sure thing."

Arthur lit the cigarette with his lighter. The airman drew hard and long three or four times. As he exhaled, a cloud seemed to lift from his face.

"Thanks, matey. I can't light it myself." He took a hand from his pocket and showed it to Arthur. It was shaking violently. "I-I'll be all right now."

Billy came back from the parachute section with disgruntled satisfaction, holding a parachute pack.

Arthur went out to the toilets. He pushed open the door to the only vacant booth to find that some poor bugger had vomited over the seat. Arthur walked back to the locker-room. The impending bowel movement could also have been his imagination.

When the first Bedford lorry rolled up on the tarmac outside the locker-room, Billy tugged Arthur violently by the arm. Several other crews shied away like frightened, nervous horses.

"Drives like a fucking maniac," Billy said by way of explanation. "He makes that lorry do everything but a slow roll."

They boarded the second. Arthur vaulted as nimbly as his dress would allow into the empty Bedford. Ernie clambered up on to the tailboard pitching headlong into the back of lorry. The last man to board had a brown-paper parcel. Billy said, "Wotcha got there?"

"Empty Brylcreem jars. We're the Brylcreem Boys.

"When we're over the target, these go down the flare chutes. When Jerry finds these, he'll know the Brylcreem Boys have paid him a visit."

"Christ Almighty! This war's getting to some people."

The lorry lurched into motion. There were three crews inside, plus equipment. It trundled slowly past the bomb dump, its screened headlights making little impression on the gloom. The hangars and the complex of station buildings receded, perhaps for the last time. They moved out on to the peri-track which ran parallel to the railway line to March and St Ives. They were nearing the front line where all men are equal.

A voice in the murk said, “On the news they said that the Japs are moving forward again.” Billy retorted, “Well, if you see any around here, give ’em a kick up the arse from me... and the Brylcreem Boys,” he added with a burst of terse, mocking laughter.

A couple of minutes later when the driver called S-Sugar, everybody out, they had arrived. The lorry pulled up and Arthur and his comrades climbed out under the wing of a gigantic Stirling. Painted on the side was a seal balancing a ball on its head. Beneath the wing the ground crew waited in a huddle round the battery-cart. One or two of the men took a last minute leak. The Corporal in charge of the ground crew came over with a clipboard and gave it to Ernie. The latter stood like a stooped monument and cast a jaundiced eye down the list of signatures on form 700. Corporal Worral assured him that the kite was in perfect trim and would fly on two engines if the worst came to the worst. Ernie said he hoped to Christ that the worst wouldn’t come to the worst and added his own name to the others. S-Sugar was now his, on loan, hopefully for the next four and a half hours.

The crew of S-Sugar moved towards the aircraft. Earlier that day Arthur had felt like leaving a message with someone, to be read out after his eventual demise as proof that he had once existed, but that didn’t matter now; he had seen Eve. He boarded last. As he slammed the entry door shut, he didn’t look back but followed Tony down the darkened fuselage.

Hardly had Arthur sat down on the swivel seat by the bulkhead door, laid his log book and message pad on the desk in front of him and plugged in his intercom before the starboard outer engine burst into life. The generator by Arthur’s left foot started to hum and the noise of atmospherics from the receiver crackled in his earphones. Just opposite, to starboard, Tony checked the gauges. On his instrument panel, the luminous dials shone in the beam from the angle poise lamp. The oil pressure needle climbed the scale. The temperature gauge was satisfactory too.

“Starboard outer okay, Ern.”

Within minutes, the remaining engines had been started and were clattering away happily. Seconds later, the ground crew, in response to Ernie’s all-clear signal, had disconnected the battery-cart. The all-clear from the control tower followed and S-Sugar lurched forward as Ernie released the brake.

The Stirling taxied along the peri-track the way they had come in the Bedford lorry. Arthur, from the window by his desk, saw the black shapes of the hangars. On the far side of the field, other Stirlings were moving ponderously on to the peri-track, their wingtips and noses marked by pinpricks of light. Suddenly, S-Sugar jerked to a halt and a deafening roar went up from the inner engines. It died and seconds later another roar went up from the outer engines. Every rivet seemed to vibrate. Then that noise died and the enormous aircraft moved forwards again.

On its arrival at the main runway, S-Sugar flashed its code letter to the control tower. At the answering green light Ernie set the flaps for take-off and released the brake. S-Sugar crept forward again. The runway stretched away in a south-westerly direction into the darkness, slightly uphill towards a hump three quarters of the way along. To starboard, the vague sprawl of station buildings could be perceived. To port, other Stirlings waited, their engines idling.

Ernie braced himself and opened the throttles. Sugar gathered speed: over thirty tons of aircraft, fuel and high explosive hurtling down the runway at nearly l00mph. He held Sugar straight and true as their speed increased, fully opening the port throttles and compensating with the rudder to counteract starboard swing. The grass at the edge of the runway became a blur. The queue of Stirlings receded. The acceleration was terrific, the power of the four Hercules engines awesome, the shindy they made deafening. Suddenly, the occupants of the aircraft felt the slightest of floating sensations as the marker lights at the end of the runway flashed under them. They were airborne. The Stirling began its laden climb into the night sky.

2

Mrs Badesby's front parlour was lit by the light which fell from one of the curved metal arms of a standard lamp. The room was shadowy and the furniture and the thick black-out curtains appeared heavier in the gloom. What light there was fell on Mrs Badesby who was knitting in a furious, business-like fashion in one of the armchairs. Eve sat just opposite in the other. She was holding a photo-wallet tightly in her hands. She looked tense, like a runner before a race. There was a clock on the mantelpiece. Both women glanced at it simultaneously. The time was ten forty-five. Mrs Badesby said, "Won't be long now."

Eve nodded and swallowed. The long night was only just beginning.

"How did things go at the village hall?"

"Not bad, considering. Most of the best places are taken now. Some people are reluctant to have anything to do with children at all."

Eve said tentatively, as if broaching a taboo subject, "You didn't have this problem in the last war."

"That's true. The war was distant then. It wasn't until the telegrams started arriving that the full force of what was going on in France struck you. Mine came at this time almost exactly. The maid had gone home; the children were asleep. I was about to go to bed myself. I wasn't even thinking about the war."

The frantic pace of Mrs Badesby's knitting slowed. The click of the needles seemed less rhythmic.

"I've never been so shocked, before or since. I'm sorry about this. It's hardly the propitious moment."

"It doesn't matter, Mrs Badesby. I did wonder, when you talked about him in the Church Army canteen. It was bound to come up sooner or later."

Mrs Badesby was a down-to-earth, no-nonsense woman with a powerful, fruity voice; but she had compassion. She stopped knitting; her tone mellowed.

"You two are lucky to have found one another. Arthur's a wonderful man. It's a tragedy that men like him must risk their lives. You're wonderful too, Eve. Your loyalty is boundless."

Mrs Badesby glanced again at the clock.

"I'm off to bed. Don't hesitate to wake me if anything happens. I'll say a prayer for you both and I'll sleep with my fingers crossed."

She rose. Eve looked up. Her face was less tense and something like gratitude crossed her features.

"Thank you, Mrs Badesby. You are a dear."

Mrs Badesby went out closing the door behind her. Eve heard a soft padding sound which faded away somewhere above her head. Then there was silence. Never, ever had she felt so alone. She opened the wallet in her lap.

If Arthur wasn't with her, then the next best thing were the photos taken during the life of sorts which they had shared since that chance meeting in the spring of 1939. The first photo she took out was their wedding photo. There was a framed enlargement on their bedside table. It was always unpacked first and made anywhere they stayed into a home. Arthur was in uniform. She wore a smart dark suit, a white hat and a matching fishnet veil. She had another photo with the best man and witnesses. Eve was trying to recall their names when the distant drone of the first Stirling taking off reached her ears. Her body tensed. There was a small pencil stub in the wallet. Eve made a mark on the wallet sleeve. She looked at the clock. It was ten minutes to midnight.

3

S-Sugar had slogged its laden way up through the low banks of cloud and was now flying at 14,000 feet over the North Sea. Ernie had coarsened the pitch of the propellers and the massive Hercules engines were making marginally less noise than at take off. The pilot's voice came over the intercom.

"Pilot to Wireless Operator; get up in your turret, Arthur, then we'll test the guns."

Arthur noted the time in the margin of the beige page of his log book, unplugged his intercom and oxygen leads and proceeded aft through the bulkhead door. After climbing the steps to the turret, he took the limp canvas seat and stretched it across on to its hooks, plugged in his leads again and reached down into his boot for his cocking toggle. Seconds later he called his captain.

"Mid-Upper Gunner to Pilot. In position, Ern."

"Okay, gunners, test your guns."

A rapid succession of staccato roars accompanied the streams of 5 in 1 tracer as they were hosed out into the night sky. They fell away in a slender, graceful arc then disappeared. The pungent smell of cordite in their nostrils, the gunners quartered the night sky through the immaculately polished perspex of their turrets. They were in the bomber stream now, an enormous corridor of aircraft, perhaps twenty miles wide, at staggered heights, strung out between Eastern England and the Upper Rhineland. Over one thousand bombers were said to be up that night, but so vast was the black canopy above them that the gunners saw nothing.

"Enemy coast ahead."

It was Robin's voice over the intercom. Ahe[illegible] Dutch coast, the intricate pattern of the Rhin[illegible] Rotterdam, squat, dark and ugly in the blackness. [illegible] were flak batteries, searchlight belts, German rada[illegible] canon shell. Ernie touched the rudder bar and the w[illegible] started to roll. The gunners rotated their turrets, c[illegible] space around the aircraft, redoubling their vigilanc[illegible] the navigator's compartment, Elton took a Gee fix and, comparing it with the visual he had just received, checked his wind speed. At the engineer's station, Tony peered through the darkness at his gauges, whilst under the vast cockpit canopy, big Ernie Watson sat at his controls like a sack of potatoes, his eyes never still, performing a non-stop circle: compass, ASI, horizon, moon, compass again. Occasionally, however, they did rest on a small withered object stuck to the windscreen; a four-leafed clover, something the ground crew never failed to find each time Sugar was on ops.

Ernie allowed himself a cramped smile before letting his gaze return to the horizon, the moon and the non-stop circle.

"Look, Ern, the bloody sun's coming up already. I knew we should've started earlier."

Robin had been looking at the eastern horizon for the past ten minutes. The dull red glow was at first only faintly discernible and Robin, perplexed, had elected for silence. Now, however, there could be no mistake.

"It isn't the sun." Ernie's voice was toneless. He had recognised the glow for what it was. "It's our aiming point. It's Cologne. The Outriders have got to them. Ernie continued in a harsher vein. "No more talking. Gunners, keep your eyes peeled or we'll have a fighter up our arse."

As if to make a point, Ernie banked the Stirling more steeply. Arthur turned his turret beam on and back again, squinting through the sight graticule which glowed dull red between the breech covers. Now and then, lines of tracer laced the sky to port and searchlights wavered uncertainly. In the rear turret, Billy, the night hawk, scented fighters but saw nothing.

Then, from his vantage point, Arthur saw white particles of fire spewing out like sparks from an invisible grindstone, followed moments later by several squib-like tongues of tracer. The flashes died away and seconds later the night sky was ripped open from below by an explosion. Billy's voice over the intercom - "Fuck their orrible luck" – helped Arthur to put the pieces in place as he blinked out into the black void. In the freezing cold of his turret he felt sweat run down his back and had to quell a surge of gratitude. The poor devils couldn't have had a chance. In the east, the glow became brighter and brighter.

4

Eve had moved into Mrs Badesby's armchair and was sifting carefully through her pile of photos. The light from the single bulb bathed the photos in a yellowish glow. The uppermost photo was of the two of them standing next to Arthur's car. He always drove like the wind, trying to overtake the car in front. That was Arthur, full of life. He would do anything dangerous, like playing rugby. The first time she had seen him play, she had been frightened: a lot of big men in muddy shorts pushing and fighting one another to get that silly ball and Arthur so small. But he was tough. Whenever he got the ball he ran in zigzags, ducking and weaving like a mischievous imp, and those big men couldn't get him and several times he sent them crashing to the ground with low tackles. The next photo was taken before the outbreak of war in his parents' back garden. Eve examined it carefully. She wore a short cotton frock and Arthur a blazer, collar and tie. The photo was sobering; it belonged to another age. The man who had come home earlier that evening hadn't the same face. The soft features had gone; strain and uncertainty had etched lines on his forehead; even the skin across his cheekbones seemed more taut.

The harsh contrast between past and present forced her eye from the Velox prints to the clock on the mantelpiece: it was half past one. A spasm shook her little body. In a sudden burst of resolution, she rose, put the wallet and photos on the table and went out into the hall. There, she put on a hat and coat and went outside.

Standing in the garden near the apple tree, Eve looked up at the vast expanse of night sky sprinkled with the shining dust of a thousand stars. The flatness of the surrounding countryside gave it limitless dimensions. It needed no conscious effort to imagine that the same dark canopy sheltered Arthur and the others. Its enormity was frightening, yet, at the same time, comforting. As she gazed skywards, two ragged strands of cloud moved across the pitiless face of the moon. As a little girl, Eve hadn't liked the moon; she didn't like it now either. Its face, golden and impassable, imparted a certain callousness, as though unmoved by human suffering. The stars, glinting like minute pieces of broken glass, were reassuring. They made her think of Bethlehem, the Three Kings, the manger, warm straw, peace, hope, goodwill. Standing alone in that back garden, eyes raised to the heavens, like a small child in front of a gigantic Christmas card, Eve prayed again, pulling her coat about her small shoulders as she did so. Eventually the chill night air forced her back into the parlour. When she looked at the clock on the mantelpiece, she saw it was two o'clock.

5

Following the red glow, Sugar, like the other bombers in the main force, converged on the city from due west. They crossed the outer defences, jinking through tripods of searchlight beams and flak bursts. They saw some poor buggers in a Whitley coned and shot to pieces over the outer suburbs just before the thin tracer of the railway line slid under them. Intercom silence was broken. Oohs and ahs and crackling superlatives bore witness to the scene below. Cologne was like a medieval vision of hell, an inferno of fire, smoke, explosions and blinding flashes.

There were aircraft everywhere: above and below, to port and to starboard, their bellies lit up by the fires blazing below. Some flew straight to drop their bombs, others weaved to avoid the probing fingers of light, the orange flashes and the ragged puffs of smoke hanging about in their wake. In the centre of the city, the red of the blaze told old hands that the incendiaries had guttered and the fires had taken hold. The Outriders had done their work well. The Neumarkt was no more.

Arthur saw the Rhine, Hohenzollernbrücke and another fret-like, smaller bridge upstream. The spires of the cathedral appeared momentarily as a thermal wind tore a gap in the curtain of swirling smoke when a Hampden passed below and to port. Arthur caught a momentary glimpse of a stick of bombs falling from above before they hit the aircraft. It disintegrated with a whomp that was audible over the shindy of the Hercules engines. Pieces of glowing orange flame dropped beautifully earthwards. Seconds later even the glowing fragments had been engulfed in the palls of smoke which chased one another over the city and nothing remained of either aircraft or crew. It was then that Sugar was coned. Ernie pushed the control column forward, the act of a desperate man. The Stirling tipped like a man plunging into a swimming pool.

The city they had come to destroy no longer existed; there was only blinding white light, screaming engines and the crump of flak shells exploding, tearing into the fabric of the aircraft, making holes where nobody wanted them. Arthur's stomach passed up through the top of his head. His body became weightless. At the flare chutes where he had been endeavouring to drop leaflets, Tony had pitched headlong and was vomiting freely.

The altimeter showed 12,000 feet, 11,000, 10,000, 9,000. Still they fell. On the bomb-aimer's prone-position couch, Navigator PO Elton Emerson saw Cologne surge crazily at him. He closed his eyes and waited for kingdom-come. The needle on the ASI crept up to 300mph - 8,000, 7,000, 6,000 - Ernie pulled at the control column, his expert eye never leaving the ASI. Arthur saw the elevators move. The dive became less steep, their descent less like something out of a nightmare. Once again his feet rested on something firm. Ernie felt pools of sweat under his armpits and the small of his back felt damp. He wheezed slightly into his mask. The altimeter reading was 4,000 feet. The Stirling had levelled out.

At first, Arthur had lost his bearings. Then, as he saw the Rhine pass under them, he noticed the light flak, alternate orange, green and red balls, like roman candles only much more dangerous. They floated skywards bursting with a flash and a crack, too close for comfort. Ernie jinked and weaved, but not soon enough.

It was Tony who saw the fire first. He was returning on wobbly legs from the flare chutes. He screamed at Arthur pulling at the latter's flying jacket and harness. Arthur gave the alarm over the intercom before tearing out his leads and climbing down from his turret with the speed of a weasel. Tony produced extinguishers from somewhere and after an eternity of fumbling and stumbling they attacked the blaze. The co-pilot and front gunner came aft with extinguishers and blankets but the flames leapt and danced seemingly oblivious to the white curtain of carbon dioxide spray. They licked and twisted perilously near the oxygen bottles.

They still had four high-capacity bombs on board and one general purpose. Outside the flak was intensifying around the wounded bomber.

6

It was ten past five. Eve drew back the black-out curtains. The first rays of dawn were bathing the eastern sky in a soft glow of pale crimson. She still held the wallet in her hand where she had marked the take-offs, the four early returns and the other returns between four and four thirty. All the aircraft dispatched had returned except one.

Eve shivered. Was that aircraft Arthur's? Logic told her it could be. Her emotions told her it couldn't. Hadn't she prayed, hoped, put her trust in God, in fate, in kind Providence? It had been the worst night of her life. She felt so helpless. She wanted to do something but there was nothing she could do except what she had been doing all night.

Eve stood frozen for some ten minutes, like time itself, before deciding to go into the front room. She had got as far as the hall, still pondering the imponderable when, without any warning, she heard the muted rasping of a key in the Yale lock. The door opened. Arthur was there.

For a second Eve was paralysed, then she squealed and threw herself at him, almost knocking him over. She squeezed him and kissed him with all the violence and passion in her body.

"Thank God! Thank God! Thank God!"

Arthur could only stay for a while; the exigencies of service demanded that he be back on the station by eight. They went back into the parlour, which was cosier and brighter now and collapsed on to the settee. Eve lay in Arthur's arms. For a short time the young couple would know perfect bliss. The sun was already above the horizon, lighting up the fields and meadows, chasing away the shadows of a night of terror. One op was over. The next was as far off as it could be.

"Did everything go all right?"

Arthur thought of the flak and searchlights, the palls of smoke, the white light, the flames licking around the oxygen bottles and the searing heat.

"It went fine," he said quietly.

"One aircraft didn't return."

"It landed at Waterbeach. The crew are safe."

Eve squeezed Arthur with sheer joy. Later, when he had gone, she mounted the stairs and went to bed. Sleep came immediately; a temporary respite. Her prayers had been answered.

CHAPTER THREE

1

If Captain Hughes hadn't had the idea of renting the waters of Codicote Mill from Lord Marchington to breed river trout, Freddie Buckingham would never have left King's Lynn and come to settle in the neighbouring village of Kimpton. That had been in 1925. Freddie had been eighteen, staunch, true and conscientious, a man to realise other men's dreams.

Freddie would catch the trout in season and squeeze the sperm and the spawn out into trays. The sperm would fertilise the spawn and when the trout were about two inches long, they would be put in tanks to grow further before being put back in the river. The finished product would be sold to the highest bidder.

Wastage had to be eliminated from the natural process; so had predators. Pike were a perennial menace. That was why Captain Hughes furnished Freddie with the Mannlikker. This rifle, of German manufacture – something Freddie preferred not to think about – proved to be a potent weapon. It had a telescopic sight and fired bullets the size of small artillery shells. Freddie soon became adept at picking off pike and anything else that threatened the enterprise which had become something of a joint venture: Captain Hughes supplying the capital and business contacts and Freddie virtually everything else.

In 1938, Freddie's prestige as a marksman was further enhanced when he shot a marauding osprey on the river. Lord Marchington got to hear about it – there was very little his Lordship didn't get to hear about, as a military man he felt it was his duty to keep himself informed – and had the osprey stuffed and mounted. It prided its place in Lord Marchington's study: a true trophy of war.

The Thirties saw Captain Hughes's optimism vindicated and Freddie's Herculean efforts rewarded. They would have gone from strength to strength, but the international situation worsened. Everyone talked about the war which was certain to come. In the summer of 1939, Captain Hughes moved from Codicote and Freddie left the River Keeper's cottage outside Kimpton to move with his wife and young son into the Lodge at Codicote Mill and enter the service of Lord Marchington. After fourteen years he had nothing, except the Mannlikker, and moral ownership of a stuffed osprey.

2

The announcement on the radio by the Prime Minister of the declaration of war that sunny Sunday morning in early September 1939 galvanised Freddie into action. He went through the bungalow and outhouses and collected every piece of weaponry he could find. He moved with a firmness and resolution that he felt the occasion justly warranted. After twenty minutes he had collected a 2.2 rifle, two 12 bore shotguns, an air rifle, an air pistol and, his pride and joy, the Mannlikker.

Peter, five years old, had watched in silent fascination. Puzzled by his father's behaviour – what he had just seen didn't fit into any previously structured pattern stored in his brain – Peter trailed into the kitchen where his mother was preparing Sunday dinner.

"Mum, Daddy's got guns and things in the middle of the sitting room floor. Why's he done that, Mum?"

"We're at war now; we've got to defend ourselves," Freddie said indignantly when his wife challenged him in a querulous tone.

"You silly man," she said – she always called him a silly man when she chastised him – "You'll get us all killed."

"But we're at war," Freddie said, pointing to the wireless.

"Well, you'll have to join up like Arthur."

"But I can't do that today, it's Sunday. We have to do something today," he protested.

"If you want to do something, you can dig some potatoes for dinner."

"I can dig potatoes, but what about the war?"

"You can write to the recruiting office this afternoon. The post goes this evening. They'll get it tomorrow," she called after him as he disappeared out of the door.

Five minutes later, Freddie was back with the potatoes swilled with rainwater from the tank in the garden. Olive took them from him and went into the kitchen.

Freddie went back into the sitting-room. His wife's voice reached him through two open doors.

"Arthur was called out on Friday when the emergency was declared."

Freddie sank down into his armchair and stared disconsolately down at the assortment of weaponry at his feet. The news, not that it was news really, did nothing to raise his spirits. His angular features were creased in thought. What a fool he had been! He should have joined the RAF reserves in May like Arthur; now perhaps it was too late. They'd be having a war without him. The bloody Hun would be coming up the village street before he'd even got a uniform on. Still, he could always write to the recruiting office. He was silent for some moments before announcing loudly, "I'm going to volunteer as an air gunner."

The skin covering Freddie's face became less taut and his body seemed to relax in the wake of a decision of great moment.

That afternoon, Freddie forwent his customary dominical forty winks - you could hardly sleep when there was a war on - and wrote to the recruiting office in Luton. A month of anxious waiting followed, during which time Freddie managed to convince himself that his services were unwanted, before a buff envelope of an official nature lay one morning on the newspaper in the Mill kitchen. Freddie was to attend a medical examination at Hendon.

A week later, Freddie, dressed in a thick tweed suit whose seams strained to contain his muscular form, found himself in a doctor's waiting room among a group of pale willowy youths, whose faces still bore traces of adolescence. In the surgery, Freddie stripped and the doctor, taking his stethoscope, looked respectfully at the squat, rock-hard body before him. It conjured up visions of awesome explosive power. Freddie first felt a twinge of doubt when the stethoscope lingered in the region of his heart. The doctor looked puzzled as though, in examining a structure previously considered indestructible, he had discovered a weak link. He backed two paces, held the stethoscope in one hand and pursed his lips as if thinking of some suitable formula of expression.

"I'm afraid your heart isn't strong enough for military service."

It wasn't until he came home that evening that Freddie fully recovered his power of speech.

The conjugal hearth was the forum where Freddie poured forth his many troubles. Olive was used to her husband's complaints, normally turning a deaf ear or chastising him in her usual manner. That evening, however, she was as shocked as he was. It was unbelievable.

"I'm no good," Freddie said, crestfallen.

"Perhaps he's made a mistake," his wife volunteered, without much hope, but with genuine concern.

"He seemed sure enough. He said going up in an aircraft would be my death."

"You'd best tell Lord Marchington tomorrow when you see him."

Freddie's problem put Lord Marchington in a spot. On the one hand he felt duty-bound to help a loyal servant serve his country; on the other, Buckingham's incapacity meant that he would be staying at Codicote at a time when world events were causing ripples on hitherto calm waters: the kitchen-maid had given in notice and the gardener and parlourmaid were growing increasingly restless.

Lord Marchington stood tall and erect at the window of his study which ran along the western gable. He gazed out over the mottled ochre pebbles of the drive, the rose beds, the river splashing by over its pebble bed and the croquet lawn burnt and dry after the heat of September. Although it was early October, the Indian summer of that year had lingered on and the days were still warm enough for the gardener to be in shirt sleeves when he pruned the roses.

As he watched the gardener's dextrous manipulation of the secateurs, Lord Marchington made up his mind with the suddenness of a man who relies on intuition rather than reasoning. There really could be no argument. As Lord Lieutenant of the County, he was under a moral obligation to do everything in his power to help a man serve his country. Codicote Mill would just have to go to the dogs; he'd send the parlourmaid to the front line if necessary. It seemed impossible that a man of Buckingham's strength could have a weak heart. Anyway, there was always a chance that this medical wallah was wrong. A specialist would be in a position to say exactly what the trouble was. He went over to the writing-desk and picked up the phone.

If the visit to Harley Street brought Freddie little joy, it certainly cleared up the mystery of his ailing heart. That evening on returning from London he gave Olive chapter and verse.

"I got a murmur on me heart. He said the walls of me heart are too thin, that's why it's weak. He asked me what illnesses I'd had as a child. I told him, the usual ones and then that attack of rheumatic fever. That would'a done it, he said. I'll have to tell his Nibs tomorra'."

"Well, at least you know what it is."

"What's the use? I'm no good."

Freddie looked morosely out of the window. The gathering dusk and the darkening sky mirrored the state of Freddie's soul. His whole body drooped with disappointment. The distance between him and Arthur had become infinite. There was no hope left.

Cut to the quick, Freddie nursed his wounded pride through the period of the Phoney War. He followed Arthur's career with more than a passing interest; first at the Luton Training Centre, then at Bombing and Gunnery School. In January, with snow coming in all its fury, Arthur was posted to Scotland to serve in a Blenheim fighter squadron. Freddie plotted Arthur's progress, and, indeed, what his own might have been had fate ordained otherwise. Spring saw Arthur promoted to sergeant and the war awake from a state of torpor. The Germans invaded Denmark and Norway. Holland fell. The Belgians surrendered. Freddie suffered vicariously for the woes of the BEF in France. Each morning at the breakfast table he would be bent over the paper poring over maps, diagrams and reports from war correspondents. They didn't make encouraging reading.

"I'm bloody worried," he would say shaking his head dolefully.

"There's nothing any of us can do about it," Olive retorted one morning at breakfast.

"What's to become of us?" Freddie bleated. "We'll be invaded."

"Will the Germans come over, Mum?" Peter sat chewing bacon rind on the opposite side of the oval table which filled the kitchen. "Will Daddy use the Mannlikker if the Germans come? Will he kill them with it, Mum?"

Olive Buckingham had no answer. The future was so black it hardly bore thinking about. News bulletins and newspaper reports shrouded the situation in euphemistic language: withdrawals, regroupings, fierce fighting, heavy losses on both sides. Lord Marchington's features, however, put up no such smokescreen. On the contrary, his face was as black as thunder and of late he had given at least one member of his staff the rough side of his tongue. Much of his time at home was spent in his study, but as often as not he was away and judging by the way he drove his Bentley out of the gates, leaving ugly gashes in the gravel as he slewed violently round the corner, his engagements must have been pressing.

"Will Dad use the Mannlikker, Mum? Can I watch?"

Olive Buckingham collected herself.

"The Germans won't come this way. We're in the country. They want the towns and the factories."

She made an effort to sound convincing. The explanation seemed to satisfy the boy who turned his attention back to his bacon rind.

Freddie ate his fried bread, fried tomato and rasher of bacon in a ruminative silence. He'd show the buggers if they showed up. He had his arsenal behind the bathroom door. During his moments on the lavatory he'd worked out how best to use each weapon: the 12 bore at close range, in the bracken on the heath nearby, or in any piece of densely-wooded countryside; the Mannlikker, still his most potent weapon, could be used for sniping. One of those artillery shells could penetrate a helmet he was sure and it had a telescopic sight. Freddie was unsure how to best use the 2.2 rifle but he'd think of something. He finished his breakfast, swallowing the last piece of tomato and fried bread, quietly confident that he would be equal to whatever the future had in store.

When the Local Defence Volunteers were formed, Freddie viewed it with the disdain of a man who, having set his sights high and failed, will have no truck with anything less. The trauma of his medical rejection was now no more than a dull, intermittent ache. He had the Mannlikker and his own plan of defending his part of England should the Hun choose to strike. The LDV was for lesser spirits. Lord Marchington, however, decided to take Freddie to task over the latter's apparent indifference to what was being heralded as democracy's answer to Nazi aggression. Before calling Buckingham into his study, Lord Marchington, in the manner of a military man, formed a plan of attack. It would be ill-advised to haul his manservant over glowing coals. Besides, failing that medical must have come as a bitter blow, especially to someone as fit and strong as Buckingham was. The LDV was a poor second when one had set one's heart on an air-gunner's brevet. He decided on a tactical approach: a description of the situation, grave national peril, importance of action, essential to mobilise every available man, then he'd come to the point, decisively and cogently. There was a knock at the door. Lord Marchington, who had been standing bolt upright at the window, hands behind his back, swivelled sharply on his heels.

"Come in," he called.

Freddie entered and shuffled to within a respectful distance of his Lordship.

"Buckingham, this country is at war and we are coming off second best. The British Army has to be rebuilt from the ground; all our equipment is in France. We've no tanks, no artillery. We're lucky to have men in uniform. The situation is grave." He dropped his voice. “I don’t need to tell you what will happen if the German Army gets one foot over the Channel.”

Freddie shook his head.

“Of course, all hope is not lost,” Lord Marchington continued, in a more optimistic vein. “The Hun isn’t here yet; always got the Channel.” Lord Marchington paused as if the thread of his discourse had taken a wrong turning somewhere between Calais and Dover. At length he went on, “I’ll come straight to the point, Buckingham. You’re a conscientious man, reliable, but this business of your heart is a *fait accompli*; nothing we can do about it. There is, however, a way out: the Local Defence Volunteers.”

Freddie made a movement with his head indicating he had heard of the LDV.

“If there is an invasion, we’ll need every available man – volunteers, of course.”

Lord Marchington cast a steely glance over the croquet lawn, now verdant after the rains of spring, and beyond to the hawthorn hedge which bounded his property to the west. He swivelled round again.

“Volunteers, Buckingham. We are mobilising the initiative of the British people in the face of the great dangers which beset us. Each volunteer will undertake to serve forty-eight hours a month. We are creating a tactically-mobile force to meet the exigencies of an invasion.” Lord Marchington walked over to the bookcase where the osprey stood. “You’re an excellent man with a rifle, Buckingham.” He looked up at the osprey which seemed to fix them both with a beady, predatory stare. “Just think, Buckingham, might bag a few Germans.” Then, in a sudden burst of joviality, he added, “Pity we won’t be able to have them stuffed!”

Freddie grinned appreciatively.

“You’ll make a first class soldier, Buckingham, and you might well see action sooner than you think.”

Two days later Freddie was sworn in and signed on for the LDV. He received an armband. A uniform and a Short Enfield would follow later. With invasion a near certainty he would soon be in the front line. Freddie felt a deep satisfaction of acceptance. He was part of the war effort.

3

Freddie's new lease of life continued. In the months that followed he was everywhere, running between the kitchen, Lord Marchington's chamber, the garden and the river bank with unflagging energy. When the siren sounded at night, Freddie, forestalling the approach of German panzer - sort of bloody underhand thing the Hun would do: come in the middle of the night - leapt out of bed as though propelled by some unseen force, got into his battledress and pedalled furiously along the lanes to Stoneheaps Farm at Kimpton, his bicycle lamp flickering feebly at the shapes surging at him out of the darkness, to draw his rifle and assemble.

Freddie was the pillar of his unit, but he had an Achilles heel: square-bashing was not Freddie's forte. Arthur, himself a bundle of energy, resolved to help Freddie and each time he came home on leave, Arthur would drill Freddie hard with the 2.2 rifle. Arthur's raucous tones were deafening in the confines of that front room, reverberating against the window panes, bouncing off the walls. Peter hid behind the settee, his hands over his ears. Eve and Olive watched in awe from the doorway. Freddie tried - he would have done anything for Arthur, for Arthur was the greatest human being who had ever lived - but in his keenness he became flustered. In the end, in a tangle of arms, hands and rifle, he dropped the latter damaging the butt. It was the only blot on a perfect record.

Two years passed. Invasion fears subsided. German tanks rolled into Russia. The war became a dark tunnel with no light at the other end and no possibility of return. It was a period of unrelieved gloom. Then, on the first day of June 1942, Freddie went to work tingling with excitement and expectancy. He prepared breakfast at the Mill, impatiently waiting for the crunch of cycle tyres on the gravel outside which would herald the arrival of the mail and the daily papers. The newspapers would bring confirmation of the previous evening's news bulletins: after two years of stagnation and setbacks, Arthur and the RAF had struck back.

The papers usually arrived just after Freddie had finished serving breakfast, after which he would go home for half an hour to have his own breakfast, bringing the papers and the mail with him. Freddie normally had a hearty appetite but that day he paid scant attention to the inner man. Seated at his place by the door, he read aloud the headlines as if addressing a public meeting: "One bomber every six seconds, two thousand tons of bombs in ninety minutes. The ruins of Cologne are hidden under a pall of smoke, rising 15,000 feet after the first thousand bomber raid in history."

Olive left her sink, and wiping her hands on her apron, joined Freddie at the breakfast table.

The Daily Express showed a black belt with thousand small white stars on it. There were numerous allusions to Piccadilly Circus in both the papers Freddie had brought home. The Daily Mail had a drawing of a pall of smoke 15,000 feet high dwarfing Ben Nevis and St Paul's which had been included on the diagram. Apart from a graphic account of the raid, there were subsidiary articles: Cologne, a city of misery; German radio's account of the raid and the BBC's broadcast to Cologne: 'We harden our hearts!' Engrossed, Freddie stared at the headlines and diagrams for several minutes then ran his eye over the rest of the news. It was of a miscellaneous kind: a wages dispute at a colliery in Wakefield, food riots in Paris, German firing squads working on Sunday in Prague and a short article about a woman shot dead in the Belsize district of London. Viewing the situation with satisfaction, Freddie folded the newspaper and turned his attention to the piece of fried bread and the rasher of bacon on his plate, both of which were covered in something vaguely akin to rime.

"This is cold," he said, prodding the fried bread with his fork.

"What do you expect? You've been reading the paper for twenty minutes. I can warm it again if you like."

Freddie shook his head.

"We've got to save gas," he said.

He took half of the rasher of bacon, folded it deftly with his knife and fork, cut a chunk out of the fried bread and placed both it and the half rasher in his mouth.

He chewed thoughtfully for a moment, then said, "Arthur must have been on that. He must have been."

As the bacon and fried bread slid down his throat, Freddie felt pride well up inside of him at the thought of his sister-in-law's husband meting out to the Hun their just deserts.

"Serves the buggers right," he said, "Serves the buggers right."

Freddie devoured the remains of his breakfast in two large mouthfuls then wiped his plate clean with a piece of wholemeal bread. He drank his tea – that was cold too – and went back to work his head held high. In the Mill kitchen, he took out a tin of polish, a rag and a stiff brush with a gleaming varnished handle from a box under the sink and disappeared into the darker recesses of the house. He climbed a dingy flight of stairs and opened a door into Lord Marchington's private chamber. The room was furnished in a spartan fashion, befitting one who has had his character shaped at public school and RMA Sandhurst. A Victorian mahogany clothes-press ran almost the length of one wall. Freddie opened the clothes-press and took out a military uniform from one of the drawers. He laid the trousers on the bed and started to brush the shoulders of the braided jacket with firm, vigorous strokes.

"One bomb every six seconds, one thousand bombers in ninety minutes. Serves the buggers right," he muttered to himself over and over again. "Serves the buggers right."

CHAPTER FOUR

1

Morning prayers at Oakington were held at nine each morning in the briefing room. Attendance was compulsory for all aircrew unless they had been on operations that night later than two o'clock. The Squadron Commander presided.

Wing Commander John Truex was twenty-four years old. After two completed tours on Hampdens he had a DFC and a nervous twitch over his left eye. He was one of the lower vassals in the military hierarchy: a knight in shining armour whose chivalry and code of ethics in war had been tarnished and blighted in the aftermath of the Industrial Revolution.

Truex had special responsibility for air crew and was respected by them. When he addressed them, his comments were apt and cogent, never resented. Although he sometimes had occasion to criticise, he was never slow to praise good airmanship. That particular morning, June lst 1942, in the backwash of the Cologne raid, he commended Flight Sergeant George Hicklin. George, who with Ernie and Benny Goodman formed a pilot triumvirate in the Sergeants' mess, came from Nottingham, said 'buzes' instead of buses and had a grin like the Cheshire Cat. That morning he looked pale and haggard. For those who had seen his face at breakfast, the Wingco's words filled in a lot of detail. George had been attacked by three night fighters NE of Antwerp. He had jettisoned his bombs and, after a plunging, twisting, turning nightmare punctuated by flashing tracer and the crash of canon shell, had succeeded in evading his predators.

Another feature of morning prayers were the Wing Commander's pep talks. That day Truex talked about the near do, the moment of truth when a cool head and presence of mind might mean the difference between this world and the next. Truex's tone was grave, his glance steely and unwavering; life and death were, after all, at the heart of the matter. He conceded that luck was important (knowing nods from the old hands), but insisted that a professional approach to the job in hand could be instrumental in increasing an airman's or a crew's chances of survival (more nods). Survival-orientation was the phrase he coined.

While Truex spoke there was a respectful silence, bordering on reverence; no movement, no coughing. This man was their leader, someone they knew, who flew with them into battle. The Group Captain had accompanied Truex to morning prayers. He sat slouched in one of the armchairs on the dais. He gave his seal of approval, a benign nod. He couldn't have put things better himself.

The Wing Commander finished on a prosaic note: the business of the day. Given the success of the Cologne raid, it was a racing certainty that this mighty air armada would be used again within the prevailing full moon period. He promised that they would be operating that night with every available crew on the battle order. The Flight Commanders would have more information later on.

That success and the full moon must inevitably mean a repetition of the saturation formula – a new concept in aerial warfare – came as no surprise to anybody with the possible exception of Billy Hamilton who was far too preoccupied with his own concepts of warfare – daylight bombing, beam guns, knocking the Hun out of the air – to even spare a thought for the moon or the bomber stream. At breakfast, there had been conjecture as to the target. Some favoured Hamburg, others Frankfurt whilst the Jeremiahs of the squadron for whom Benny Goodman appeared to be the chief spokesman, thought that the saturation formula would be tried on Happy Valley. Billy didn't care. As they filed out of the briefing room at nine forty-five, he hissed to Tony, "It'll be too bloody dark, whatever happens."

2

Truex and his Group Captain left the briefing room by the door at the side of the dais. Both men disappeared into the Groupie's Vauxhall Cresta. Its motor coughed into life and it rolled sedately away down the main road of the 'drome. Air crew started to make their way out to dispersals where, on the pans, the Erks had begun their daily toil.

The Base Commander's office was one of a complex at station HQ just inside the main gate. Truex followed his Group Captain into the room watching him as he took off his hat and threw it with a deft nonchalance on to a convenient peg.

The Groupie went over to a window and closed it.

Truex cast an eye round the office: two studded armchairs, a desk littered with the debris of bureaucracy, the inevitable green filing cabinet, the floor covered with good, strong Air-Ministry lino, dark brown and ubiquitous. From the top of a cupboard an electric fan stared out impassively over the room. As the Groupie turned, Truex glanced out of the window. A low, flat grassy area ran gently down to the peri-fence and the railway line to March and St Ives. Beyond, the fruit trees were slowly losing their blossom in the breezes of early summer. The Groupie motioned to an armchair.

"Sit down, John. Make yourself comfortable – if you can. Most uncomfortable bloody chairs I've ever sat in." The Groupie perched himself on the edge of his desk. "Pity you didn't make it to Cologne."

"I'll have better luck next time I hope, sir." Sitting deeply in the armchair, Truex felt uncomfortable. The Groupie towered over him.

"You were very good at morning prayers. I admire a man who can command respect and you certainly can."

The Groupie was impressed, but not over the moon.

Truex sat impassively letting his CO go on.

"You set an excellent example. Difficult to define what leadership is exactly – easier to recognise the quality in someone. It's a gift, I suppose. God given. Your predecessor had it; you've got it too."

"Thank you, sir. Let's hope my efforts won't be entirely in vain. As it is, I don't rate my crews' chances of survival very highly. Most of them won't live long enough to become adept at flying or surviving."

"Don't take it so hard, John. We've all got to hope, each one of us. Hope's all we've got. I'm not a deep thinker. Doesn't pay to be in wartime, or any other time as far as I'm concerned. Don't you reflect too much either. I'm in charge of this camp, God help me! I notice things. You're taking the war too seriously – in the way a saint or martyr might. Be committed by all means, best way of getting through a war to my mind, but there's no place for those who reflect or worry too much about moral issues – not here or in any other theatre of war. There'll always be wars, have been since time immemorial. God only knows why – greed I shouldn't be surprised. Anyway, we don't deserve anything better, so that's what we get."

"Who's we, sir? Those boys out there? They're the best people in the world. I love them. I'd do anything to save the life of just one of them."

The Groupie rose like a man who meant business. He placed himself next to Truex, his body bent so his head was close to Truex's.

"I know you do, John. That's what I like about you. That's what the men like, feel, instinctively. That's why they like you. Listen, John, unlike most people on this station I'm not a conscript: I'm a regular. That chair," the Groupie waved a finger at the chair, "represents twenty-five years of my life. Twenty-five years to get a command.

"What does it mean? I'm at best a country squire, meting out justice, arbitrating, deliberating, mediating, and at worst I'm a wailing wall. There are barrack-room lawyers in the airmens' mess complaining about the number of peas on a plate, PC Plod of the Cambridgeshire Constabulary is on to me about servicemen riding their bikes without lights and I've got farmers phoning the Base complaining that their hens aren't laying because of low-flying aircraft. And those men aren't joy-riding: they're flying to orders. Twenty-five years!" The Groupie waved another cursory hand at the chair without taking his eyes off Truex. "In the Twenties and Thirties I was becalmed. I used to wish for war. Anything! Just to get things moving. Now it's finally come, I'm too bloody old. How long have you been in the RAF, John?"

"Nearly four years, sir."

"Wing Commander after four years! That's what I call progress. How do you explain it?"

"I beat the rush at the beginning of the war. I've completed two tours. I've survived. Others haven't been so fortunate. There's nobody I mustered with still alive, as far as I know, except for a couple of bods in POW camps."

"It is an ill wind, isn't it? Look, John, play your cards right and you can be an Air Vice-Marshal by the end of the war, and you'll still be young enough to get out and do something else. You can do it, but you've got to fit into the system, otherwise you'll just be put out to grass. There'll always be wars, John, we've just got to make the best of a bad job."

The Groupie straightened his body and went round his desk to his swivel-chair, leaving his wing commander in the wake of his rhetoric. He sat down.

"Do you know how I'd stop wars, sir?"

"No, but I'd be interested to hear."

"I'd conscript differently. I'd take fifty year-olds first. When they were killed off, I'd take forty year-olds and when they were gone, thirty year-olds and wait until last before calling up twenty year-olds. That would do the trick, you'd see. No more wars."

The Groupie was sitting back in his chair. There was a smile on his face. He seemed to have forgotten the Twenties and Thirties. The innuendo in his voice was ill-disguised.

"Suggestion from young radical. All right, let's implement it tonight, shall we? Put me on the battle order; after all, I am forty eight."

"That's not what I meant, sir."

"I know it isn't. No, to be honest, I've been feeling a bit peeved about missing the Cologne prang. Bit like missing out on history. Favourite subject at school, history. Not that I went much on underlying causes and all the bloody intrigues – too much like the Air Force that – no, kings and battles, that was my thing. I suppose I'm a bit of a romantic at heart. Armies were smaller in those days. Field Marshals and monarchs even had a different contact with their men.

"They led them into battle. Top Brass nowadays are confined to bunkers behind the lines. Sign of the times. Still, if Nelson could get his arm shot off, then it's up to me in the name of fairness to risk something."

"Very well, sir. In the mess there's no one laying odds that there won't be a thousand raid tonight. The moon is still right and the thousand force is still marshalled. My guess is Essen."

"Mine too. It hasn't been bombed for nearly two weeks."

"I'll put you on with Flight Lieutenant Reavely. He's a good man, on his second tour. Will that be all, sir?"

The Groupie looked forlornly over the paperwork on his desk then up at Truex. "Yes, John. See you at lunch."

Truex replaced his headgear, saluted smartly and left.

Truex's office was in a single-storey brick building on the 'drome which also housed the offices of the Section Leaders and Flight Commanders. As Truex entered, his aide, Flight Lieutenant Dewsbury, came through from an adjoining room.

"HQ's just been on the scrambler, sir. They've just heard from Group. War on tonight. One guess as to the target."

Truex and Dewsbury exchanged looks of those who share the same gift of clairvoyance. Truex said, as if there could be no doubt, "Essen."

Dewsbury smiled. "Right first time, sir. Maximum effort."

3

As far as Wing Commander Truex was concerned, events leading up to the second thousand-bomber raid were very similar to the first, except that that night he would be an observer and the Base Commander would be going along for the ride.

As dusk gathered over Oakington, the crews made their way down to the locker-room. Truex went down with them. He knew that tension affected his men in different ways. Some became very quiet and subdued, collecting themselves for what was to come and sparing any extra thoughts they had for their families, children, if they had any, and wondering if it would be their turn to die tonight. Others became boisterous as tension demanded an outlet. There must have been a lot of tension in the locker-room. When Truex entered, the hubbub was general. Reavely was in a corner adjusting his parachute harness. As Truex picked his way over to him, snatches and threads of conversation detached themselves from the buzz of voices. "The best of British luck to one and all." "Happy Valley here we come – Christ Almighty!" "Glory, glory what a helluva way to die!" "The stars said in this morning's paper that today would be my lucky day." "Well, in about half an hour's time you'll be able to tell 'em they were fucking wrong." The retort came from a stocky, blond gunner who had a DFM ribbon. Truex reached Reavely.

"All the best tonight, Eric. You've got a special cargo and I don't mean the bombs."

Reavely had a quiet manner. He was upper class, minor public school, the quintessential officer; just the right amount of dignity. Even the terrible ordeal he was going through at present was having no outward effect. He smiled at Truex.

"Thank you, sir. We'll all do our best. Just wish the weather forecast was a bit more optimistic."

There was the sound of lorries drawing up on the tarmac. Truex gave one or two more smiles of encouragement then went outside.

Crews were already climbing into the Bedford lorries. A large, ungainly figure lumbered out of the locker-room followed by his crew. He clambered into a lorry. It looked as if he were scaling a mountain. He half fell into the dark depths at the back of the vehicle. There was a laugh from someone already inside. The figure swore, Canadian accent, before regaining his posture. Two more crews climbed aboard before the lorry lurched into motion. Truex turned.

The Groupie was standing beside him.

"Good evening, sir."

"Evening, John."

The Groupie's Vauxhall Cresta was parked a short way off on the tarmac and, as though in obedience to some unseen signal, the two men started to walk towards it. Truex noticed that the Groupie's erstwhile swagger had been replaced by the firm, stoic steps of a man walking out to face the vagaries of a capricious destiny. He felt he should say something, words of succour to a condemned man, but could think of nothing. When they reached the car, the Groupie gripped the door-handle tightly and turned so he faced Truex. He spoke.

"This is what comes of being so bloody romantic. I've been thinking about Nelson all day. That was a hell of a bloody war too. The poor devils below deck, if they survived, became either deaf, hunchbacks or raving mad. For the first time in years I've felt my age. I must have been bloody daft in France. We all must have been." The Groupie looked forlornly up to the sky like a man who has lost all hope. "Weather isn't up to much either."

Truex looked up too. The sky was black and forbidding.

"It might be better over the target. Anyway, sir, we can't just stooge around, we've got to try and hit the Hun hard. We'll have to hope for the best."

"That's the spirit, John. Hope for the best. That's what I told you today. Don't forget it. You're young and you're lucky. Just play your cards right. I've always believed in you but never more than now. All the best."

Before Truex had time to answer, the Groupie disappeared into the Cresta. Just as it moved off into the darkness the last lorry left for dispersals. Across the field the first lorries were proceeding in fits and starts past the pans. In the distance there was the sound of a driver crashing his gears and a faint howl going up from inside. Truex turned and started towards the control tower.

The Groupie joined his crew just as Reavely was signing for the aircraft. He looked up at the Stirling: it was colossal. His gaze rested on the enormous port main wheel before moving slowly over the wheel house panels flaring out just above the tyre and following the girders of the two-stage undercarriage into the darkness under the port wing. It was as if the Station Commander were seeing a Stirling for the first time. The wing root was so thick that a man could almost stand inside. The propellers were higher than a man's head. The knot of fear inside the Groupie's stomach loosened as he craned his neck.

"Good evening, sir. Nice to have you with us," Reavely greeted his CO with an unusual combination of heartiness and deference.

"Good evening, Flight Lieutenant. Bloody great things, aren't they? Makes you wonder how they get off the ground."

"Taking off's quite an art, sir, but flying's easy. The Stirlings handle beautifully in the air; a gentleman's aircraft if ever there was one. We'll be boarding now, sir."

"Very well, Flight Lieutenant. You're the captain."

They passed under the port wing and climbed the white metal ladder up to the entry door. The last man in lifted up the ladder and slammed the door. The pan was empty save for the battery-cart and the ground crew.

From his position in the control tower, John Truex felt like a man in the back row of a theatre gallery, a one-man audience watching a gigantic spectacle. The length of the peri-track the angular Stirlings broke into movement, like enormous prehistoric birds whose vulnerability had relegated them to furtive nocturnal activity. The aircraft rumbled ponderously forward building a queue along the track parallel to the railway line. The leading aircraft reached the runway and flashed its code number. At the answering green light it moved out from the wings on to the stage. Truex felt a slight spasm of cramp in his stomach. Taking off with a full bomb load was never easy; for the unlucky ones it would be their last take-off before oblivion. S-Sugar was first. That was Watson. His take-off was perfect. No suspicion of snaking. If he couldn't climb into a lorry without falling over head first, he could fly an aircraft. Reavely's was perfect too. That would please the Groupie, if he even noticed. The Duty Officer stifled a yawn, logged the take-off and phoned it through to the ops room. While aircraft flashed their code numbers in the foreground, the spectacle was enlarged as the early take-offs, small pinpricks of light at their extremities, slogged their way aloft against the decor of the night sky.

The Wing Commander stayed in the control tower until the last Stirling had completed its soggy climb over Cambridge. The take-offs had gone well. Even the younger pilots were coping well with the Stirling's tendency to swing to starboard. Throttle gently was the secret. He'd mention that next time at morning prayers. It was always nice to start with something encouraging.

4

"Front Gunner to Pilot. I think that's the Rhine down there, Skip."

Even as Stirling D-Dog swam up to its assigned height, patches of white cloud had slid by the aircraft, ominously thickening to a dense layer by the time they reached the coast. Flying over this thick continent of snow, the bomber stream, invisible from the ground, had proceeded east aided on tracking by Gee. Now, however, with the usual visual fixes absent, location of the target was difficult. The thin silver thread of the Rhine, discerned through cloud and haze, had been the first visual fix since England. Cloud and the industrial haze which hung perennially over the Ruhr had defeated them. The pyrotechnics of the first thousand-bomber raid two nights before would not be a feature of the second. From the co-pilot's seat, the Groupie peered into the uncommunicative darkness, straining his eyes to the utmost for a glow, however faint, but there was nothing. He shifted irritably in his seat, like a man with cause for complaint.

The navigator twiddled the knobs of the Gee set inserted into his table. Four pips appeared on the cathode ray tube. He turned the knobs again, centralising the pips on the strobe time base and read off the co-ordinates on the coarse and fine scales. Using the co-ordinates, he plotted their position on the Gee lattice chart on his table.

"Navigator to Captain. Reckon we're near Duisberg. We follow the same course for another ten or fifteen minutes."

"All right, Navigator. Gunners, keep your eyes peeled. Anything on the ground? There should be fires somewhere."

The gunners rotated their turrets and tightened their vigilance. The attack pattern was a facsimile of the Cologne raid. An advance wave of bombers was to light up the target in the opening phase with batches of incendiaries. The second wave had loads of either high explosive or 41b incendiaries.

A voice crackled over the intercom.

"Fires down below."

The Groupie peered sceptically out of his side window through what he thought was a break in cloud cover. Lights twinkled far below with the white incandescence of diamonds. As he looked, there were flashes from the ground in the vicinity of the fires and searchlights bounced their hammerheads off the clouds. The voice crackled again. It seemed to be a long way off.

"Incendiaries. Just been dropped by the looks of them."

"This is it everybody. The target-marking force has put those there; let's see if we can do the same."

"Might not be Essen," the navigator crackled.

"Doesn't matter. We can't stooge around here all night; we'll have to make the best of a bad job. There are flak batteries down there so it must be something worth defending." Reavely turned his head briefly and his voice crackled on, "No concentrated bombing tonight. The weather's beaten us."

On his couch, the navigator looked through the wires of his bomb-sight. They were almost over the twinkling lights now. The Groupie looked with academic curiosity at the small puffs of black smoke exploding round them. Every now and again probing fingers of light cut ominously through the night. The Stirling rocked slightly as the flak intensified, snipping small pieces out of the port wing.

"Keep her steady. Bit further. Not far now." Slowly the sprinkling of white spots crept into the bomb-sight. D-Dog was being buffeted like a ship on a stormy sea. "Keep her steady."

Reavely fought with the controls as the black puffs multiplied, hanging about the starboard wing, building a thin, ragged carpet. A searchlight beam came dangerously near, but the cloud cover, if it had broken the concentration of the bombing, was also confusing the defences on the ground. The navigator pressed the release switch and the batches of 4lb incendiaries fell in a prearranged sequence from the bomb-bay.

It happened as the contents of the last container were being released. The cockpit was filled with blinding light and the Groupie felt the aircraft jump violently. He blinked and for a moment understood nothing. The gabbling in his earphones seemed to come from another world. He stole a glance at his captain, then, above the roar of the engines, there was a thunderous crash and the Stirling lurched violently as if it had received a tremendous uppercut from an invisible sledgehammer. The control column flew out of Reavely's hands, he gripped it again, recovered and steadied the aircraft. The heavy crump was still ringing in their ears when a second crash was heard and the Stirling reared like a frightened horse. Reavely's body shuddered. He might have been in the throws of a seizure. Pieces of flak had torn through the fuselage shattering the pilot's right leg below the knee. D-Dog yawed to port. Gripping the wheel, Reavely applied pressure to the rudder pedal and the stricken Stirling started to weave.

"Flight Engineer to Pilot. We've been hit. Port outer engine u.s.; we're down to three engines."

Reavely fought to bring some order to the swirling mists in his brain. In intense pain, he banked the aircraft to port trying to compensate for the increased power on the starboard side. The interior of the Stirling became dark again. Outside, the night air was clear and calm.

"Pilot to Engineer. See what you can do about the fuel. Navigator, the quickest course home and I don't care where it takes us."

Waiting for a new course, Reavely had the distinct impression that his right flying boot was filling with blood. He released pressure on the rudder and the aircraft turned slowly. He tried to twiddle his toes but without success. For a brief moment his eyes left the dull glow of the instruments and he stole a glance downwards. He still had a leg for what it was worth.

"Navigator to Pilot. 285 degrees. That'll take us over Rotterdam – not that it'll matter tonight."

As the navigator's voice died in the earphones, the pitch of the three remaining engines became more muted. It was the Groupie who saw that the starboard inner had stopped. For the first time that evening, the Base Commander's voice was heard over the intercom. Reavely responded immediately.

"Navigator, a course for the nearest friendly country: Holland, Belgium or France."

The reply was immediate. "Alter course 20 degrees. 265."

Reavely reset the compass. The pain in his leg was excruciating. D-Dog was down to two engines. If attacked, he would be unable to manoeuvre the aircraft. His whole body was sweating. They were unlikely to get far on two engines and even if the kite made it home, he certainly wouldn't. The Groupie or even the flight engineer might well be able to fly it, but neither could cope with landing. He sucked in oxygen more rapidly. So this was it: the Wingco's moment of truth: Flight Lieutenant Francis Eric James Reavely, twenty-nine years old, would fail to complete his thirty fourth trip. Fighting to steady his voice he said, "Pilot to crew; we won't get far on two engines; the others might well have been damaged too. You're to prepare to bale out, but don't jump until I give the word."

At their stations, each member of the crew clipped on his parachute pack. The Groupie left his seat, took a pack from the stowage rack at the end of the navigator's compartment and returned to the steps which led down to the forward escape hatch just aft of the bomb-aimer's couch. He sat down heavily. Now, he knew what the letters FTR chalked up on the board in the ops room meant in practical terms. His gaze was fixed on the hatch. Beneath it was darkness and an agonising drop into nothingness. It was then that the Groupie realised that both his hands were shaking. He looked furtively round at the shadowy shape of the navigator. He was sitting at his table, intercom lead still plugged in. Two minutes later the noise from the engines changed again and Reavely, his steady voice giving no indication of the terrible pain he was suffering, gave the order to bale out.

There was a flurry of activity. The navigator pulled out his oxygen and intercom leads and rose. The sliding doors to the front turret opened and the dark shape of the front gunner emerged. He took his chute from the stowage rack by the couch, clipped it on and in what appeared to be the same movement, flipped up the attachments to the forward escape hatch. As it plummeted away into space, cold air gushed into the aircraft and the Groupie saw the gunner disappear through the hatch like a rabbit down a hole. The navigator came up behind him and the Groupie rose. Gripped by an inner calm, he proceeded with firm steps down to the hatch with the confidence of one following a well-trodden path. He went down on all fours and rolled out through the hatch.

Oakington's ex-Base Commander pitched sickeningly into darkness. The initial rolling sensation confused his senses. Desperately he started to count but he jumbled the numbers. Ten came after five like a magic formula and he pulled the cord. There was a whoosh, something flew up in front of his face and a sudden, unceremonious jerk slowed his fall. He had floated – God only knew where he was – under a billowing canopy for what seemed an eternity when out of nowhere, he perceived trees and fields. The ground surged up at him as if in belated answer to a prayer. The Groupie landed feet together and rolled over in an untidy heap. He lay still on his side for several minutes. The grass was soft and wet and the night uncommonly mild. When the beating of his heart had slowed and he had collected himself, his first thoughts were for Flight Lieutenant Reavely.

Reavely was holding D-Dog in a shallow dive to keep the one remaining engine above stalling speed. He had counted five members of his crew out through the forward hatch but had no idea of the fate of his rear gunner. He called over the intercom: a voice in a roaring wilderness. The pain from his right leg which was exerting pressure on the starboard rudder was so intense now that it failed to produce the earlier psychological and physiological effects; instead it had become the source of some strange, masochistic pleasure. Alone on the Stirling he had no thoughts for the ground crew, old friends of five months standing who would wait in vain on the dispersal pan before wending their way dejectedly back to their billets; a kite gone west, friendship brutally severed, nor for his own crew now they had baled out. Now, he had to get out. Please, God, let me get out. Reavely let go of the stick and the aircraft went into a steeper dive. He tore off his mask from its studs, rose from his seat and turned, dragging his shattered leg after him. His face, taut and grey, glistened with sweat. His head pounded. In front of him the navigator's compartment sloped steeply. The parachute stowage was an infinite distance away on the other side of the navigator's table. He should have asked one of his crew to help him on with his pack, but it hadn't seemed important then. With an effort that made his head reel and his heart throb, he painfully climbed the navigator's compartment to the chute stowage, took the remaining pack and clipped it on. He turned like a man guided only by instinct. Above him the heavens rotated and once he fancied he saw the horizon. He lurched back the way he'd come over a carpet of charts and maps towards the steps leading towards the hatch. He had visions of frying in his own fat. He had to get out. A clean death was all he asked. The steps were precipitous, but down there was escape. Please, God, help me! A clean death, that's all I ask! He took the first steps then fell, helplessly, reeling over. The hatch, a black cavernous hole seemed to swallow him whole. A rush of air swept over his face and Reavely, clawing frantically, found the cord and tugged. The chute opened immediately, took his weight for a brief second, then he hit the ground. Seconds later, as he lay on German soil – he had come down near Sölingen - Reavely heard a deafening explosion rend the night air which put the pain in his wounded leg into temporary abeyance. Four hundred yards away, D-Dog had crashed into a railway bridge. The echo dying in his ears and the subsequent weaker detonations of exploding ammunition gave the pilot confirmation of his survival; but, as he was to tell his crew later that day, it had been, like victory at Waterloo, a damned close-run thing.

5

The first Stirlings arrived back at Oakington a couple of hours later. Dropping out of the sky and crossing the flare path, they landed uncertainly on stalky legs epitomising, it seemed to Truex in the control tower, the fatigue of those on board. After watching the first half-a-dozen landings he decided to go over to debriefing.

The interrogating officers, eager perhaps for a repeat of the Cologne raid, looked pained as they put their usual questions to men whose tiredness was etched in their very features. Between sips of rum-laced coffee they told their tales. Some had bombed on ETA (estimated time of arrival), others on fixes. One or two had visuals through gaps in the cloud cover: glimpses of the Rhine, flak, twinkling lights; one gunner claimed he had seen a canal. S-Sugar bombed on a fix, Elton thought west of Essen, possibly Duisberg. Arthur and Robin saw sticks burning in the target area and take hold. Billy, fuming over another night of lost opportunity, reported dull red fires.

After debriefing crews repaired stiffly to their messes. In the Sergeants' mess, the first arrivals tuned the wireless to the control tower's frequency and listened with subdued expectation for the return of absent friends as incoming aircraft called for landing instructions. Newcomers dropped in in twos and threes, sitting awhile, waiting for news before going into breakfast. After an hour the board in the ops room had return times for every aircraft dispatched expect one.

Arthur cycled straight home, leaving camp as a man might abandon a sinking ship or leave a blazing building: explosive power in every push of the pedals. For Eve, the night of torment and anxiety had been longer than the previous one. The starless sky and the banks of cloud had put an infinite distance between her and Arthur. Just after five, the muted rasp of Arthur's Yale key and the twist of his wrist bridged infinity and delivered her from the purgatory of waiting.

6

Truex finally decided that all hope was out with the crew of D-Dog when he went into the ops room just before nine later that day. Their loss was not just tragic, it was vexing too. They were old hands, the most experienced crew on the squadron. Their getting the chop made survival and death appear to be little more than the effect of the spin of a providential roulette wheel, scuppering much of Truex's thinking.

On reflection, however, and somewhat illogically, Truex felt that whatever hope there was lay with the Groupie. The Groupie was the type that won a Christmas draw, a raffle at a fête, or found bargains in the most unlikely places. For him there were always convenient pegs, doors, windows, parking places. If he stood alone on a deserted London street under an ominous sky, a taxi would wing in from somewhere. Perhaps convenience would stretch to a quirk of fate, such as a tree, a haystack, a water course and perhaps his good fortune would benefit others in Reavely's crew. If he had baled out, he would most likely be taken prisoner. Truex wondered what the Hun would make of him. He would certainly give them plenty to think about; he was a real Englishman.

CHAPTER FIVE

1

D-Dog was only the beginning. Throughout the month of June, the Bedford lorries rolled like tumbrels out to dispersals. Seven more Stirlings failed to return. It was a terrible, nerve-racking time. The descending darkness made everything worse, at least Billy thought so; he blamed everything on the dark, but he wasn't alone in fearing the shadows of night.

The Upper Rhineland was the most frequent target, with Emden running Essen a close second. Nearly sixty aircrew were posted missing. Others came back dead, or with wounds so terrible that, even if they didn't prove to be fatal, they would leave the bearer incapacitated or crippled for life.

The Brylcreem Boys went early that month. Trapped by G forces, they plunged to their deaths in a blazing coffin somewhere between Duisberg and Essen.

Sometimes, a crippled Stirling would make it back across the North Sea to crash land in England and airmen died in fires or explosions, either on landing or when trying to rescue trapped or unconscious comrades from the wreckage. The countryside was littered with the wrecks of burnt-out aircraft.

Crews came home and told of miraculous escapes. George Hicklin, coned over Emden, found himself upside down with the bombs still on. The next day in the mess, he couldn't recall how he had escaped. Two trips later he wasn't so lucky. It was a night fighter this time.

His crew baled out, but George made the ultimate sacrifice. The Cheshire Cat grin perished in a blazing ball of fuel and magnesium.

Gunners were particularly vulnerable. Benny Goodman had two near dos, on both occasions coming home with his rear gunner dead. The first time there was no problem removing the dead man from the turret. Ten days later the starred perspex obscured the view of what was inside. The flight engineer already had an inkling. When he had tried to lift the gunner out of the turret, the head had come away from the body. He must have been badly shot up. The ground crew had to lay a tarpaulin under the turret and call the fire tender. The flight engineer was sent to Uxbridge.

Replacement crews filled the gaps. To the survivors, these new arrivals seemed to be getting progressively younger. The RCAF sent numerous airmen, which pleased Ernie who, although serving in the RAF – he had been living with his grandparents in York when he joined up – always claimed blood was thicker than water. The Canucks were great gamblers; so were the Aussies who were equally numerous. Some nights, when ops were scrubbed very late, the Sergeants' mess looked like a gambling den. Ernie was always in the thick of things: at the billiard table, which was used for crap games, or by the piano, like a rock amidst a bubbling sea of blue serge. Billy sometimes sang, but never played cards – he had trouble with spades and clubs. He was seldom in the mess, reckoning that it was a dead loss staying on the station anyway. He was dead right. Anybody hanging around might end up on ops, replacing a sick airman or someone who had cracked under the strain, like Benny Goodman's flight engineer. While the money lasted, crews went into Cambridge. Getting in was easy, there was always plenty of transport. Getting home was harder. In another day and age it might even have constituted a problem, but such was the transitory nature of existence that most airmen, even the ones who on duty had imbibed their wing commander's precepts of care and circumspection, off duty took temporary leave of their senses. An undergraduate bicycle was pinched with no qualms at all and dumped just as unceremoniously after use. The number of bicycles littering the environs of Oakington station early mornings was always a reliable indicator of the previous night's intake in Cambridge.

On the 12th the King and Queen, accompanied by the AOC 3 Group, visited Oakington. No one had ever seen the station looking so tidy. The lawns had been manicured, the flower-beds weeded and there wasn't a piece of litter or a fag-end to be seen anywhere. All aircrew were lined up on the tarmac in front of the hangars except for Arthur's crew who were inside one.

The Royals shook hands with every member of each crew and chatted with some. They came into the hangar last. The King was wearing the uniform of Marshal of the Royal Air Force and each member of the Royal Family had an escort. The Flight Commander introduced Ernie to his Majesty; Ernie presented his crew. The King saw Billy's DFM and asked him if he'd shot down a fighter.

"One and a half, Your Majesty," was the reply.

At times like these Billy tended to exaggerate his importance as defender of the realm. Truex probably thought so too. He was nearby and put the record straight, explaining to his Majesty that one-and-a-half meant one and a possible, that Flight Sergeant Hamilton had claimed three and that the Royal Air Force was always restrictive in confirming kills. He looked Billy straight in the eye and said with controlled rage, "And the same rules apply to everybody."

Arthur was standing next to Billy and caught the full force of the Wingco's blast. He swore that Truex would have summarily tried Billy and gladly had him shot if he had had the power to do so.

Arthur shared few, if any, of Billy's ideas except for the one about hanging around on the station. If his crew were on stand-down, Arthur was on his bike and first away. He spent his time with Eve. Eve loved Cambridge. Certain quarters were raucous, but there was peace and quiet too. In the warmth of early evening they would follow the footpath along the Cam, through the colleges: St John's, Trinity, Caius, King's, inevitably ending up on Market Hill where in the Victoria cinema, the palliative flickering images temporarily effaced the grim reality outside. How Arthur wished that life could be like a film where a power which arranged all things was woven into the fabric of the story and whose end always justified faith in the future, hope for better times to come.

But even the silver screen could remind Arthur of his occupation. One evening in June, Arthur and Eve saw 'Aloma of the South Seas' at the Victoria. The theme of the film was an arranged marriage between Dorothy Lamour, in floral necklace and sarong, and the son of a local chief; a man she had never met and who had spent fifteen years in the United States. The betrothed pair met one day by chance, neither knowing who the other was. It was a humorous scene and, although it bore no resemblance, it took Arthur back to 1939 and his first chance meeting with Eve. Several times during the film, Arthur glanced at Eve out of the corner of his eye; she was in rapture, cushioned on a dream. Even he was beginning to enjoy it, then later a technicolor volcanic eruption had a realism he could well have done without: fire and lava cascaded earthwards in enormous lumps, smashing into the ground, disintegrating on impact. Arthur thought of Cologne. The spell was broken. Emerging into the twilight of evening on Market Hill, they were met by the scene of about a dozen air force bods all trying to pile into a taxi. Further along the street a newsbill announced in bold letters the cost of the war: £12,000,000 a day. It was June 17th 1942.

The previous night, Arthur had survived a trip to Essen, and that night, a stand-down for most, three crews of freshmen would soon be starting for St Nazaire. They would hear the roar of aircraft engines as they lay in bed. There was no escape.

Sometimes, however, Arthur's buoyant optimism held sway. Lying in bed at night with Eve's heavy breathing punctuating the stillness, he would list factors favouring his survival as others might count sheep. There were parachutes and the distance between his turret and the rear escape hatch wasn't great; they had four engines and the Stirling showed an amazing capacity to absorb battle damage and still remain airworthy. Ernie and Elton were both first class. They were an experienced crew. Wasn't survival also a matter of routine? Perhaps death wasn't ineluctable.

Arthur was always careful to temper both his optimism and pessimism when talking to Eve. It was pointless dissembling, he reasoned, for Eve would have to live on after his death. It was perhaps this that preyed on his mind most: what would become of her if he died? It would lie outside his power to help her. They had discussed this eventuality in the halcyon days of coastal patrols. His father had had a legacy drawn up, ensuring Eve of an income if she became a widow. At the time it had seemed he was merely being provident, the legacy being a simple form of insurance; now, however, a month of night bombing had cast ominous shadows over his longevity.

Eve, for her part, had a faith in the power of God to arrange everything. It was this faith, nurtured since childhood, which gave her the strength to stand the terrible strain of waiting each night Arthur was away.

She prayed, her little hands clasped in supplication, and the fact that almost every night ops were on one aircraft failed to return, and that others too had next-of-kin praying for them did nothing to daunt her belief that everything would work out. Such was her commitment. Such was the intensity of her love.

2

One evening when Arthur and the others were on stand-down and the attractions of field, lane and hedgerow offset the urban delights of Cambridge, the young couple followed the road which ran past their house away from the village towards the river. It was a pleasant walk. Willow trees stood like sombre sentinels, isolated, or in clusters above the flat East Anglian countryside. The road, which was higher than the ground on either side, crossed a large field where a pungent-smelling plant was growing, similar to cabbage but with long stalks and small leaves. Eve said it was kale. There were a few sequestered houses, a small stream where the trunk of a large willow grew horizontally out of the bank at a right angle to become vertical, an avenue of unkempt hawthorn bushes and a raised grassy bank where cattle grazed. On the other side of the bank was the river.

If the jetties, boats and punts, the grassy banks and the footpaths along the Cam made it warm and open to human pleasure, then the waters of the Ouse, wide, deep and foreboding, gave Eve the impression that they embodied the unknown. She shuddered slightly and squeezed Arthur's hand. They looked across the river at the restaurant on the far bank, the stately willows and the long thick grass, then returned to Stowe across country using the church spire for orientation. They reached the road which led out of Stowe by plunging through the field of wheat by the walled churchyard. From there, they half ran, half trotted back to the village, down the main street to finish their ramble, breathless and laughing - Arthur had picked a strand of wheat and was tickling Eve's ears with it - at the pub, The Happy Angler, a stone building with small windows looking out on to the pavement and street.

3

Paula Gilder worked as barmaid at The Happy Angler. Responsible and well-organised, she was the landlord's right hand. She was in her late twenties, tall with a sumptuous figure. Customers didn't see her hips, thighs and plump, shapely calves, but her bust and shoulders were enticement enough. The tight fit of her clothes betrayed a body which was becoming more lavish with each year that passed. Her hair was tied in a bun which gave her features a prim aspect. To men who saw her body first, and most did, the hard face was a challenge. Still waters run deep. At least, PO Elton Emerson thought so. He was in the bar when Arthur and Eve entered. Paula's features softened when she saw them.

There was an exchange of greetings. Elton ordered – he insisted – then a clatter of skittles and a throaty roar took Paula round to the public bar.

Arthur and Eve went directly to the far corner and slumped on to the interior-sprung seat which ran the length of the wall. Elton, having drawn a blank, joined them. It was then that Billy and Tony entered.

Billy, in a mellow mood for once, saluted PO Emerson in a fashion which suggested that the latter had recently been promoted to Air Commodore. With Tony in his wake he stamped over to the corner, casting a cursory glance at the bar as if he had expected to find something there. Paula's statuesque figure glided majestically round from the public bar and Elton went solicitously up to her. When he returned a few minutes later, Billy and Tony were furtively scrutinising Paula.

"We've come down to check out the barmaid," Billy said unashamedly.

Billy and Tony's errand – it was Billy's really – and Elton's obvious interest, set the course for the rest of the evening. Elton's cultured, soft-spoken elegance hid a genteel passion. He admitted to a weakness for voluptuous women. Billy's passion was earthier. He admitted to a weakness for anything in a skirt. The two men exchanged notes. Elton said, "A magnificent woman, magnificent. I could really fancy her."

"Fancy her? I could hardly get me arm round her."

"That's what I call a woman."

"You're all right, navigator. You'd need a map and compass in bed with her just to find your way around."

Eve felt a reprimand was in order. She admonished them both with mock gravity.

"You mustn't talk about Paula like that. She's a nice woman, refined."

Elton said, "I find her refinement titillating too. Still, Eve, you are right; it is poor form to talk about one woman in front of another."

Billy, still genial – it must have constituted a record – said, "There's no one who can hold a candle to you, Eve. Give us a kiss."

He rose, bent over towards Eve and pecked her on the cheek. He proposed a toast. “To the belle of the ball.”

They raised their glasses and Eve, in her summer frock with her hair set in a quiff, radiated happiness as only a beautiful woman can do when she’s the focus of attention of four young men in uniform. Arthur squeezed her hand.

“Billy’s right. You can knock spots off anybody.”

Arthur enjoyed the evening. He didn’t give a damn about the sexual innuendoes. It was infinitely preferable to the shop talk of near accidents, shaky dos, crashes, and failures to return which as realities of their working lives tended to dominate conversations between air crew.

Paula remained aloof, except when Tony bought his round. Her features melted into a coy smile. She flushed and put a hand up to her temple as though brushing away an offending strand of hair. Tony lacked the perception to realise Paula was making a pass. His experience was limited to the workings of aircraft. The workings of the fairer sex were as yet a closed book; but before the end of that summer, the book would open and the pages would flick over at an alarming rate as he experienced the delights and deceptions of the sexual life.

By closing time, Billy had found cause for complaint. The WAAFs on the station were friendly enough, but could do without it. His voice was full of the disappointment he always showed after an uneventful op. Elton mentioned the Nissen huts on the edge of camp, WAAF quarters they were, and Billy’s ears pricked up. He was game for anything after a few pints. Tony, last man out, counselled prudence. He didn’t hear Paula come round from the other side. Her wistful gaze followed him out. Weeks later he would see her again, but in far different circumstances.

4

They parted quickly. As the three airmen disappeared up the street, Arthur thought he heard the word Nissen hut mentioned quite clearly at least twice. Perhaps a raid of a different kind was being prepared. Arthur and Eve crossed the deserted street. An owl hooted from the direction of the churchyard and the shadowy figure of a cat moved stealthily along the pavement.

Later, Arthur and Eve made love not without a certain gay abandon, as if uncertainty and death belonged to another existence. Arthur lay on his back, Eve sat astride him. Later, when Eve had reached her climax, they lay back. It was then that the war once again reasserted itself. Eve's body tensed and she gripped Arthur's hand as the rumble of aircraft engines gradually filled the room. Arthur said, "Freshmen. They're bombing St Nazaire tonight. Should be a cushy number, although you never know."

Three aircraft took off at one minute intervals. Eve rolled over on to Arthur. She put her arms round him. "We're safe here," she said. "We're lucky people."

Eve fell asleep first. Arthur stared up at the ceiling as he always did, waiting for sleep to come as it would in the small hours. Lying there, listening to Eve's heavy breathing, he took stock. Apart from the Cologne raid, they'd had no problems; although not once had they really seen the target. Not that that was important as far as he was concerned. It was all very well for these keen bods to throw heart and soul into the war: they didn't have families. He tried to be conscientious, to do his job, but his interests lay elsewhere. He had completed eight ops, a little more than a quarter of a perilous journey at the end of which, he tried to convince himself, lay the promised land. Yet, he asked himself, what was this fabled country? It had no geography, and in itself no permanence. It would be a period of instruction at an operational training unit, not unlike the ones he had already done, which for the RAF was a convenient pigeon-hole from which he could be plucked when the occasion demanded. After nearly three years, the war showed no signs of ending. Perhaps it would go on for ever. Perhaps, if he were still alive, they'd be living in a rented room in five years time. Although thoughts like those were hardly worth entertaining. The future stretched to the next op, no further.

Arthur lifted his left arm and laid his hand on Eve's back. This was happiness: her warm body against his, the scent of her hair, touch, feeling, warmth; but in wartime, happiness was a lend-lease affair. You had stand-down nights, like this one, periods of leave if you lived long enough, a weekend pass, compassionate leave if you were lucky; in return you leased body and soul. His generation had been bloody unlucky, there was no denying that. It was like being struck down with an incurable disease: you had to live with the fact. Just occasionally, by a miracle, it would disappear; sometimes one was incapacitated; most often it was terminal. Yes, there was no doubt about it; fate had been cruel. They had all been bloody unlucky.

5

One aircraft failed to return from St Nazaire. It was hit by flak just after dropping its load of bombs and went into an uncontrollable dive. All on board perished. The nineteen-year-old pilot had joined the RAF straight from school. It was his first trip. The Stirling plummeted into the sea at roughly the same time as Arthur was falling asleep.

CHAPTER SIX

1

The end of the month saw two raids on Bremen, heavy cloud making necessary bombing on fixes. On both occasions, a Stirling failed to return. On the last day of June, S-Sugar undertook a square search. Some poor buggers had ditched in the drink and Arthur's crew were to look for life-rafts or any sign of wreckage. The strawberry season was at its height and each crew member boarded with a punnet in his hand.

They took off just after eleven, shattering the stillness of a summer's morning and sending three girls, who had been sitting on a fence just outside the camp perimeter, toppling over backwards in a flurry of billowing skirts and a tangle of legs. The Stirling climbed steadily through patches of fluffy cumulous cloud. The crew sat at their stations in shirt sleeves and Mae Wests as the iridescent sunlight penetrated the immaculate perspex. Tom Campbell, the new wireless operator, sat in the co-pilot's seat. Elton lay on the bomb-aimer's couch flanked by a chart and a punnet of strawberries. He had a bird's eye view of the placid countryside as it slid beneath him. From his turret, Arthur commanded an even better view: the fens giving way to fields, and roads converging on Norwich like the spokes of a wheel. He popped a fat strawberry into his mouth and crushed it against his palate. As the juice and meat filled his mouth, the pleasure was as sensuous as the opiating heat of the turret. He turned the bar, the turret swung beam on to starboard and a shower of gold fell from the sky.

Presently, they reached the coast: a flat arc trimmed with a line of white breakers. The azure sea sparkled below and brought back memories of Coastal Command. He was higher than any man had hitherto been; in another sphere where war didn't exist. Wasn't this why, in 1939, he had joined the RAF? For the first time he wished that Eve could have been with him.

The search was a parenthesis, an intermission in the nightly drama of area bombing. It also proved as fruitless. When they had arrived back at Oakington and had showered and changed, they repaired to the mess. It was then that Tony had mentioned the week's leave which they were due for and which had already been the subject of hesitant discussion. They all had tentative plans.

Robin and Tom had discussed a fishing holiday in the West Country where Robin's parents owned a guest house and a small fishing boat. There, if all went well during the next few days, they could spend what might be their last week of freedom in tranquillity.

Ernie would be staying with his grandparents in York, doing nothing, which suited him fine. For Eve and Arthur, the problem was equally simple: they would spend three days each with their respective parents, perhaps a fourth with Eve's, most of which could be spent with the Buckinghams.

Tony and Billy planned to spend their leave in London with Tony's parents. Tony had spent his last period of leave at home in a state of semi-shock after his overshoots. In many ways, he had no wish to go home. Seeing his guv'nor and mum, telling them the news - what news there was - took him about half an hour which left him with six days and twenty three and a half hours to kill, minus travelling time. Billy, for his part, said that he was damned well going to get his meat in if it was the last thing he ever did and that he knew of a place which was cheap and where the skirt was all right. Tony found Billy's terminology obscure, but nodded his consent anyway, thinking his comrade's company would be just the ticket.

On principal, Bomber Command aircrews on operational squadrons were entitled to one week's leave every six weeks. Whether they got it or not depended on operational exigencies. As July began, the offensive became an onslaught. Most aircrew were all in. The terrible strain of fighting fear and nerves all day before each op was taking its toll. Some days, ops were scrubbed as late as five o'clock, mostly due to the weather, sometimes because of an unserviceable aircraft. Days like these were the worst. The reprieve was only illusory. The op would have to be done at a later date and the worst part of any op was the waiting.

To cope, a phlegmatic disposition was useful. Ernie Watson was quite a philosopher. One day, on one of their rambles, Arthur and Eve saw some cows huddled in a corner of a field. Eve said there must be something up and they went over. They saw an untidy heap of blue serge. It was Ernie sound asleep by the hedgerow, oblivious of the bovine curiosity which his presence had aroused.

Billy Hamilton, however, had no such disposition. He belonged to that strata of humanity to whom daily routine has ritual significance. As the build up continued, Billy suffered accordingly. Once, they were actually waiting for the Verey light take-off signal from the control tower when an airman came cycling towards them frantically waving a piece of paper as if it were a telegram announcing the capitulation of the entire German army. That cancellation was heartbreaking. Billy was too angry to even fume. That might have been the straw that broke his back. The next day, outside the flight offices, Billy's nerves snapped. The gathering storm had broken.

The group of officers and NCOs lazing about on the grass in front of the Nissen hut didn't hear the origin of the argument. It wasn't until they heard someone howling and raving that they turned towards the source of the commotion. Billy was standing in front of Squadron Leader Kilpatrick, the Padre, waving his arms and shouting. The torrent of words suddenly ceased as if someone had raised the arm on a gramophone and Billy shouted, "Piss off!" He stormed off in the direction of the billets.

Tony heard about the intermezzo in the mess before dinner. His comrade was nowhere to be seen. It was late that evening when he saw Billy again. Tony was lying on his bed in the billet he shared with Billy when the door opened and the latter entered.

Tony wasted no time in taking his room-mate to task. This was probably a mistake. Tony's voice had a shame-making tone. It fired the embers of Billy's discontent.

Billy and the Padre had had a short altercation about wars and padres. Squadron Leader Kilpatrick had joined the list of Billy's grievances. Billy went over to the wardrobe, pulled out his kitbag and threw it on to the bed. It was followed by a hail of possessions: clothes, shoes, shoe brushes, a cardboard box, and his toilet bag whose contents he managed to tip out on to the floor. All the time Billy ranted and raved, snapped angrily, poured forth his beefs in an unending spate: the goons at the Air Ministry, night bombing, the operational ceiling, the brownings, beam guns, the waiting, the uncertainty and always, always the fighters and the fact that his word had been doubted. Billy was venomous, but he was plaintive too.

"I bloody shot down all three. I did, I did, I tell you. There was a fourth. I'd 'a' got 'im too if 'e 'adn't cleared off."

"But the mid-upper gunner..."

"He saw fuck all. He was in a dead faint 'alf the time. Now 'e's at Uxbridge. Best bloody place for 'im. Why can't they believe you? What do they expect – me to tow 'em in an' dump 'em in front of the Watch 'ut? I'm sick! Sick! I've given this air force everything, Christ, everything! D'you hear me?"

Tony was up at the window, squeezed in between the writing table and the wall. He had been indignant. Now his hands were shaking. The little room was filling with confusion and fear. Billy was trying to pick up his toilet things with only limited success. A packet of razor blades lay at Tony's feet.

"Y-you got a gong."

"Fat lot of use that is. Listen, we're ten loads of bombs, that's all. Some of us a bit more, some a bit less. It doesn't matter to them because they play the percentages."

Billy was stuffing things into his kitbag. Tony had a sinking feeling in his stomach; things had taken a nasty turn and might never be the same again.

"What's going on, Bill?"

"I'm clearing out."

It took a second for the news to register. Tony took a step away from the wall. "What! Christ! AWOL? You'll be court-martialled."

"If they catch me, which they won't. Look, the instructor at gunnery school, he had a bull whip, been in the Spanish Civil War, he took me aside one day and said, 'You're not a good gunner, you're outstanding.' That's not a line-shoot; that's the truth, but what fucking use am I here? You could as well 'ave Betty Boop in the rear turret, or Toby Twirl or somebody. I'm clearing off."

"W-where?"

"Ulster, then south of the border. They're neutral." Billy was ready. He stood erect and indomitable. "Good luck, then."

Billy's tone was hollow and mocking. It suggested that even if Tony got lucky - which was unlikely - the luck he got would be insufficient to save him from certain death. He might have been abandoning Tony on the burning deck of a sinking ship. Tony wanted to speak but there was a bottleneck somewhere in the region of his larynx. He heard a door slam and suddenly he was alone.

Tom lay awake most of the night, in the forecourt of death. He had just dozed off, when he was abruptly woken by a knock at the door. He opened his eyes to see the Senior Station Warrant Officer peering round the door. The latter announced good tidings in a baleful voice.

"Your room-mate, Flight Sergeant Hamilton, appears to have spent the night in the ante room. One of the mess orderlies found him there, sleeping like a log. Funny thing was, his kitbag was on the floor beside him."

The Warrant Officer stared in incomprehension at the fully-dressed figure lying on top of the bed.

Tony looked drowsily up at the middle-aged face then across at the empty bed. "We got in late. Billy couldn't get up the stairs."

The explanation appeared to satisfy the older man. The door closed. Tony wondered what the hell was going on.

Tony was first down to breakfast that morning. Billy came and sat opposite. They ate a round of toast in a sheepish silence, then Billy spoke.

"I chucked my bag over the fence, walked out of the entrance past the barrier, then I couldn't find my bag again. Must have chucked it too far out and then walked past it in the dark. In the end I didn't know where the 'ell it was. It's pitch dark out there. It took me about an hour and a half to find it and by then I was so bloody exhausted that I chucked it back over and came back. The sentry looked at me as if I was a lunatic." Billy drank some coffee and took a huge mouthful of toast. "There's another reason too." Billy spoke with an embarrassed reluctance, like a child owning up to a parent. "I couldn't do it." He drank some more coffee. "Don't you want to know why?"

Tony nodded.

Billy looked furtively around him as if walls had ears. The dining-room was sprinkled with blue serge figures sitting in twos and threes at the long tables. Mess orderlies sailed gracefully back and forth carrying silver tea and coffee-pots.

"While I was rummaging about after that bloody bag, I started thinking." Billy took a deep breath. "I felt as if I didn't belong on the other side of the fence. To tell you the truth," he blurted, "I couldn't leave you and Arthur, and the others. We'll just have to sit tight and see what happens."

A warm wave of relief penetrated Tony's body. Colour suffused his cheeks. But if his confession was tight-lipped, Billy's contrition was nonetheless somewhat unnerving. Billy should be aggressive, temperamental, rumbling like a distant storm.

"We'll stick it out then – together?"

There was just a trace of anxiety in Tony's voice.

Before Billy could answer, an orderly appeared in the doorway to the dining-room and called, "Telephone for Sergeant Lovett." The murmur of voices lulled. Billy looked round the vast dining-room. The orderly called again. "Sergeant Lovett? Telephone."

"He must be on the lovettory." It was Billy's voice; a raucous clarion call. Tony laughed loudest. Billy was back.

2

When leave didn't materialise due to operational exigencies, Arthur and his comrades got a second wind. At the beginning of July they flew to Bremen. A couple of days later they undertook a gardening trip to the Frisians. One morning in the second week of July, nine crews appeared on the battle order, among them Arthur's. The target was to be Wilhemshaven.

The flat-roofed brick buildings at Oakington were already losing their colours in the gathering dusk as Ernie Watson's burly figure tumbled out of the lorry on to the dispersal pan. Elton followed him, clutching at his bag as if it were a lifebuoy. Billy was last off. He slouched, disgruntled, over to one of the Stirling's huge main wheels and gave it a perfunctory kick. He stood looking at it in an attitude of sullen indifference.

Tony and Tom passed under the vast ceiling of the port wing to the belly and fuselage of the aircraft. Tony put out a hand and ran it along a line of rivets.

The kite had done twelve trips and represented stability and permanence more profoundly than the runways, the hangars or the camp buildings. The aircraft shared their fate; while it lasted, they would. The Hercules engines, the wiring; the hydraulics and the riveted armour plating were their lifeline. There was a dull thud as he hit the fuselage with his gloved hand. Not a mark anywhere except for the five flak holes sustained in the Cologne raid over a month ago. He had made a special study of the metal patches riveted over them only that afternoon. S-Sugar had stood on its pan, nose held high in lofty indifference to the feverish activity on the ground below. It was being bombed up for the night's raid and Tony had been in the company of Squadron Leader Kilpatrick.

They had discussed amicably the previous week's intermezzo. Fragments of what the Padre had said came back to him. "No question of your comrade being put on a charge – difficult moral question -- beware of glib answers - collective responsibility - collective guilt."

He had spoken, in the eloquent terms of his pastoral function, of the terrible events of their time in which they were all, regardless of moral considerations, forced to participate. He was not, himself, a brave man and had asked God in prayer to be spared this demanding pastoral task. It was one prayer which the Almighty, in his infinite wisdom, had seen fit not to answer. This was the worst of all wars: the waiting, the uncertainty, the uneven tenor of discomfort. His heart went out to Flight Sergeant Hamilton. He prayed for him each day as he did for every man on the squadron.

Their walk together had taken them very close to S-Sugar under whose belly armourers, stripped to the waist, had been bending over the bomb trolleys fastening carriers to each bomb with their crutch keys. In the little time left before briefing, Tony had explained the process of bombing-up to the faint clanking accompaniment of the low-geared winch inside the fuselage. He doubted whether the Padre was interested, but the subject had seemed safer than the metaphysics of religion.

The sight of Billy's solitary, brooding figure standing alone a short way aft of the rear turret looking at the barrels of the four brownings which protruded ominously from the perspex canopy brought Tony back to the present. Billy wasn't the same. Since that night in the armchair, he had been strangely silent. The torrent of swearwords and abuse, his fuming restlessness, seemed to have ebbed like his own energy. With Billy like this, the future hardly bore thinking about.

Tom Campbell broke Tony's train of thought. Tom's crew had gone missing two weeks back when he'd been forced to stand down because of sickness. Since then, he'd been Sugar's wireless operator leaving Arthur free to operate the mid-upper turret.

"Halfway tonight; fifteen more ops and I can start cheering."

"I'll keep my fingers crossed, for both of us," Tony said.

They turned and walked over to the others who were standing by the battery-cart. Along the peri-track, the noises of the lorries grew fainter. At each dispersal, men stood in huddles exchanging last minute doubts and confidences. Just as Tony and Tom arrived, their huddle broke up in a flurry of movement. Ernie gave the clipboard back to Corporal Worral and they boarded.

Billy took farewell of the others, swearing as he climbed over the tail spar, squeezing past the ammunition tracks to disappear into his lonely outpost aft. Arthur was next in position. He stowed his parachute and climbed up the three steps of the metal access ladder as nimbly as his dress would allow. Ernie was last. He enthroned himself in front of the lifeless instrument panel preparing himself mentally for what was to come. He had completed twenty seven trips; in the darkness of uncertainty, light glinted at the end of a tunnel of thirty operations; but he tried to put this out of his mind. He had to. A miss was as good as a mile. A moment's distraction, inattention or a cruel quirk of fate and all would come to naught. Tony came up to his shoulder.

"Tanks and pumps on, Ern."

Ernie slid back the side-window and gave the thumbs up sign to the mechanic at the battery-cart. The starting procedure went like clockwork. After the all-clear from the control tower, there was a hiss of air and S-Sugar jerked forward, then steadied to a slow trundle, swaying and lurching along the peri-track like a huge bird whose ungainliness on the ground gave no notion of its grace in the air.

Sugar was third in the queue for take-off. A short way from the main runway, they stopped and Tony cast an eye over his gauges. He went fore as Ernie ran up the inner engines. The needles on the booster gauges crept up to 30" static. The two men eyed the rev counters. The inner engines were giving power. The process was repeated for the outer engines, then, as the noise decreased, the dark shape of the first Stirling sped down the runway, lifted its tail and on reaching the hump, sailed over the peri-fence. Two minutes later, the second Stirling was airborne. Sugar took up position and flashed its code letter. The answering green light followed almost immediately.

From his turret, Arthur surveyed the railway line and the dark shapes of the stunted fruit trees beyond. To the south-east, he discerned the angular profile of the railway station on the edge of the village. He swung his turret, and the low mounds of the bomb dump, the control tower and the hangars slid past. At the end of the runway, Arthur glimpsed faint pinpricks of light. Ernie opened the throttles, port marginally ahead of starboard. There was vibration and an awful shindy from the straining Hercules engines. This was the moment when Arthur always wondered if they would make it off the ground. Ernie opened the starboard throttles and increased pressure slightly on the rudder bar. The noise increased and the camp buildings receded and fell away as Sugar's tail rose and she became airborne. There was noise in Arthur's earphones: "Climbing power, wheels up, flaps up." The laden aircraft gained height and slowly banked to starboard. Down below to port, Arthur detected the silvery line of the Ouse. Eve was down there in another world, praying to God that he ordain that her world and his should meet again. Arthur crossed his fingers and added his own prayers to hers.

The laden slog continued. Ernie coarsened the pitch of the propellers, the noise decreased and the needles on the rev counters dropped slightly in response. Half of a pale, insipid moon shone through the cockpit canopy, giving the visible parts of Ernie's glistening grey face a lurid pallor. He put his mask up to his face and switched on his mike.

"Everything okay?"

A succession of affirmative grunts followed.

"Pilot to Navigator. Base to Cromer, track 045?"

"045 it is, Ern."

Ernie set the gyro compass to 045. He turned the wheel slightly and the compass needle moved to between the parallel lines on the glass. Ernie wheezed with relief. Flying six people over a hostile distance was a serious business. Taking off was over and done with. The flight out over Cromer and the North Sea was next. It was the easiest part of the op; tiredness and fatigue had not yet gnawed their way through the outer edges of his vigilance. The flak, the searchlights and the unnerving pyrotechnics of the target would come later; so would the possibility of fighter interception, and if they were fortunate, the long haul home and landing. But Ernie anticipated nothing. He had learnt early on never to look beyond the next moment of darkness. In this way, the hell of an op was broken up into bearable fragments.

Ernie's life had been something of a hell too. A shambling alp of a man, he had always been big and clumsy; the type to lurch into door frames or knock expensive china ornaments off rickety tables. Early on, he had learnt that, for his part, locomotion was a question of external propulsion. He had crossed a series of life's bridges on a variety of vehicles: a Harley Davidson, ridden through the pine forests at the tender age of eleven, tractors and bulldozers driven just as lawlessly in his early teens; later, cars, lorries, buses. In 1938, he crossed the Atlantic to work in Britain and became a weekend flier in the Volunteer Reserve. Now, still on his broad beam, where he had been all his life, he was captain and pilot of a Stirling bomber.

They had been climbing for ten minutes when Ernie, whose memory was a diary he carried about with him, allowed himself the luxury of a smile. He put his mask to his face again.

"Heavy breathers turn off microphones. It's like flying with a pair of bellows snorting in your ears."

The altimeter registered 6,000 feet, the ASI 145mph. It was then that the unexpected happened, like the arrival of a thief in the night, unannounced, with no warning. Billy was nearest to the accident, but he didn't see the blunt nose and the port wing detach themselves from the darkness. The clatter was deafening, though, and the jolt almost smacked him through his perspex. He wondered what the hell was going on. Arthur saw everything, however: the shape, the red sparks, the flash which preceded the violent lurch. From his crow's nest he watched thunderstruck as a shooting star plunged earthwards leaving a trail of fire. Its fall terminated in a soundless explosion.

To Ernie, it felt as if the control column had been momentarily torn up by the root. He didn't need to see the giro horizon to know that the Stirling had levelled out and was dipping its nose. It shuddered and wobbled. He pushed the rudder pedals, port and starboard, and turned the wheel. Sugar yawed, the wobble seemed to stabilise then return. He took a hand from the wheel and fastened his mask. The Stirling lurched again and Ernie fought with the control column.

"What the hell was that bang?" Ernie spoke tersely as if someone on board were responsible. "We've got no rudder and not much elevator. She's not climbing anymore: she wants to dive."

Arthur took his gaze from the glowing mass to starboard and let it fall on the shattered tailplane.

Again he saw the shape, the sparks, the flash. He filled in the details that Ernie's deductive powers couldn't provide.

"Ern, Arthur. Something's just hit us; twin-engine job, Wimpey, I reckon. It must have lost an engine. It went into a dive. Just seen an explosion on the ground. No parachutes."

Ernie's voice was calm and composed. He gave the order to bale out.

"I'll hold the kite as long as I can on one elevator. Get your chutes and go!"

Arthur was down from his turret with the speed of a ferret. He snapped his pack on to the hooks of his harness with hands that trembled slightly and proceeded aft. He had already removed the ventral escape hatch when he saw Tony and Tom come careering down the bucketing fuselage. The aircraft lurched violently to starboard. Arthur lost his balance. Tony and Tom crashed over like a pair of skittles. Arthur rose, took up his position and looked briefly down into black inky nothingness. For a moment he thought he was going to vomit. He braced himself and tipped out headlong into the gush of cold air. He spun agonisingly and helplessly and made a frantic attempt at counting. He pulled the cord, his pack flew up and brushed past his face. He felt a solid jerk, a slight pain in his groin and suddenly he was dangling from his webbing with a canopy blossoming above his head.

Apparently motionless in space, Arthur became aware of a strange silence. As the dark shape of the Stirling grew visibly smaller, he fancied he saw a speck detach itself from the tail, fall some way then slow down as a canopy deployed. Billy had got out. He watched Billy for some time before taking stock of his own situation. Mentally, he went through the landing drill: knees together, slightly bent, collapse in a heap on hitting the ground, be prepared to release harness quickly if windy. He had just run through the drill a second time when he saw the ground beneath him. For a few seconds it came no nearer, then with a rush came up and hit him.

He lay for a moment before picking himself up and unclipping the parachute. The grass was wet and there were patches of damp on his battledress. Looking around, Arthur saw that he was in a field and not two hundred yards off he perceived the outline of a detached house. He collected his parachute as best he could and started on unsteady legs towards it.

When Arthur got to the house, he knocked at the front door and waited. When a second knock brought no response, he followed a gravel path around to the back of the house. He stopped and thought for a moment, turned and peered around him. He saw a well-ordered kitchen garden, well-cut grass verges, well-trimmed hedges. The house obviously wasn't deserted although the occupiers might be away on holiday. As far as he could see there wasn't another house for miles. It was the crunching of his feet on the gravel that gave him the idea. Clutching at his bale of washing with one arm, he bent down and scooped up a handful of gravel with the other. The clatter of the small stones against the upper storey window was deafening. For a moment, Arthur thought he had broken a pane. Then a light went on and a moment later the window opened.

An irate-looking woman in a red dressing-gown peered down into the darkness. Arthur quickly explained his predicament. He wondered if they had a telephone.

It took a moment for the news to sink in. Then the woman turned and Arthur heard a shrill voice say, "Bruce, there's a poor man in the garden. He says he's lost his bomber." She came back to the window, once again gazed down to make sure that what she had seen really existed and said, "Don't go away, we'll be right down."

The woman in the red dressing-gown threw open the front door as if welcoming a long lost relative. "You poor man," she said in the same shrill voice. She beckoned him in and closed the door. Her husband was hovering on the staircase. "Where did you say you came from?"

"RAF Oakington."

"Bruce! Telephone RAF Oakhampton!"

"Oakington," Arthur corrected her.

"Oakington, Bruce, Oakington!"

She spoke in rasping tones like the commandant of a regiment. The telephone stood on a small table in the hall beneath a long mirror. Bruce lifted the receiver off the hook without a word. The woman turned her attention back to Arthur.

She ushered him into one of the armchairs opposite the fireplace. Arthur sank thankfully into it. From the mantelpiece, a brass owl fixed him with a glassy stare. The woman went out into the hall where she whispered tersely to her husband that the poor man had been through a terrible ordeal and she was going to get him a cup of tea.

Arthur collected himself and listened intently. Above the clank of the kettle lid and the gurgle of water he heard the husband's quiet modulated tone on the telephone and gathered they had been on the other side of the A142 between Ely and Bury St Edmund's when the collision occurred. He looked round the room. Apart from the usual trappings of comfort there was an escritoire in one corner. The polished writing slab was down revealing a multitude of small compartments. From the gun turret in which, minutes ago, he had been firmly ensconced bound for Germany, he had plummeted into another world. Only his flying gear and his still throbbing heart told him it hadn't been a dream.

The woman in the dressing-gown entered with tea, bread and jam, imperiously, like the Queen of Hearts. Arthur half-expected her to shout 'off with his head!' Instead she smiled, like a benevolent nurse. It wasn't until Arthur tried to take the tea that he discovered that his hands were shaking violently. The Queen took the cup from him and put it on the table.

"You poor man," she said again. "Come and sit up at the table."

She put her hand under Arthur's elbow and led him to the table. Arthur slumped down again. The woman patted his arm and smiled.

"I've made you some jam sandwiches. Home-made jam. I didn't bother with margarine; Bruce says it tastes better without."

Arthur noticed it had gone quiet in the house. He wondered where Bruce was. Perhaps he'd fallen asleep or been stuffed into a teapot.

Bruce entered diffidently.

"I've got through to Oakington. They seemed very relieved that you were safe. They're sending someone to pick you up. I've given them directions, though I'm not sure which way they'll come, probably through Ely. I should imagine they'll be the best part of an hour. Of course, you're welcome to stay here," he added with a hurried glance at his wife.

"I'm very sorry to have troubled you like this."

"Oh not at all, not at all," the red woman said. "We've all got to do our bit. We'll leave you to your tea. I've made a pot so don't hesitate to ask for more. Oh dear!" She put up a hand to her mouth. "Do you take sugar? We do have some, but my husband and I don't take it."

Arthur smiled and said he wouldn't mind a spoonful if that was all right. The woman smiled back and retreated, ushering Bruce before her. Even out in the hall her harsh whispers were clearly audible. "The poor man's suffering from shock; it's only to be expected, he's been through a lot. It's this war," she went on, as if only she could be expected to understand, "It's terrible. I'll give him an extra spoonful."

Arthur took a sip of tea, lowering his lips to the cup. It tasted good, but the paper thin slices of bread and jam had no appeal. The woman came back with the sugar bowl and spoon. She beamed fondly as Arthur took two spoonfuls. She departed again leaving the bowl on the table. The sugar made Arthur think of his comrades and he wondered what had become of them.

He drank two more cups of tea. The woman stayed with him while he drank the third cup. She sat on the edge of an armchair looking as if she were dying to say something. Bruce came in too and perched himself gingerly on the edge of the other armchair. The woman talked for the next half an hour.

They had a daughter – gifted girl – wanted to be an actress – overcrowded profession – tried to dissuade her – strong-willed – couldn't tell her anything – had to bang her head against the wall – taken a job in a factory – quite well paid – working there with a friend – safety in numbers – one never knew – war put all accepted social and moral standards in abeyance – made careers difficult too – doing her bit – had to do one's bit – good experience – all experience useful – life a great teacher – couldn't guess what she was doing – think of the porch steps – incredible coincidence – marvellous to know they work – Sylvia would be thrilled – something to tell her workmates...

She was still talking when the noise of an engine and a sharp knock at the door told Arthur that deliverance was nigh. Arthur rose. As he made for the door, the Queen of Hearts just had to throw her arms round his neck and kiss him. Bruce gripped Arthur's hand with surprising vigour and shook it violently, emotion choking in his throat. Amidst these fond farewells Arthur almost forgot his parachute. Forty-five minutes later when the Hillman pick-up jerked to a halt in front of the building which housed the locker-room, the woman's shrill voice was still ringing in his ears like a persistent echo.

When Arthur walked into debriefing, Robin was the only one to have arrived back. He had been lucky. Landing by the side of the main Cambridge Ely road, he had extricated himself from a hedge and got a lift directly to camp. Tension eased as the others dropped in one by one: Tony, Tom, Billy, Elton. Billy made most noise. His arrival coincided with that of the coffee urns. He claimed he had walked a good ten miles with only one boot and explained volubly to the red-faced WAAF wheeling in the trolley that if he'd wanted to walk, he'd have damned well joined the bleeding army, whereupon the Interrogating Officer, whose voice had the calm modulation of the long suffering schoolmaster, asked Billy if he would like to take a seat.

"Be a bloody pleasure."

He hobbled over to a chair and collapsed demonstratively on to it with a grunt of self-commiseration. It was then he noticed that Ernie was missing.

Elton told his story. He had floated down perilously close to some power lines and after an ineffectual attempt at steering landed on the edge of what he thought was an army camp. He had given the camp a wide berth and walked across hedgerow and field for about half an hour until a white object in a field made him freeze. Thinking it was a bull, he had been about to retreat when he had noticed that the object had a familiar aspect. On closer inspection he had seen it was the parachute left behind thirty minutes earlier.

The story should have provoked mirth and an allusion to the fact that Elton was a navigator, but their captain's whereabouts was a source of unease. Pilots seldom baled out. They helped themselves to coffee. The Interrogating Officer scribbled one or two notes. It was then that the Wing Commander breezed in.

His news was both good and bad. He took the good news first. Flight Sergeant Watson was safe. A gentleman in Forely Fen, seething with the indignation of the property owner whose seclusion has been violated, had phoned the camp. Their captain had gone through the roof of his greenhouse and landed on an orange plant the gentleman in question had been nurturing since 1931.

There were laughs as the tension of the night dissipated. Billy forgot his blistered foot and howled, "That's Bomber Command, the work of years annihilated in an instant."

Truex continued, "You'll see him in the sick-bay. He's got some cuts, superficial, nothing serious. The kite crashed in Mildenhall Fen; write-off, like the greenhouse. The bad news is of the other aircraft. You collided with one of the Group's Wellingtons. It seems it went into an uncontrollable dive. All on board perished, I'm afraid."

The official confirmation of what they were already fairly sure of still came as a shock. There were shudders and one or two low whistles of commiseration. The Interrogating Officer said, "This confirms Flight Sergeant Johnson's report, sir."

Truex nodded and went on. "It's nice to see you back, boys. It's a great relief to us all. Tomorrow you'll be seeing the MO for a check up. There'll be no question of you going up again before your leave is due. You'd better get some rest now."

3

Eve was sitting on the bed in the upstairs room which they had at their disposal. On the bedspread in front of her lay all the photos she had of Arthur, two dozen or so, arranged in the manner of a game of patience. She had positioned herself so that with only a minimal movement of her head she could see the clock on the bedside table and the square of night sky through the windows of the darkened room. The photos, the passage of time, and the night sky where Arthur's fate would be decided, were all she needed to keep him safe. Several times that night, in the terrible silence of that slip of a room, she had turned over each photo so that they were all face down. Then, she had called up in her mind's eye a certain photo and tried to turn up exactly that one. She had done this until each photo was face up and she had been able to discern her loved one's face in the darkness two dozen times. She reasoned, with the illogicality of one at the mercy of fate, that as long as she turned up the right photo then the spell she had woven would hold.

The rasp of a key in the front door lock was only the faintest of sounds in that upstairs room, yet it disturbed her passionate rite, struck a discordant note in her nocturnal vigil and filled her heart with a strange, inexplicable terror. Something was as it shouldn't have been.

She rose, her gaze sweeping automatically over the clock. It was two. She scurried out on to the landing. Arthur was at the foot of the stairs. Her thumping heart leapt. Understanding nothing, she ran down the stairs into his arms.

It was the first time Eve had had her husband in bed with her after an op. Arthur had told her of the night's adventure. They lay in silence sharing the same thoughts, searching for consolation. At length, Arthur said, "We won't have to go up again before going on leave. The Wingco said so tonight, so we can confirm our plans."

Eve squeezed his hand and endeavoured to get even closer to him than she was, snuggling up, running her hand over his flat hard stomach and up over his warm bony chest.

"It'll be wonderful to get away from here, darling, even if it's only for a week."

For Eve, it felt as though she had become a child again and was looking forward to Christmas: the crib, the twinkling lights in the shops, the tinsel, music, holly, mistletoe, the tingling cold, the warmth and goodwill. The week would soon pass, she knew that, but waiting and anticipating were sensations in their own right. Eve was satiated and opiated by hope and expectancy. Arthur would be hers for a whole week. No one else had prior claims. They would be free. Her hand was on his heart. Her breathing became more stertorous.

She had fallen asleep.

Arthur stared up at the ceiling. At that particular moment he felt happy without being able to explain why. To do so might demand intimate knowledge of the innermost essence of happiness. Certainly it wasn't because his hold on life was any less precarious. Even though he had survived tonight, which those poor buggers in the Wimpey hadn't, it might prove to be no more than a temporary reprieve. In any case, his eleventh op had been officially aborted and didn't count towards his tour. He placed his hand on Eve's which still lay on his chest. Happiness, he supposed, was when things were running normally. It consisted of simple things: life itself with its trials, deceptions and joys; of hearing that there would be a tomorrow, a day after tomorrow, a next week; a future which one could count on. That was what they had, a week; one week's leave; a stay of execution; happiness. He, too, fell asleep.

PART TWO

CHAPTER ONE

1

Tony Reeves viewed the week's leave with mixed feelings. It was always nice to see one's parents, but since becoming a flight engineer on one of the new four-engined jobs, he had become aware that his relationship with them, before so intimate, was no longer the same. His last leave had come in the wake of three accidents he had had in April and early May. He had talked unobtrusively about his two overshoots and of a third near do when Ernie Watson had been forced to drop thirty tons of aircraft with faultily rigged aileron controls on to a runway from fifty feet - the jolt had nearly killed them both - and his guv'nor and mum had listened with parental concern, but without any real understanding of what he had experienced. He inhabited a different world. He came home like a voyager returning from a distant continent whose task is to describe the landscapes of countries like Ecuador or Brazil to those who have never been there. The world of Tony and of his comrades was one of cold, fatigue, endless nerve-racking waiting; it was claustrophobic, shadowy and nauseating; a world which by its very nature defied geography and over which hung perennially a cloak of sudden fiery death.

Billy Hamilton, although a Londoner, had little acquaintance with the part of London where he found himself now, and as the two young airmen walked along the quiet street discussing the best ways of making use of seven days' leave, Billy cast suspicious glances about him, hobbling a few paces then turning around in his tracks as if expecting an ambush. He saw over the balustrades into the leafy gardens where, behind thick foliage, rows of late Victorian houses stood aloof at a respectful distance from the street. There was little evidence of bombing. Here, for some reason, they were behind the front line.

Further along the road, the houses were replaced by shops: antique dealers and galleries mainly and the two men crossed a wide street which had a rural air; quaint houses and shops with windows of thick glass, before penetrating a street where four-storeyed terrace-houses with basements below street level stood neatly in line like soldiers on a parade ground. They had walked about halfway along the street when Tony stopped in front of a flight of five steps which led up to a portico.

"This is it," he announced proudly.

Billy let his kitbag slide to the ground and craned his neck. "All of it?" he asked incredulously.

"Not really. We've got junk in a lot of rooms. I think these houses used to belong to rich people. There are still bell-ropes in the bedrooms. The top rooms are pretty small, servants' rooms I should think." Tony pointed to the two first floor windows which had wrought iron balconies. "We live on that floor."

Tony and Billy went up the steps and the door opened as if by magic. Tony's parents stood like a guard of honour on each side of the doorway. Tony's father, tall, thin and bespectacled with a mop of greying hair, patted Billy on the back, took Billy's right hand and shook it heartily. Tony's mother, small and sparrow-like, pecked Billy on the cheek.

"We're so glad Tony's got a friend. How nice of you to come." She ushered them both into an enormous living-room. "Douglas came home the moment he got your phone call. He was so excited."

The large room was cluttered with disparate pieces of furniture which might well have been acquired in a piecemeal fashion. Sideboards, tables and shelves were encumbered with ornaments: gilded jugs in rows, in descending order of size; vases, brass knick-knacks, china figures, pewter mugs, silver ashtrays. The walls were covered almost entirely by prints of old Masters in heavy gilt frames and in every conceivable place stood clocks of different shapes and sizes, arranged in such a fashion that there was nowhere one could sit without seeing the time. The heavy curtains framing the sash windows enhanced the impression of an Aladdin's cave.

"Please sit down."

Douglas waved a hand in no particular direction and after a moment's hesitation Billy followed Tony through a wilderness of polished mahogany to the window and a pair of armchairs placed either side of a Turkish ottoman. Billy sat down, uneasily, like a man unused to domestic comfort. He glanced furtively around him. A print hanging on the wall above his head caught his attention. It depicted a man in tight breeches and knee-length stockings looking forlornly at a violin, the strings of which were broken.

"I work for an estate agent," Douglas said cheerily, pulling up two chairs and sitting down opposite Billy. "In my business you pick up quite a few odds and ends."

Billy nodded. "You're not kidding."

Mrs Reeves sat down opposite her husband. "We hear of your exploits on the news."

"Bomber Command in action. It's very often the Upper Rhineland," Douglas chipped in.

"Essen," Billy said balefully. "They only send us there because it's so heavily defended. You never see much because there's always so much haze. Waste of blinking time going there."

The afternoon was not a success. Billy, perched on the edge of his chair seemed moody and ill at ease and the conversation was punctuated by painful silences. Every quarter the clocks chimed, though not in unison. One would start, the others would follow suit, vying for supremacy until, after several seconds of discordant chiming, silence was restored as suddenly and abruptly as it had been broken. At the mention of each new topic, the conversation spluttered momentarily into life then guttered like a dying flare as Billy muttered short, cryptic, sometimes unintelligible replies. After one particularly long silence, Tony's mother said, "I expect you boys have got a lot to talk about, so I'll leave you and get some tea."

With the exit of Mrs Reeves, the conversation got some sort of second wind. They discussed Cologne and Billy, sitting hunched on the edge of the chair, told Douglas about the fighters he had shot down.

"I can sense those fighters, but the damned things just won't come. I reckon they're avoiding me. I shot down three that night. You've got a sight graticule; it glows dull red. That's what tells you how far off they are. When they fill the graticule, that's 400 yards. You can fire then, but I wait. Course, it's not easy. Some of them, some of the blokes, fall asleep I reckon. I don't, I'm like a 'awk. Got three that night. Nobody believes me, but I got 'em. I reckon there were more, but they didn't dare come in. Now they know who I am. They saw the letters of the aircraft, S MG. Now they're avoiding us."

Tony was sceptical. Billy saw his comrade shake his head.

"Don't look like that. Look, we lost eight kites in July. Something must be getting them. Nobody's been around as long as we have. Well, how do you explain it?"

Tony couldn't explain it and didn't get the chance to try. Tea was ready.

Tea was a sumptuous affair. Mrs Reeves must have emptied the larder of everything she had been stockpiling. Pride of place went to a huge pile of small triangular salmon sandwiches with the crusts cut away. Mrs Reeves confided, like someone bursting to share a secret, that she was going to make a bread pudding the next day.

They ate their tea. Billy attacked the plate of salmon sandwiches like a man who hadn't seen food in years. As the pile diminished, he started to thaw. He smiled several times at Mrs Reeves who said, "You've a good appetite, Billy. I like a man I can feed."

Douglas said, "More tea, Billy?"

"Ta. You get starved in that turret. It's cold, cramped too. You feel like one o' these salmon. We baled out yesterday. I left a boot in the turret."

The faces of Tony's parents clouded over with concern. The threat of sudden violent death had encroached upon the suburban gentility of the large living-room.

Douglas said, "Tony mentioned it on the phone. You collided with a Wellington, I believe. Terrible! When he phoned, you'd just seen the MO."

"He was hopeless! I showed him my foot. I'd walked about ten miles on it, and he said - nothing I can do about that. There are some goons in the RAF. I wanted that boot back. It's in the rear turret, so all they got to do is pull it out and then mail it to Oakington. We haven't got time for that - he said. It's a good boot. I'd worn it in. I mean, that boot meant something to me. Him, he didn't give a damn. You risk your neck, right, and they can't do a simple thing like looking for a boot. Makes you sick! No wonder we're losing the war!"

Later the two boys went out. Billy dumped his kitbag and had a quick swill. In his tunic, he was spruce and debonair. They only had a week; there was no time to waste. The dog was scenting the rabbit.

Tony's parents stood at the door rather in the same manner as they had done when Tony and Billy arrived. They stood under the portico, waving. Their son and his comrade might have been embarking on the first stage of a journey to the Antipodes.

2

The two young airmen proceeded down to Notting Hill where they boarded an eastbound bus. Sitting in the front seats on the upper deck, they looked in meditative silence at the handiwork of their German counterparts as the torn vistas of West London slid by. The bus jerked to a halt opposite a shattered side-street. There was a crater in the middle of the road and the windows on both sides were boarded up. It was peculiar, Tony thought, that while certain areas were unscathed, others looked as if they had suffered a minor earthquake. He leant across the aisle to Billy.

"Reckon Jerry bombs like we do, Bill; they see flak, or explosions, or most likely a fire, then bomb on that. A fire's a great aiming point at night," he reasoned dispassionately.

Billy nodded but said nothing.

After various detours, they arrived at Oxford Circus, alighted opposite a gutted shoe shop and threaded their way through the ruins of Central London, Billy hobbling and loping, Tony taking enormous measured strides. They stopped at a barrier. Beyond was a deserted, blackened street. A sandwich-board with a police notice stood uncompromisingly in the middle of the road just in front of the barrier. They turned and made another detour. At the end of the next street sandbags were piled high outside the entrance to an air-raid shelter. Around another corner a notice board was attached to wooden supports outside some official building. There were the usual exhortations including an RAF poster. 'You must not let this opportunity pass – Join the RAF!' Billy stopped in his tracks and howled, "Join the RAF for a quick death."

Tony wasn't amused.

They walked on along depeopled streets. Once, on seeing a gaping hole on the other side of the street, Billy said, "I don't know if the place still exists."

There were more detours then Billy stopped abruptly halfway down an unscarred street, gave a whoop of triumph and heaved open an ill-fitting door. In a stride, the two Sergeants had left a twilight world of devastation for a smoky, shadowy, dimly-lit underworld where shady figures loitered at the bar or sat around in huddles walled in by black shutters. Tony followed Billy over the sawdust-strewn floor to the bar.

"Beer's all right here," he said and, as if to allay any misapprehensions Tony might have had, added, "We're going to have some fun tonight. I got friends here."

He clenched a fist and brought it up in an uppercut. The barman was a swarthy individual with a broken nose and two cauliflower ears. He came along the bar and Billy ordered. Tony understood nothing.

They went over to a bench which ran along the wall and sat down. Tony drank deeply from the glass.

"You were right. The beer's fantastic." He smiled, for the first and last time that night.

Presently, Billy motioned to two girls to come over. They loomed out of a thick fog, coarse, giggly and painted and placed themselves between the two airmen.

The one next to Tony had short dark hair, a large mouth and was wearing a short white cotton frock which hung loosely about her thin angular body.

"I'll have a gin and orange, ducky." She addressed him with a familiarity that belied her years. "They got plenty o' gin 'ere." She dug him in the ribs and shrieked coarsely like a witch in a Grimm's fairy-tale.

Tony swallowed and turned his head. Billy had already put his arm round his girl and seemed to be in the act of boring his nose into her ear. Tony rose and went up to the bar with a heavy reluctance.

"Ta." She snatched the drink from him, took a huge gulp and banged the glass down on the table, half-empty. "I needed that. Go' a fag? I'm aht at the moment."

Tony fished up a packet of cigarettes from his pocket.

"Oh ta." She lit the cigarette, exhaled a cloud of blue smoke and laughed again, uncouthly. "Fags and booze, wot keeps me goin'. Yuh need somink while this war's on, donyuh? Keeps my figure down too." She patted the hollow where her stomach should have been and prattled on, cackling like a hen. "You'ra sergeant then. Known alotta sergeants I 'ave."

Tony grunted affirmatively. Discomfort rose in him like nausea. He lit another cigarette and cast an eye around the room. Billy was explaining to his girl how he'd shot down the fighters. He could do that being a gunner. Priming exactor throttles or logging fuel consumption was hardly the meat and drink of passionate conversation. Through the haze he perceived several khaki uniforms.

The door jerked open and a shaft of light momentarily vanquished the shadows as two sailors entered looking as though they knew exactly what they wanted. The girl chattered on, oblivious of Tony's reticence.

"Mosta me friends prefer silors. Don't mind meself, as long as the persn's nice. Wos yer nime?"

"Tony."

"Mine's Priscilla. I'm nineteen years old, gotta bruffer and a sister. Me bruffer's eleven. 'e's an evacuee, in the country. Likes it, 'e does. I work in industry, munitions. Bin there for a year." Priscilla chattered on in short sentences, giving information about herself. She might have been answering a questionnaire. "Course, we're not s'posed to talk abaht it." She moved her head closer and Tony recoiled as her carious breath tinged with alcohol wafted over his face. "We work undergrahnd. Good money, it is. Two bob an hour. Wot you get?"

"Not much for the job we're doing," Tony said sourly.

"Yuh don't 'ave t' tell me. It's all the sime t' me. Just trying t' be pleasant." Priscilla stubbed out her cigarette and lapsed into a sullen silence.

"Want another drink?"

"Oh, ta. Sime agine." The girl recovered some of her perkiness.

"What you having, Bill?"

Billy unwound himself from his partner. "Same again, Tony."

When Tony returned, Priscilla was examining her face in a hand mirror. "I got a spot comin' on me nose. Wanna look?"

"Not particularly."

"Why d'yer fink people get spots?"

Tony shrugged. He was wondering what time they'd get home.

"Don't talk much, do yuh?

"No."

"Perhaps yer a man of action." She nudged him and gave another coarse laugh.

Later, the two men went out to the gents: cracked, stained porcelain and a malfunctioning cistern. Standing at the urinal, Tony heard the clank of a coin followed by a metallic bang. Billy came to the next basin.

"Packet of three," Billy said, adding cryptically, "You never know." He opened a sachet and slipped a smooth packet into Tony's hand. "We're going somewhere else," he said.

They left the stench of urine for the fug of the bar. The girls rose. Priscilla said with a shrill giggle. "We're goin' somewhere first; you never know."

They trotted out through a door marked ladies and Tony wondered what it was that nobody seemed to know.

3

The room where Tony and Priscilla found themselves was almost entirely taken up by a shamelessly large double bed which sagged in the middle like a hammock.

The only other pieces of furniture were a wardrobe and a washstand with a chipped ewer and a cracked bowl. Black-out shutters were propped up against the foot of the iron bedstead. A layer of plaster-dust covered everything except the bed. The girl pulled back the bedclothes, revealing a well-worn, yellow-stained bed-sheet.

"Wi yer unzip me?"

Tony reached out and without moving his feet, unzipped her. He was standing between the blackout shutters and the window. Outside, the skyline of the city was darkening against the red glow of the evening sky. He hadn't the vaguest idea of where he was; the confusing geography of a shattered city, the gathering gloom and the incessant prattle of the two girls had thwarted his attempts at orientation. At first he had tried to keep track as they had turned corners, but the innumerable detours and the air-raid shelter signs with their arrows had given him the impression of going round in circles. At last, when even the arrows had disappeared, the feeling had been unmistakable that the four of them were nowhere at all.

Eventually they had stopped at a large house, not unlike Tony's own home. Billy's girl had pressed a button and a bell had jangled somewhere in the back of the house. The door had been opened by a dishevelled individual wearing carpet slippers, shapeless corduroy trousers and a threadbare jacket. There were long black hairs hanging from his nostrils. Billy had given him some money and all four of them had clattered up the carpetless stairs and creaked along the landing to the rooms they occupied at that moment.

"In't yuh gonna git undressed then?" Priscilla, looking angular and anaemic, was standing naked except for a pair of frilly panties. Her sallow, translucent skin was criss-crossed with thin blue veins.

"Yuh look as if yer rooted to the spot. Yuh can move abaht if yuh wanna." The girl stretched out her arms and her small, pear-shaped breasts shivered imperceptibly.

The ensuing silence was suddenly broken by the faint twang of bedsprings from the other side of the wall. Billy was getting his meat in. In a nearby street a car horn sounded. To Tony it came from a great distance, across a world he had once belonged to, but which, because of circumstances apparently beyond his control, he had been forced to forsake. In the gathering gloom the girl was undeterred.

"We'll 'ave a cuppa in a minute." She pointed to the dark shape of the gas ring by the boarded up fireplace. Tony sank down on to the bed.

"I wouldn't mind one now," he said weakly.

"I don't mind tea after, but not instead."

Tony looked up at the ghastly, skeletal female standing before him. He thought of the mess orderlies at Oakington. They were real ladies. They wouldn't be seen dead in a place like this. The twanging from the adjoining room became more frantic. Priscilla heard it too.

"Your mate's a caution, in' 'e? When we left the pub, 'e said 'e oughta bin on submarines. Up periscope! Gawd Almighty! Up periscope! Sounds as though 'is periscope's up all right, eh?" She flopped down beside him on the bed. "Where's your periscope then?" She thrust a hand between Tony's legs.

Tony jumped and the French letter fell to the floor. Priscilla's loud, silly laugh filled the shabby bedroom. That did it! He was getting out! He pushed the girl to one side, rose and rushed out without looking back.

4

"I couldn't do it, Bill. She looked like a consumptive."

"What d' expect for half a bar, Veronica Lake? The rooms cost money too – quid each."

"Wasn't bloody worth it."

"You're bloody telling me."

The discussion continued as they walked along empty streets. The cool evening had lain the dust of the warm day. Night had fallen. The wail of the first siren was impending.

"We'll have to go somewhere else," Billy said.

To Tony, the news came like a blow in the stomach. Somewhere else! Only last night they'd baled out of an aircraft. They could easily have been killed. Just then he wanted to lose Billy, forget he ever existed; but he couldn't. He was committed to Billy for a whole week. Like a mariner adrift in a boiling sea, he'd no choice but to hang on and hope. He looked obliquely at his comrade. Billy's face was dark and sullen. He couldn't go home with him like this. He had to protect his parents, come what may. His mum had worked hard for that tea and was planning things for the coming week. In desperation he tried to talk. Perhaps words, well chosen, could mellow Billy.

"Look, Bill, I don't think your idea was a bad one, getting a couple of girls. They weren't unattractive, I suppose, but mine was so bloody conceited. Do you know, she earns more money than we do?"

Tony's words only partially achieved their desired effect. Billy's sullenness gave way to anger. He stopped in his tracks. "Well, that's what I've always bloody said. We're the only people not getting anything from this war; except for a sore arse and a quick death."

Billy started walking again with heavy, lop-sided steps. Tony followed. An air-raid warden looked askance at them: two blue serge figures hurrying through a shadowy landscape of rubble and gutted buildings. They turned a corner into an unravaged street. Halfway along it, a group of people stood blocking the pavement. From a half-open door a shaft of matt orange light penetrated the gloom outside. A taxi winged in from nowhere and a woman wearing a long dress tried to shove a man in a dinner-jacket into it.

The man was protesting in a slobbering voice, "I've never been so insulted in my life."

The woman said, "You have, but you were too bloody drunk to remember anything about it."

Billy, unmindful of the scene on the pavement, said, "Let's go in here."

He was following his hunter's instinct which led beyond the half-open door. Before Tony had had time to protest, he found himself on the other side of the door. As it slammed shut, the first siren started to wail.

"Oh, we've got the Air Force here tonight, have we?" The voice came from a heavily made up woman sitting behind a table. Her dress might have been bought in a jumble sale. She was smoking a cigarette in a holder.

Billy reached for his wallet like a man unwilling to take no for an answer.

"That's right. We're both Air Vice-Marshals. What's the damage?"

"Oh really! We are honoured! Ten shillings each, please. You buy your drinks at the tables."

Billy threw down two ten-shilling notes. The evening was proving expensive. A thick-set man with a mop of dark hair and a dark jowl caught Billy's eye. He was standing behind the painted woman. He stared at Billy and Billy stared back. Dark Jowl turned his head first and Billy proceeded triumphantly down a flight of stairs into the well of the building.

Dark Jowl bent over the painted woman. "You shouldn't have let them in. The Boss don't like uniforms."

"Likes money though, doesn't he? Anyway, I thought they looked smart enough. Blond one was a real good looker. Looked as if he could handle himself too."

"We'll see about that. I'm getting help."

At the foot of the stairs, Tony looked out over the crowded dance-floor, a mottled sea of evening dresses and dinner-jackets.

"I don't think this is our type of place, Bill."

"They let us in, didn't they?"

"I didn't like the look of that bouncer either."

"Don't worry. Every able-bodied man's in the Forces. He's probably got a wooden leg."

As they stood there, a waiter walked past. He held a silver tray on which there was a pile of banknotes. They caught Billy's eye. He grabbed one and held it up like a child examining a strange object.

"Ten quid," he whistled under his breath.

The waiter was a small man dressed in tails. He had the air of an arrogant penguin. He clearly did not associate Billy with the class of clientele he was used to serving. He snatched back the note. Billy snarled, "We wanna drink."

"If you sit down, you'll be served," he snapped.

At the top of the stairs, Dark Jowl surveyed the scene. He clenched the banister rail and his knuckles whitened. By his side stood a man even bigger and uglier than he was; a cross between Boris Karloff and King Kong.

Billy sat down heavily and the basket chair groaned in protest. Tony looked round uneasily at the well-coiffured, opulent society among which fate had cast them. The nearest thing to a serviceman in this place was the band, dressed in military uniforms with red sashes around their waists. They were putting down their saxophones for the interval.

"Well, what's it to be?" The waiter stood before them. Confronted with an unpleasant task, he wanted to get it over with as quickly as possible.

Billy boiled with indignation. "We'll have a couple of pints, and don't speak like that to me, I don't like it."

Tony whispered. "Take it easy, Bill. This doesn't look like the sort of place where you buy pints." His eyes scanned the tables: ice buckets, soda-water siphons and small glasses.

The waiter returned. He banged down two glasses. "Two halves. That'll be ten shillings."

"A dollar a piece! Daylight fucking robbery! That's more than we earn in a day." Billy's voice rose above the murmur.

Blood rushed to Tony's face as heads turned. All day he had felt like a canoeist navigating fierce rapids, but the current was getting stronger and he was getting weaker.

The lady at the adjacent table stared at Billy. She was pale with blonde hair and thick arms. She wore a white evening dress in some shiny material. Billy saw her.

"What are you staring at? There's nothing wrong with this uniform."

The gentleman at the table replied. He was sleek, well-groomed and was dressed in a dinner-jacket. The two of them might have just stepped down from the top of a wedding-cake.

"I don't think it's the uniform the lady objects to as much as the language of the person in it."

The haughty, sententious voice placed the two airmen at the edge of a cataract. At any moment they would plunge helplessly over into a foaming abyss.

Dark Jowl had released his grip on the banister and was coming down the stairs with slow, measured steps. He was followed by King Kong. The two men's eyes never left Billy.

"I hadn't opened my mouth at first before that bastard started looking down his nose at me." Billy waved an agitated arm in the direction of the waiter. He took a step and snatched a note from the waiter's tray. "I looked at this because most of the people I know are dead and gone before they've even earnt ten quid. I'm wondering where the 'ell this sort of money comes from."

By this time every eye in the place was on Billy. He was swearing and gesticulating wildly. People craned their necks, others rose. The two bouncers had reached the bottom of the stairs. They looked like men about to indulge themselves.

Unabashed, the wedding-cake figure started up again, his tone only slightly mollified. "I just think you might mind your language when there are ladies present."

"Nobody tells me to mind my language when I'm over Germany in the middle of the night."

Tony wanted to crawl away and die. "Billy, for God's sake let's get out of here before it's too late. These people aren't like us."

But Tony's last despairing effort was already too late. The first bouncer was a step away from Billy. They had tipped over and were falling helplessly into oblivion. Dark Jowl took a pace forward and grabbed Billy by the scruff of the neck.

Tony raised a reproving finger and opened his mouth to protest. There was no need. Rage had given the squat, powerful rear gunner a lunatic's strength. Ducking and twisting his body, he tore himself free and from the crouch he found himself in, drove his left fist into his adversary's midriff. Dark Jowl wheezed and dropped his guard. Straightening his body, Billy smashed his right fist into the man's lower mandible. The bouncer crashed across the nearest table.

A shock wave of screaming, tottering women, tinkling glass and overturned chairs seemed to spread from the devastation at Billy's feet. It was then that King Kong moved in.

Tony shouted, "Hey! Two on to one is definitely not fair."

He took a step forward but found himself flying backwards. When his world had stopped moving, he looked up. Billy was boring in with combinations of short punches pounding King Kong to the body and head. He was raving and bellowing like a madman. Pandemonium had broken out. The guests were screaming and wailing, moving in a tidal wave towards the stairs. King Kong fell as Tony rose giddily to his feet. Billy aimed a wild kick at Dark Jowl who was endeavouring to get to his feet, then he picked up a siphon.

It was then that Tony's recollection of events became confused. He heard a muffled roar but couldn't place its source. A crack appeared in the ceiling, lengthened and branched out. A soda-water siphon crashed into the shelves behind the bar, but the tinkle of glass and Billy's howl of triumph were drowned as an enormous piece of plaster detached itself from the ceiling and crashed to the floor followed by a chandelier. As Billy dispatched another siphon towards the bar with another yell of unfettered rage, two policemen arrived at the head of the stairs. In the street people were pouring in panic from the club and an ambulance, a police-car and two fire-engines had arrived.

5

Tony Reeves sipped at his hot tea. From where he sat, through a doorway, he could see a gap between the houses opposite. It was difficult to say what had been there before. The debris had been cleared. He looked at the boards on either side of the door. The blast must have destroyed the windows of the small café. The top floor was missing too, and a shaft of light penetrated the murk through a hole in the ceiling. Tony glanced over the passage to the counter. His own dark, harassed reflection in the cracked glass of the display case stared back at him. He put his hand up to his chin and felt the stubble on his face. He looked down at his uniform; it was covered with a fine grey dust and a button was missing from his tunic. The woman behind the counter eyed him with suspicion through the display-case: an unshaven, unkempt serviceman cut an incongruous figure. Tony felt something akin to gratitude for her attention. She represented respectability, the world of his guv'nor and mum, the world he belonged to, which he had temporarily abandoned during the course of twelve chaotic hours. The woman behind the counter turned her head away, perhaps in disgust.

Tony had been released from detention just before dawn. He fancied he still smelt of disinfectant. Civil charges were to be levelled against Billy after which he was to be handed over to the military authorities.

In the police car, Billy had sat grim and unsmiling, his left hand nursing his swollen right fist, to all intents and purposes having worked off his anger. At the police station, however, the situation had been only marginally better than at the club and might have been considerably worse but for the timely intervention of Tony and the two police officers. The Duty Sergeant had foolishly admonished Billy for his behaviour, invoking as an argument the stripes on Billy's sleeve. Billy had reached out and grabbed the Sergeant by the lapels dragging him half over the desk.

"Don't tell me what these stripes are for, I bloody earnt them. How d' you get yours – arse crawling?"

The cells had been full of the usual collection of drunks and itinerants who moaned and groaned as Billy continued spitting venom in the cell block.

"Shut yer blinkin' row."

"Can't yuh let a body sleep?"

The cell door clanked shut. Tony collapsed thankfully on to a bunk. Billy raised Cain.

"D'you know what gets on my wick? D'you wanna know?" Billy was bent over Tony. He eyes were wild and staring. There was a swelling over his right eye, his tie was askew and his collar button was missing.

"No, tell me," Tony said in a tone of voice from which hope was all but gone.

"Us getting the chop and that fucking waiter still being alive. That's what. Look, if those bastards in that place've got so much money, they can go and fight."

"What do you expect? That's the way it is. Lots of people have been bombed out, lost their homes, belongings. Christ, there are people getting killed crossing the road in the blackout."

"What about those bastards tonight? There was more money on that tray than we'd see in a year, if we lived a year. We're in the wrong racket. Where the 'ell do they get it?"

Tony shrugged. "Rich parents," he suggested. "Anyway, perhaps we'll survive."

"Some fuckin' hope. Although with my kind of luck I'll probably just get crippled for life." Billy, who had begun pacing back and forth again, like a wild man, stopped suddenly and stuck his face into Tony's. "I'll tell you one thing, if I survive this war, there's going to be a fucking revolution in this country and I'm going to lead it."

"Good luck."

Billy fell back on the other bunk, exhausted. Tony lay face down on his, his arms covering his face. His hands were shaking. His heart had been thumping for the past hour. For the first time since childhood, he wanted to cry. The word nightmare wasn't strong enough for what he had been through that evening. That slut of a girl, that club, that pig of a waiter and now this, a prison cell. This was worse than those overshoots. Nobody he had met since leaving home would pass muster in society he called decent. That waiter ought to be taken to Germany and kicked out over the target; it would serve the bastard right. Billy was right, things were unjust, but what could one do? Going to war against everybody led you nowhere. Just over twenty-four hours ago they had been listening to the Wingco telling them how necessary it was to get some rest. This was the first day of their leave and now this had happened. How could they possibly hope to survive? And what about his parents? They'd be wondering where he and Billy had got to. They might well be waiting up. Christ, what a mess! Heavy breathing reached Tony's ears. Billy had fallen asleep. In about ten minutes he'd probably start shooting down fighters in his dreams. Perhaps, Tony reflected, in view of what had happened, that was only fair.

Tony screwed up his eyes as he moved from the claustral gloom of the café out into daylight. He viewed the shattered street. In a crumbling world, he felt himself crumbling. He put on his forage cap – it was a miracle he still had it – and started to walk along the street in a direction he hoped would take him home. He wondered what he would say to his parents.

CHAPTER TWO

1

When Arthur woke that July Sunday, the soft sunlight of early morning was penetrating the small window high up in the bedroom wall, gilding a patch of wallpaper above his head. Eve, on whom the strident call of the cockerel had passed unnoticed, slept on unaware that seven days' grace was drawing to a close. As Arthur lay by her side, he was reminded of how time had passed. The night they had spent together after he had baled out, the collection of the pass from the orderly room, the train journey and the thought of the seven wonderful days to come. He had celebrated his twenty-sixth birthday, possibly his last. Tomorrow at eight, the deadline expired, the Stirlings would be waiting and the battle for survival would recommence.

From the scullery came the sound of water gurgling, an enamel bowl scraping against a stone sink, a latch being lifted. Through the half-open window, Arthur heard the crunch of footsteps on the gravel outside. Eve's father was going to feed the chickens. A door opened just across the landing. There came the sound of slow measured footsteps. Eve's mother was picking her way down the precipitous winding staircase. Eve's movements told Arthur she too was waking.

"I'll get you some warm water to shave with in a minute," she said in a muffled, sleepy voice.

Arthur kissed the tousled mop of hair visible where the bedclothes ended. "There's no hurry. I could lie here all day."

There was a flurry of movement and Arthur found Eve on top of him, fully awake. "Lazy monkey. You can't lie here all day; it's church for you, my lad; eleven o'clock. We're all going. Mum's orders."

"What does Pa say to that?"

"He doesn't mind really. It gives him a chance to go into the pub on the way home."

Arthur rose and went to the window. He placed his forearms on the sill, rested his chin on his fists and looked out over the garden and the field of gently surging wheat beyond. A thin column of smoke rising from the far end of the garden told Arthur that Pa was making good use of the cover which the hen house afforded him. He turned to Eve who was sitting on the edge of the bed. "We'd better get cracking. Pa's stolen a march on me. He's already smoking his first pipe."

"He's got to pluck a chicken for dinner. I'll get you some hot water." Eve took down her dressing-gown from behind the door, hurried into it and skipped out of the room and down the stairs to the scullery.

Twenty minutes later, Arthur was sidling down the garden path towards the hen run. A thin, wiry figure in a soft felt hat, waistcoat, collarless shirt and dungarees was plucking a white fowl. At the sound of footsteps he looked up, smiled through uneven, nicotine-stained teeth and held up the chicken by its legs like a trophy of war. It's neck hung limply and though its eyes were open, it saw nothing. Arthur shuddered and forced his gaze down to the white feathers which covered the mud of the hen-run like a carpet of snow.

"You stole a march on me, Pa. You got in your first pipe before me today."

"Lots to do today, Arthur; church, whole family." He increased his speed and the cloud of descending feathers thickened as the body of the Sussex white was progressively laid bare. "Going back tonight, then?"

Arthur sucked at his brier and nodded with gravity.

"Been nice having you both, Arthur. Enjoyed every minute we have."

"Been nice staying, Pa."

When the chicken had been plucked and drawn, they took a pipe together, in silence, sucking on their briers, drawing in each breath with studious care. When they got back to the house, breakfast was ready.

After breakfast they all helped with the preparatives for lunch. Pa dug potatoes and cut a spring cabbage; Arthur helped Eve pick peas and Ma got the chicken ready for the oven. Afterwards Mother, who was captain of the ship - nautical terms were in vogue since their youngest son had joined the Navy - ordered Arthur and Father to the galley. The two men sat happily in the sun-drenched yard, Arthur shelling peas in a colander while Pa spud-bashed.

They changed for church. Arthur put on his tie and tunic; Eve a summer frock and cardigan. Ma wore a floppy hat and an almost ankle-length cotton dress with a pattern of enormous flowers. Pa, despite the increasing warmth of the morning, chose his normal attire: a well-worn dark suit, thick waistcoat, starched collar and trilby. Mother put the chicken in the oven and they set off.

Bankside, the rough-cast, semi-detached house where Eve's parents lived, was situated at the entrance to the village of Codicote where the road from Welwyn suddenly steepened. A massive oak stood like a sentinel at the corner of the front garden by the small gate. Steps led down the grassy bank to the pavement.

The four of them moved up the Great North Road which formed the village high street. Arthur and Eve strolled hand in hand several yards behind the old couple. Arthur's professional gaze quartered the village street: a straggle of terrace-houses built at the end of the last century; in the gardens, roses bloomed and clusters of ox-eye daisies and global thistle stood waist high. Nothing moved. The dominical tranquillity of the village belied the turmoil of the world outside.

Presently, the gardens gave way to shops, the post office, the village hall, a transport café and five pubs which Ma claimed were five too many. They passed the first pub. A large sign, an enormous brass bell, hung high above the pavement. Ma looked up and scowled. After passing the fifth pub – a fifth scowl from Ma – they took a right turn, following a footpath through the fields which led out on to the road to Knebworth. St Giles's church lay a short way along this road, beyond a low wall of grey flint and mortar. They entered the churchyard through a lych-gate.

Whilst harbouring few, if any, anti-clerical sentiments, Arthur had never been a regular churchgoer. For him a church service was essentially a round of standing, sitting and kneeling of which he much preferred standing. Eve, however, if not completely conversant with liturgical praxis, was at least capable of anticipating the main lines of the service and Arthur willingly let himself be led. They followed the Epistle and the Gospel in the prayer-book and as their eyes moved along each line an acoustic distortion of the text reached their ears from across a wasteland of pews and flagstones. From time to time he stole glances at Eve's parents. Ma's features were set hard, as if she had heard it all before and had merely come to check that the Vicar was doing his clerical duty. Pa's expression was indeterminate, but Arthur was inclined to believe that spending a sunny Sunday morning walled in by stained-glass, stone walls and chilly flagstones and listening to largely irrelevant information was only done in the interests of conjugal harmony.

The few sermons Arthur had heard had been occasions to let his mind wander. Only intermittently did words or phrases penetrate his consciousness. That morning was to prove something of an exception. The Vicar had placed an apple on the edge of the pulpit. It caught Arthur's attention almost at once. He found himself listening.

"...the blossom is important, pleasing to the eye, to the touch, to the senses. Which one of us has not, at some time, stopped and looked at an apple tree in blossom, a delight to the eye, a joy to behold; one of the truest, most simple delights of nature, apple blossom. But, my dear Christian people," the Vicar raised a finger and let a warm, pastoral glance move from one side of the church to the other, "What are we waiting for?" He picked up the apple and held it up for inspection. "We are waiting for the fruit, my dear people, the fruit. Now, the question I put to you all today is, what is the fruit of our lives here on earth?"

Arthur glanced surreptitiously from side to side. Ma had the same inscrutable look; Eve was listening intently, her hands clasped in supplication; Pa was eyeing the apple.

"The fruit of our life here on earth is the life of the spirit, the life hereafter. Our life on earth, with its trials and tribulations, sorrows and joys, is our preparation for the life of the spirit. In doing God's will, obeying his commandments, in the accomplishment of the daily round, the common task..."

At that point Arthur wanted to raise a hand. What happens to the fruit if the blossom gets destroyed – by night frost, for example? It was then that Arthur parted company with the Vicar's train of thought. He found himself thinking of frosty nights, flak and cannon shell, the will of God and the Armageddon that he and the RAF had unleashed from the skies on to the city of Cologne. The sermon prompted more questions than it answered. How many frosty nights over hostile German cities were he and his crew supposed to endure and how many people would willingly forfeit forty years of life to jump the queue for the Kingdom of Heaven? His mind wandered back to the High Street that very morning and to Ma and Pa. He guessed they were both a bit over sixty. Ma had given birth to eight fine children; they'd worked hard; had no more than the simplest of life's pleasures. He would have given anything to wander the same path with Eve, but there was always the war to cast a black, shadowy question mark over one's longevity. It was the war, Arthur felt, that turned the Vicar's sermon into something in brackets, not strictly applicable to the real world.

The Vicar continued on his pastoral theme, digressing to talk of the flowers of the field, Solomon in all his glory, and briefly on the ephemeral nature of all existence. He seemed to be making frequent reference to the flowers decorating the church, but by this time Arthur had completely lost the thread of the Vicar's reasoning.

After the service, the congregation filed out in twos and threes. Arthur said, when the four of them were halfway to the lych-gate, "Well, the only thing I understood about that was the collection."

Mother scowled and Eve gave him a look of stern reproval. When they got out on to the road, the two women went on to prepare dinner. The two men were walking casually down the road when Pa stopped by a stile.

"We'll go this way, Arthur." They climbed into a field. "Follow me, Arthur."

Arthur wondered what was going to happen.

The old man walked along the edge of the field for about twenty yards, then stopped. There was a small hole in the hedge between a hazel thicket and a hawthorn bush. Pa went down on all fours and put his head and shoulders into the hole. He emerged with something dark and shiny. Arthur grinned; at last something made sense.

"You're a fly one, Pa, but you'll need a bottle opener."

The old man put his hand into his jacket pocket. "Here you are. There's one for you too, Arthur."

Arthur got down and rummaged in the undergrowth until he felt something cold and hard. He rose. "That's the stuff to give the troops, Pa. Brown ale; cold too."

"Mother Nature, Arthur; keeps things cool."

They sat down in the long grass. Arthur opened his bottle, Pa took out his pipe and tobacco-pouch. "I promised Mother I wouldn't go into the pub and a promise is a promise."

"You're right there, Pa."

"Mother's a good Christian woman. Reads the Bible on Sunday afternoons."

Arthur had taken out his pipe and was filling it. "What about you, Pa?"

"I likes me beer and me baccy, Arthur."

"What did you think of the sermon, Pa?"

Pa drew on his pipe. "Don't remember much about it. Fine apple, though."

Arthur took a swig of ale and smiled.

They lapsed into one of those silences which are born when words are superfluous. They sat in the short tufted grass by the hedgerow alternately swigging ale and puffing at their pipes. The weather had been glorious for the past month and that day was another beautiful day in a summer which never tired. Everywhere the ripening corn danced as the gentlest of breezes sent ripples through the fields of wheat and barley. In the hedgerows, insects buzzed and hummed, darting between the last lingering petals of the dog roses, hovering before the clouds of blackberry blossom: the fruits of this life. Arthur took another swig. Cool velvet ran down his throat. He said with a certain wistfulness, "It's great to be alive, Pa."

Pa said, "You're right there, Arthur; it certainly is."

2

When the two men arrived back at Bankside, dinner was on the table in the small dining-room adjacent to the scullery. The chicken, roasted and golden, had been placed in the centre of the table. It was flanked by steaming bowls of vegetables and golden brown roast potatoes. Mother came in with parsley stuffing and bread sauce.

"I wanted to carve the chicken, but Father wasn't here." There was a note of reproach in her voice. She disappeared into the larder to reappear seconds later with two bottles of brown ale. "I hope you didn't leave those other bottles where they could do any harm, Father."

Arthur was taken aback. "Walls have ears, Pa!" he said with a laugh.

Pa, carving knife and fork in hand, looked unperturbed. "Mother is as sharp as a ferret, cunning as a fox and as wise as an owl, a wonderful woman."

He carved immaculate slices of chicken. Ma said grace, then they helped themselves to roast potatoes, vegetables, stuffing and bread sauce.

The meal was delicious. Globules of fat floated on the surface of the thick, rich gravy, the spring cabbage melted in the mouth, the peas were sweet and the roast potatoes, steeped in the essence of the chicken, had fluffy white interiors. They ate with a care bordering on reverence. Arthur couldn't remember having eaten anything better and suggested a toast to the womenfolk. Pa said that Mother was the finest cook that had ever breathed and that there wasn't anything worth cooking that Mother couldn't cook. Eve would follow in Mother's footsteps. They raised their glasses, Arthur gave Eve a peck on the cheek and prayed inwardly that he would be around to taste the fruits of her labours.

After dinner, the intention had been to go straight down to the Buckingham's but Eve took her box camera from her bag. She said, "We've got time for a photo. I've got one picture left."

The previous day, standing around the oak, they had taken seven snaps. Mother had come out in response to a call from Eve and taken two pictures of Eve and Arthur together in each other's arms, leaning against the massive trunk. That day they took the last photo.

Mother held the camera – Father thought she was becoming a very proficient photographer – and Eve, Arthur and Pa stood on the other side of the small lily pond, so that Mother had the afternoon sun at her back. When Arthur had carried out their case and bags to the car, it was time to say goodbye.

Eve embraced her mother and father. Her eyes moistened. She knew what she was going back to. Arthur kissed Ma and then took Pa's bony right hand in his, feeling Pa's enormous strength as he playfully tried to outgrip his father-in-law. Arthur knew as he squeezed the old man's callused hand that the odds were against him squeezing it again, but Flight Sergeant Arthur Johnson was a brave man. He turned to Ma.

"Now look, Ma. That chair in the dining-room; you keep it warm for the next time I'm home. I'll be back – don't forget."

He kissed Ma a second time, raising a finger of mock admonishment, lest she forgot.

Mother was close to tears. "I'll keep it warm, Arthur, don't worry. God bless you, dear."

"And the next time you're in church say one for me."

Arthur and Eve were at the gate. Arthur was well aware that he might be stepping out into oblivion. Next to resolute, fear-conquering optimism, humour was probably his best weapon.

"You'd better say one for Pa too!"

Ma said, "I'll say one for both of you, God bless!"

Pa said, "It's been wonderful having you. We'll keep our fingers crossed."

Arthur and Eve were walking down the steps. "Do that, Pa," Arthur shouted.

Ma and Pa stood under the boughs of the great oak, their arms raised as their youngest daughter and son-in-law drove off through the empty village slumbering in the heat of early afternoon.

3

When the young couple arrived at Codicote Mill, they found Olive pottering about on her rockery. Freddie was over at the Mill baking a cake. Olive came down the steps to the courtyard and gave them chapter and verse on Freddie's culinary misery. Baking was the bane of Freddie's life – a thorn in his flesh, another cross for Olive to bear. The problem had its roots partially in the war – what problem didn't? – a household of twelve each of whom had to contribute a twelfth of each ingredient from the supply made available by ration coupons, and partially in the principals of equality and justice adhered to rigidly by each member of the household. On hearing of Freddie's plight, Arthur lost no time in going over to the Mill, not actually to work, but to act in a supervisory capacity and to give his best friend what moral support he could.

The twin doors to the kitchen would have enhanced the decor of a conservatory. Arthur peered through the glass panels. He saw a battlefield. On the large table, kitchen scales and a large enamel bowl were beleaguered by an army of jars with screw-on lids. Eggshells, a beater, items of cutlery and crockery lay scattered like material discarded in the wake of a hasty retreat. The Aga, an enormous metal fortress, took up almost the entire wall opposite the door. Freddie was bent down in front of the oven doors. Arthur entered and was hit by a wall of heat. Freddie rose, beads of sweat on his forehead and turned. His face cracked into an enormous smile.

"Arthur!"

"Freddie Buck!"

The two men went into something between a clinch and an embrace, swinging one another round like wrestlers. They broke. Arthur surveyed the littered kitchen.

"Christ, Fred! What's happening? Panic on? Feeding the five thousand or something?"

Supervision was unnecessary. A sympathetic ear was all Freddie needed. Arthur listened to a tale of woe: rationing, mucking about, twelfth of everything - except the eggs - anthracite short, Aga playing up, garden overgrown, river infested with pike, place upside down, everybody complaining, flies, heat and his Nibs coming home tomorrow - that was why he was baking the cake. It was a bugger, a real bugger.

Arthur dusted flour off his uniform and shooed away a recalcitrant fly - the kitchen was full of them, as if corpses were putrefying somewhere.

"When are you going to be finished, Fred?" Arthur sounded concerned.

"I'm ready now, Arthur; just got to wait for the cake, clear up this mess. Half an hour, three quarters to be on the safe side."

Arthur suggested that he and Eve take a constitutional. They'd be back in forty-five minutes or so. Freddie agreed and set about bringing order to the kitchen, like a man who has triumphed over adversity.

Codicote Mill with its rough-cast facade and high gables straddled the area between the River Mimram and the first gravel terrace of the eastern slope of the valley. Years ago, the river had flowed under the house itself, driving a wheel, but now it was forced in a smooth green hump over the confines of a sluice. It broadened its course to babble in a graceful curve between the rose beds and the croquet lawn. Passing under a footbridge, it took a more leisurely allure under the sorrowful bows of weeping willows, rippling over shallows between patches of water weed, foaming around snags and leaving the property under a road bridge.

Eve and Arthur walked arm in arm over the sluice, following the river bank past the thatched roof of the summer house, through the kitchen garden and out to the northern end of Lord Marchington's twelve acres which consisted of fields of ragged, tussocky grass. In the haze of afternoon, puffs of off-white cumulous clouds had formed, in rows, like artillery smoke on a battlefield. A little further on, the languor of that afternoon overtook them and they headed for a solitary hawthorn tree not far from the river bank. Arthur lay back and looked at the patches of blue sky visible through the spindly branches. Eve sat by his side, brushing away the occasional fly and contemplating the river as it flowed sluggishly past. Beyond, within calling distance, was the narrow road to Kimpton where, as a young girl, she had cycled to catch the Luton bus. Further along, she could make out the red brick of the River Keeper's cottage. Olive and Freddie had lived there prior to moving over to the Mill at Codicote. She had always rung her bell when she had cycled past of a morning. In the evening, as often as not, she had stopped and chatted with her older sister. In those days the war had been but a black speck on a distant horizon. Four years ago; it seemed much more; so much had happened. Now there was fighting everywhere and each year it got worse.

The sight of a swan wandering near the water's edge broke her train of thought. It flopped into the water and glided serenely upstream. "Look, Arthur, a swan."

Arthur yawned. His eyes were closed. "If it's got wings, I don't want to know about it. I'm on leave."

"It's in the river now. I think they look more graceful in the water."

"They're like the Stirlings then: graceful in the air but difficult getting up and down." It was the first mention of the Stirlings that week. Not that it mattered. He would inevitably talk shop with Freddie anyway. He slipped his hand into Eve's. She took it and lifted it up to her face still watching the effortless progress of the swan upstream to the shadow of a stunted willow. Arthur's heavy breathing made her look down.

"You mustn't go to sleep. Freddie'll be finishing soon. We'd better be getting back."

Arthur groaned in mock protest.

"You know how he likes talking to you."

Arthur knew. He knew Freddie. Freddie was his best friend. Freddie Buckingham: Englishman, staunch, true, heart of oak, courage of a lion; special characteristic: weak heart. The doctor had told him that going up in an aircraft would be his death; the supreme irony. They rose stiffly and set off back. Eve looked around briefly for the swan but it was nowhere to be seen.

4

They met Freddie, Olive and Peter by the western gable. Seeing Arthur, Peter started jumping up and down. "Uncle Arthur, you said you'd jump over the stream; where we caught the sticklebacks."

His mother said, "Don't be silly, Peter, Uncle Arthur's got his best clothes on."

But Arthur was already crossing the bridge, slipping out of his tunic as he ran. "Come on then, Peter. It's do or die, Fred."

Freddie, galvanised into action, started to run. Eve gave a squeal of delight. The company moved over to the croquet lawn.

The stream where they had caught the sticklebacks had its source at another sluice, an overflow from the river. It rejoined the Mimram by the croquet lawn. It was just above this point that the two men intended to jump, from the lawn to a triangle of grass bounded on two sides by water.

Arthur, the athlete, jumped first. His run-up was perfect. He took off a foot from the edge of the water and landed neatly on the other side of the river. The jump was at least fifteen feet. Freddie's attempt was doomed as early as his fifth or sixth stride. His baggy trousers didn't help matters. They never stayed where he had hoisted them. He hesitated, tried to regain his jerky momentum and would have fallen headlong into the water if he hadn't taken off a yard from the water's edge. He landed a foot short of the far bank clouding the stagnant water. He emerged with a thin layer of river silt covering his trousers up to his knees. "Bugger it!" he said irascibly.

"Mum, Daddy's fallen in the water. He swore too."

"You silly man; now you're all dirty. You'll have to go home and change."

Freddie shook his head sourly.

"Never mind, Fred," Arthur consoled him. "It's in a good cause."

A heavy, sympathetic silence descended. Collectively sharing the burden of Freddie's chagrin, they wandered idly over to the far side of the lawn. It was bounded by a wooden fence and a hawthorn hedge. A copper beech grew at one corner of the lawn, at the other there was a gap. It was Peter who, poking his head through the gap, saw the old horse grazing peacefully in the field beyond but it was Arthur who suggested they try to catch it. Arthur just took off. Freddie, shoes squelching, laboured in pursuit.

The task proved to be more difficult than Arthur had envisaged. They made several sallies. There were screams and cheers as Arthur, tie trailing like a streamer, reached top speed over the uneven surface. Once, they almost succeeded. The horse appeared to be cornered, Freddie had cut off one path of retreat, but it turned suddenly, shaking its head and mane in a gesture of equine irascibility. Arthur lunged in desperation at the halter, missed as the animal shied away and fell headlong. The horse cantered some way then stopped. It looked blankly at the figure in the grass. Arthur looked up from behind a tussock. Freddie was gasping for breath not ten yards away. The whoops of delight from Eve and Peter died.

Arthur said, "We'll get him next time around, Fred."

Red faced, Arthur rose. He looked grim and determined. He walked over to Freddie. The two friends conferred and devised a new strategy.

They would keep the horse as near to the hedge as possible, advance slowly, arms outstretched and at a suitable distance they would accelerate; stealth and sudden speed. Arthur said that was how lions got their prey. The horse had gone back to grazing.

The plan worked sweetly; they advanced with guile. The horse looked up, a faint trace of suspicion in its large brown eyes. When Arthur was five yards off, it turned, tossing its head in annoyance, but Freddie, arms outstretched, moving to Arthur's left, blocked its line of retreat. It turned again, but Arthur made an anticipatory dash. It was now or never. The muscles on his face tautened, veins stood out on his neck. He accelerated, lunged and gripped the halter. The horse gathered speed, but Arthur was ready. Holding the halter tightly with both hands, he allowed the horse to take his weight and drag him some yards. It slowed to a canter and stopped in its tracks with a sullen shake of the head. Arthur mounted. The others came over; Freddie lifted his son on to the horse's back. It took a few steps but then refused to budge. Arthur lifted Peter down and dismounted himself. Arthur said that the animal was a bit long in the tooth. Freddie reckoned they'd run it into the ground. They left the horse to its own devices.

Back on the croquet lawn, Peter took Eve and Arthur by the hand. "Can we play hide-and-seek now, Uncle Arthur? Go on, Uncle Arthur, please," the boy implored. "You're good at that, Uncle Arthur. Please."

Arthur had no choice. "Okay, Master Peter, I'm game, but where are we going to hide?"

The answer came like a well-rehearsed line in a theatre play. "In the woods or in the gardens, but nowhere else."

If the croquet lawn was immaculate, then what Peter called the woods was a place of confusion. It lay on the northern edge of the lawn where the grass was long and apple trees with knotty, twisted trunks grew in profusion. Along the banks of the stickleback stream, weeping willows stood in a forlorn line, their lowest boughs sweeping the surface of the stagnant water. The gardens occupied the ground between the river and the stickleback stream. Peter, who was to seek, had taken up position at the trunk of the copper beech.

He shouted, "You mustn't go over the river; it's out of bounds. I'm going to count to a hundred, then I'm coming."

The four adults dispersed. Eve, tittering and giggling, slipped away to the south side of the croquet lawn. It was as undisciplined as the north side, but the absence of trees meant it afforded fewer hiding places. Arthur went in the opposite direction. He crossed the stream by a narrow wooden footbridge and came to an area of well-kept lawn criss-crossed by flagged paths and bounded on two sides by high privet hedges badly in need of cutting. He found a hole in a hedge just opposite a sun-dial. He crawled thankfully into it and sat and awaited developments. Presently, he heard the sound of squelchy footsteps. Freddie walked by in an exhausted trance.

"Fred! Over here. There's room for a little one."

"'ullo, Arthur!" Freddie squeezed his damp, muddy frame into the hole. The hedge tilted slightly and the leaves rustled. "Not getting you dirty, Arthur, am I?"

"Doesn't matter, Fred. I don't suppose I'll wear out these trousers anyway."

Freddie looked enquiringly at Arthur. His craggy features were marked with concern.

"We 'aven't seen you since you moved to Cambridge, Arthur. 'ow's it going?" He'd been waiting for this moment for months, but somehow this wasn't the way he imagined it would be.

"I'll never live through this bloody war, Fred."

"You don't think?"

Arthur shook his head sadly.

"How many trips you done?"

"Ten. Twenty to go."

"Well, that's not bad, ten trips. That's a third."

Freddie tried to find a glimmer of hope, however faint. Casualties were a fact of life in wartime, but that Arthur belonged to the ranks of the mortal was difficult for Freddie to accept. Arthur was the very epitome of manhood; an indestructible bundle of energy. The Germans couldn't get Arthur, for Freddie was as convinced of

Arthur's immortality as he was of his own. Yet he seemed so final, so definite. What on earth was happening?

Freddie swallowed. "So you don't think you're going to make it?"

"I don't see how it's possible, Fred."

"W-what's the trouble, then?"

"Losses, Fred. There's always someone missing after a raid, and if we go one op without casualties, we lose two on the next just to make up for it."

"Get shot down do they?"

"Nobody knows. They go up and never come back. Night fighters get some. Flak gets a lot of ours because we've got such a low operational ceiling."

"Have you been hit?"

Arthur nodded. "First trip. Cologne."

"We read about Cologne in the papers; bombs by the trainload." The headlines were engraved in Freddie's memory.

"Best place to find out about it, Fred."

"But that's what the Hun deserve, Arthur. Look what they've done to London. Even out here, they've 'ad a go at De Havilland's and the viaduct at Digswell."

Arthur shrugged. "It's still not much fun watching, Fred. Couple of kites were shot up while we were there. A Hampden copped a load of bombs falling from above. One minute they were there, the next they were gone. Poor devils! That's the way it happens."

Arthur shuddered visibly. Freddie adjusted his position. The privet almost keeled over like a foundering ship. Arthur paused and Freddie pondered over what he had heard. From the direction of the lawn they heard a whinny of delight from Eve: Peter's first success.

"What do you think's gonna 'appen then?"

"Things are going to get worse. This business of bombing cities is just starting. The key word is 'press on'." Arthur told Freddie about the streaming of bombers, the saturation formula, Oakington and the carousel of changing faces. "Sometimes I wake up at night and wonder what the world's coming to; that is, when I manage to fall asleep. I just hope this war's doing some good."

Freddie was now in a state of semi-shock. Arthur the extrovert, the bundle of energy, had never been so pessimistic. The Phoney War, during which Arthur had made frequent visits from the Luton training centre – he used to come over on that service bicycle with that bloody great saddle – seemed an age away.

"D'you think they can win?"

Arthur shrugged. "Not now, I don't think so. He made his first mistake when he invaded Russia. Now he's got the Americans to contend with too. Rumour has it that they'll start bombing soon."

There came the sound of footsteps on the bridge. Arthur recognised Eve's immediately. He heard her voice too. She was chattering happily to Peter.

"The question is, Fred: how many of us are going to die before Jerry's finally licked?"

"There they are! It's cheating to hide two in one place," Peter said pointing an accusing finger.

Freddie and Arthur tried to extricate themselves simultaneously from the hedge and almost succeeded in tearing it up by its roots. When they finally freed themselves, their hiding place looked like the scene of a traffic accident.

"Your Dad couldn't find anywhere else to hide so he crept in with me. There was enough room for both of us." Arthur looked back at the wounded privet. "Well, there is now anyway. Convey my apologies to his Lordship, Fred. Anyone know where my tunic is?"

"You left it on the lawn before the jump," Eve said.

"We can go back that way," Olive suggested.

"Can't we do anything else?" Peter asked plaintively.

"We're going to have some tea," his mother said.

They crossed the bridge under the shade of the weeping willows. Arthur took over. "We'll do something after tea." He put his arm round Peter's shoulders.

"Can we play cricket?"

"Why not? But we must have tea first; even real cricketers have tea."

The boy seemed satisfied with the answer and lapsed into a contented silence.

5

When they arrived back at the Lodge, the sunlight of early evening was shining through the limes, casting patchy shadows on the browns and ochres of the drive. The women went into the house. The men went up into the garden and fed Freddie's ferrets with a plate of blood. Peter prattled happily about 'the farrets' and told Uncle Arthur about moonlight ferreting. He spoke quickly and excitedly with the child's pleasure at being able to provide an adult with information. You covered up all the entrances to the warren except one and then it was best that it was moonlight 'cause otherwise the ol' rabbit wouldn't run and the 'farret' would kill it down the hole. Arthur was pleased at the change of subject, even if he wasn't too keen about the moonlight bit.

The two men ate their tea in the living-room. Freddie, in clean attire, sat sunken in one of the two enormous armchairs. Arthur sat at the end of the settee nearest Freddie. Olive came in with a cup of tea which Arthur said was just what the doctor ordered after chasing that horse. He slapped Freddie heartily on the knee and Freddie said he was bloody exhausted. Eve came in with a plate of thinly cut bread and butter, plates and knives. Olive reappeared with a jar of strawberry jam.

"This is the life, Fred, lords of the manor."

"It's a treat to bloody sit down, Arthur."

Freddie took a plate, a slice of bread and butter and scooped two large spoonfuls of jam. He affected at spreading them over the bread and folded it double. As he took his first bite, a huge blob of jam fell on to the plate.

Olive came in and took Freddie's empty cup. When she had gone out, Freddie, who had appeased the worst of his hunger with the first jam sandwich, took an enormous draught of tea which almost emptied the cup and started up again. Arthur's transfer to Bomber Command had given him food for thought.

"What are you going to do if you come down in Germany?"

There was anxiety in Freddie's voice. His own fate might hang in the balance too. Arthur explained the escape drill: escape packs, compass, silk map of Germany, food rations.

"You're supposed to bury your harness and parachute, lie low during the day and try to move at night."

"How're you going to get back?"

"From Germany, Fred, it'd be difficult. From an occupied country it should be a bit easier because of the Resistance. I don't suppose the people there like the Germans much; let's hope not anyway, otherwise I don't know what we're fighting the war for." Arthur took another slice of bread which he covered with a thick layer of jam. "Some jam, Fred; strawberries like golf balls." He held his plate carefully under his chin a took a bite. “Last time we went up, we had to bale out.”

Freddie almost choked on a golf ball. “No!” he said shocked. He leant forward in the massive chair like a captivated schoolboy while Arthur told of the collision, the fall into the night sky, the house, the Queen of Hearts and the tea. “Well, I’ll be buggered!” Freddie said. “You’re all right then?” Freddie peered at his friend, perhaps expecting to see some bodily defect hitherto unnoticed.

“The worst bit was falling out into the darkness. They say the shock of baling out can kill you. Now I know why.”

The two women had come in now. They sat and listened in silence arms folded, from time to time shooting glances at one another as though there were more at stake than just Arthur’s life. Freddie was still entranced on the edge of the armchair. Arthur’s infrequent visits gave him the possibility of re-establishing contact with a world to which the side-effects of a childhood illness had prohibited him entry. The flower of Freddie’s hope, so brutally nipped in the bud at Hendon three years previously, now had formed side shoots which enabled him to experience, albeit vicariously, the trials of the air gunner.

“I’ll tell you one thing, Fred...” Freddie pricked up his ears like a hunting dog. “If we do get hit, I’ll be first out. I’ll be out of that bloody kite so fast you won’t see my arse for dust.”

Freddie nodded. Relief crossed his rugged features. Peter, who had sat himself on the floor between Arthur’s legs, said, “I’ll think you’ll be first out too, Uncle Arthur.”

Arthur ruffled the boy’s thick black hair.

“I’m going to be an air gunner when I grow up. I’m going to bomb the Germans.”

“No, you aren’t, you silly boy,” his mother scolded him.

“Oh yes, I am.” He put his arms up in such a way so as to liken a gun and fired an imaginary burst up at the ceiling.

“I sincerely hope that won’t be necessary, Peter, old son.”

Eve cast a furtive glance at the gilt clock on the mantelpiece. There was something inexorable about the movement of the second hand. She looked at Arthur but was reluctant to speak. Arthur drew the inevitable conclusion.

“Time flies, Fred.”

“You might be going up tomorrow night, then?”

"Perish the bloody thought, although it's possible, if they need a gunner. If I survive this war, Fred, I'm staying firmly on mother earth." He rose with stiff reluctance, stretched and stifled a yawn. "Lovely tea, Olive." He kissed his sister-in-law.

Peter had wandered out into the kitchen, taking pot-shots at the flies buzzing over the kitchen table. He came rushing back. "But you promised to play cricket. You can't go now, Uncle Arthur, you promised."

His mother said, "There isn't time now, Peter. Anyway, it's late, your bedtime, seven o'clock. It'll have to be next time. Uncle Arthur and Aunty Eve have got to be getting back."

At the sight of Peter's crestfallen face, Arthur shrugged off his lethargy. "Get the bat and ball, Peter, and the stumps." He turned to Freddie. "The war can wait, Fred; for an hour, anyway." Arthur tore out into the hall with gigantic strides. "While the cat's away the mice will play. His Nibs might well be home next time we come. Come to think of it, anything might happen."

Peter appeared cradling bat and stumps and they crossed the courtyard for the second time that day. Arthur carried the bat, Freddie the stumps and Peter skipped on ahead with the ball.

"I wouldn't have chased that bloody horse if I'd knew we was going to play cricket."

"That's not the spirit, Fred." Arthur's tone was one of gentle rebuke. "Do or die. Are you going to be Edrich or Compton? Silly question to a man who comes from Norfolk."

They reached the house and swung left. The river and lawn were just ahead. Peter was already on the lawn throwing the cricket ball in the air in gestures of wild, childlike joy.

6

The croquet lawn seemed darker and more at peace in the calm of that summer's evening. The stony façade of the house was steeped in sunlight and the river babbled timelessly just below; a running splash of gold studded with white foam.

Arthur banged in the stumps, bat vertical, using the handle. "Hope his Nibs doesn't mind us taking liberties with his lawn." He hammered in the third stump and surveyed his handiwork. "Well, if he does, it's too bad; it's in a good cause."

Freddie paced out twenty-two yards and forced the single stump into the turf.

"I'll open the batting, Fred – Dennis Compton. You open the bowling – Bill Edrich."

"I'll be wicket keeper, I'll be wicket keeper." Peter flapped his arms in excitement.

"Right," Arthur said, "All we need now are some fielders. You girls," he spoke as if he had just noticed Eve and Olive who were sauntering from the bridge on to the lawn, "Don't stand there nattering; this is serious, isn't it, Peter?"

Peter stopped flapping his arms. His features became set and earnest. "Yes, it is." He took up position in the long grass at a respectable distance from the wicket.

The field placings, being dictated by prudence rather than by the merits or shortcomings of the batsman, would have appeared strange to the purist, the position of the wicket in relation to the river necessitating the placing of both fielders in the covers. Freddie was to cover the leg-side boundary as best he could. If Arthur hit a six, which even Arthur himself judged unlikely, it would be just too bad.

The croquet lawn was a bad cricket pitch, the softness of its surface making fast bowling a thankless task, like bombing a sandy beach. That evening, however, in the failing light, discarding the cloak of fatigue which had weighed and inhibited throughout a long day, Freddie bowled like a man possessed; as though in telepathic communication with the gods. He hitched up his trousers, gave the ball a perfunctory rub and started his run from the edge of the lawn.

First ball: Freddie powered in. The ball pitched just short of a length and skidded over the short grass. Arthur brought his bat down just in time. "Good bowling, Fred."

Second ball: Freddie thundered in. The ball, of fuller length, struck Arthur's bat as he went on to the back foot. The ball went out into the covers rudely disturbing the cover fielders' tête à tête. Arthur shouted and Eve, taken by surprise, squealed and jumped into the air. The ball lost momentum when it hit Eve's foot. She turned, uttered another squeal and gave chase. She stopped the ball a foot from the water's edge.

Third ball: Freddie pounded in. The ball, the fastest yet, missed both bat and wicket and buried itself in the long grass. Peter ferreted it out.

Fourth ball: Freddie galloped in. He unleashed the ball with a tremendous jerk of his squat, powerful body. Arthur played forward. The ball, pitching just wide of the off stump, came off the inside of Arthur's bat and hit him squarely on the shin. He collapsed in agony.

"Christ, Fred, you've bloody nearly crippled me. Damned good bowling, though," he admitted ruefully.

Freddie, contrite, came flapping up to where Arthur lay. "Sorry, Arthur. Bit of a bugger."

They all gathered round Arthur's prostrate form offering words of advice and commiseration. After a while he rose and began to hobble around in small circles.

"Batsman retired hurt," he said.

Peter said, "Can I bat now?"

Arthur collapsed again. "Christ, Fred, kids are merciless."

"No, you can't, you little beggar," his mother rebuked him. "You're going to bed."

Arthur said, "You can have one over, Peter. Your Dad can bowl underarm. I'm retiring behind the stumps: the one-legged wicket keeper."

The shadow cast by the copper beech was longer now and more oblique, its tip reaching an invisible line from the wicket to the single stump at the bowler's end. The air was more chill and the shadowy areas between the willows, the greens of the lawn, the trees and the long grass were becoming darker, merging into uniformity. Only the rush of water cascading over the sluice and the ripple of the river represented immutability in a slowly changing world. Freddie stood halfway down the wicket and bowled underarm to his son. Off the fourth ball, Peter scooped up a chance to Eve who was standing a short way down the wicket. She took it smartly with a girlish whoop of delight. Arthur whipped up the stumps and they trooped back to the Lodge. End of play for the day.

The second parting of the day was as poignant as the first. They tucked Peter up in bed and Olive filled a carrier-bag with eggs, vegetables and jam. It was half past nine when they got out to the car. Arthur smote the bonnet of his 8 HP Ford.

"We're taking the wagon back. I've managed to get a tankful of petrol and a little more besides, so damn the cost, damn everything."

They were several minutes by the car, talking of this and that, putting off the inevitable. The farewell came suddenly, like nightfall after a long summer's evening. Car doors slammed, the engine fired, hands were raised and tyres crunched over the gravel, leaving brown marks, a thin cloud of wispy exhaust fumes and deafening silence. Freddie and Olive went back inside. Freddie's brow was creased in thought.

7

In bed that night, Freddie Buckingham lay staring up at the ceiling. He was back in the hedge with Arthur, but it wasn't the fragments of conversation which made him ponder, it was Arthur's attitude, his enthusiasm. There was something wrong somewhere. What was it he had said about hoping it was doing some good? That wasn't the way the news bulletins put it or the newspapers. What about Cologne? Hadn't that been a victory? Bombs by the trainload. Served the Hun damned well right. Arthur, however, didn't seem all that enthusiastic. But how could he doubt? Hadn't he hardened his heart too?

Arthur's doubts were serious, for Arthur was Freddie's alter ego; the man Freddie would dearly have loved to have been. Arthur was all that a man should be: courageous, staunch, modest, broadminded, kind, easy going - he hadn't a clue about money, he always said that if it weren't for Eve, they'd never have anything - educated, a bundle of energy, but above all, Arthur was a gentleman, not an arsy-tarsy type, but a fair player and a good loser whose yes meant yes and no meant no. But how could he doubt when the Hun had done what they had? Freddie pondered over these problems as though he alone bore personal responsibility for them. Then slowly the truth dawned, like a small seed germinating. Arthur wasn't coming back. Freddie sat up in bed with a jolt. Olive rolled over and groaned.

"Olive! Olive! Arthur's going to die."

Olive opened her eyes. "Silly man! What a thing to say!"

"It's true. I know it. He's going to die. It's a bugger, a real bugger."

CHAPTER THREE

1

Tony Reeves arrived back at Oakington like a man returning from a long exile: unsure of his welcome. The events of his evening in London with Billy had not only preceded him, but had acquired extra details which differed according to the source. His comrade-in-arms had smashed up a night-club, demolished the place entirely, held the forces of law and order at bay by bombarding them with soda-water siphons, had knocked several men unconscious and had gone berserk at a police station. An airman on jankers, weeding a flower bed in front of the Sergeants' mess, had confided to a fellow miscreant that it was a damn good job that Billy wasn't a German. Later that morning in the Wing Commander's office, Tony heard an objective account of the night's happenings.

"There are charges of disorderly conduct, assault, behaviour likely to cause a breach of the peace. A woman has lodged a complaint that her dress was ruined. Somebody else broke the heel of a shoe. Two employees at 'Sadie Jane's' were assaulted; one broken jaw, three front teeth lost, two broken ribs and an assortment of bruises and contusions."

Truex might have been reading items from a shopping list. Standing in that small office, it seemed to Tony that the distance between him and his commanding officer was infinite; not like in the briefing room before an op. The parachute harness carelessly hanging from a nail knocked into the wall opposite looked as out of place as it would have done in a court of law.

Truex stopped reading and looked up at Tony. Understandably, his voice betrayed no emotion. In the context of the war being fought from Oakington, this episode wouldn't even merit a footnote.

"Flight Sergeant Hamilton didn't wreck the establishment, although he might have done if he'd been given the chance. The raid on London was light that night, but one stick of bombs did land in that district and the premises adjoining the club received a direct hit. As the night-club is now buried under several feet of rubble, any damage done by your comrade, Sergeant Reeves, pales into insignificance. There remains the problem of the police station, but the powers-that-be are pulling strings. I daresay your comrade will be back here within a week at the very latest to face a charge of AWOL, which will probably be waived."

"Thank you very much, sir."

"I beg your pardon, Sergeant."

"I-I said thank you, sir."

"Sergeant Reeves, Bomber Command suffers a perennial shortage of gunners and Flight Sergeant Hamilton cannot fly until all charges are out of the way." Truex's voice had the cold, admonitory tone which he usually reserved for his aide when he considered the latter was lacking in perception.

"Yes, sir."

"That will be all, Sergeant."

Tony saluted smartly and left.

The crew met up later in the ante room, discussed their respective leaves and exchanged odd snippets of info. Tony gave his version of the night-club intermezzo as if he were in the confessional. Robin said he had doubted the wisdom of going on leave with Billy in the first place.

"Beats me how a bloke like that got into the RAF."

Tony looked enviously at Robin and Tom, bronzed and fit after a week's sea fishing.

"We ate some fish last week, I'll tell you. If we'd stayed one more week we'd have swum up the estuary and spawned bloody eggs."

Tom said, "One day we went for a swim with Rob's sister. She's like a seal. Beats me how she gets enough to eat in wartime. The tide was coming in, there was about one square yard of beach left and 'im and his sister had to start chucking sand at one another."

Ernie, who had spent most of his leave on his back, had most of the other news. Benny Goodman had completed a tour of operations to be posted to an OTU on instructional duties. Ernie was now the most experienced pilot on the squadron with only two trips left to complete a tour. Reavely and his crew were behind barbed wire, a fact which everyone, especially Ernie, found encouraging.

Tony rose and offered to buy a round taking out an unused book of tickets bought that very morning for half a crown. He looked morose and unhappy.

"Cheer up, mate; everything might work out," Arthur consoled him.

Tony nodded and went up to the bar with heavy steps. What a week! At every mealtime during that dreary week, Billy's vacant chair had reminded him of the events of that terrible night. It had been worse than a trip to Happy Valley. The fact that his parents shared his disappointment had only added to Tony's mortification.

The orderly put five pints on a tray and extracted tickets to the value of the goods bought.

Back in the ante room, the conversation had started to revolve around a new kite. Ernie said that it was a bugger losing Sugar like that.

Robin said, "We might get a duff kite: two halves welded together."

"I doubt that," Ernie said knowledgeably. We're the senior crew on the station now. If there are any duff kites going, which I doubt, the sprogs'll get 'em. Losses are always higher for new crews."

"You're not always sure that a new kite's not duff," Tony said, remembering the incident in April with the faultily-rigged aileron controls.

Ernie stretched his bulk in the upholstered armchair and said, "The Stirlings are all right. Four engines are better than two; they're well armoured and there's plenty of room in them."

"You'd appreciate that," Tom said. "I just wish they went a bit higher. I'd feel a bloody sight safer."

"They're good kites; handmade, like Rolls Royces. Beautiful to fly; like riding a bicycle. If the goons at the Air Ministry hadn't cut twenty feet off the wing-span, we could all look forward to a long life, or at least a longer one."

In fact, it was a week before Ernie and his crew found themselves on the battle order. One morning, as July was drawing to a close, Arthur, Tony and the others were assembled in the briefing room with about a hundred other aircrew, the previous night having been a stand-down. There was the usual low murmur tinged with expectancy. Tony was sitting in the back row, his thoughts nowhere in particular when he suddenly realised that something out of the ordinary was happening. He heard a familiar voice, a voice that had been haunting him, say something about the war being over and they could all go home. There was laughter, sudden movement and the room darkened. Tony rose too, in a semi-daze, heard a familiar name, then he saw the clenched fist above the heads and the penny dropped.

Billy's welcome was tumultuous. Boyish faces, shining with youth and innocence, older faces, although probably no older in years, creased and lined with tension and uncertainty, greeted him like the Prodigal returning. Hija Billy - Wotcha Billy - Good old Billy - Good on you, Bill - Welcome back, Billy. When the sea of serge had subsided, Billy remained still for a moment, like a rock, then started to make his way to the back of the room, his face shining with a happiness that knew no earthly dimensions. Tony remained standing watching Billy come nearer. He took a step forward. "Hija, Billy boy." There was uncertainty and contrition in Tony's voice; but the man Tony had left in a police cell smarting over treachery and injustice took him in a bear hug and lifted him from the floor. There were more cheers as Billy, releasing his grip, turned round, his right fist, the sledge hammer, held aloft in defiance. Billy's face was wreathed in an enormous smile. It lit up the whole world.

It was to be an eventful day. Ops were on.

2

The mists of early morning still swathed the few trees near the pans and the long grasses fringing the tarmac were still thick with dew when Ernie took his crew out to dispersals. The new kite which he and Tony had flown in the day before from Waterbeach was waiting for them on the pan. By some strange coincidence, its letter was B which prompted Corporal Worral, who had served an apprenticeship with a commercial artist before the war, to suggest painting a clenched fist on the side. The suggestion met with approval. Billy grinned, clenched his fist, and after playfully tapping Tony in the midriff, held it up for inspection. Tony smiled. For the first time in weeks he felt tension leave his body. He had opened a door and stepped back into the past.

Corporal Worral then asked whether he should paint flames round the fist, "to give an added impression of defiance and indomitability," he said, spitting saliva around him. The idea was not received with much enthusiasm, for obvious reasons.

They decided on an NFT for eleven thirty which would enable serviceability checks to be made on each piece of equipment. Ernie wanted to put the kite through its paces.

"No two aircraft are the same," he said, "Just like women."

Elton nodded in agreement. Without further ado, each man repaired to his station. The gunners checked gun alignment and went over the perspex of their turrets, Tony checked the tanks and Ernie spent his time under the cockpit canopy, perhaps trying to get the seat to better fit the contours of his bulky carcass.

By ten o'clock, the fist was well advanced when a tall, sandy-green camouflaged Standard 12 van lurched to a halt on the pan. Billy came up to the side of the van wiping metal polish off his fingers and asked for a mug of tea and a piece of bread pudding. The stout, blue-uniformed NAAFI employee refused to accept payment.

"I know who you are, dear. It's on me," she said in a rough falsetto.

When she saw Corporal Worral's handiwork, she shrieked her approval and said that if the kite packed the same punch as Billy, they'd knock the Hun for six. She laughed coarsely at her own wit, shaking like an enormous jelly. Everyone else congregating round the wagon laughed too. Only the Stirling, massive, lofty and silent and Corporal Worral, equally lofty on his stand, squinting intently through his thick glasses, didn't share the joke.

The NFT proved a stomach-churning affair. Ernie, with only two ops left to his tour, left nothing to chance. After the normal checks he put the Stirling through its paces, throwing the aircraft across the sky, banking steeply to port and then falling sideways a thousand feet. At times it seemed that Ernie had lost control of the aircraft until he wrenched at the controls and it soared into a climbing turn.

Emerging from the Stirling thirty minutes later, the boys were pale and wobbly. Robin staggered over to the edge of the pan and retched in the long grass. He walked unsteadily back to the aircraft and his captain.

"Why the hell did you corkscrew like that? You could have bloody killed us."

"I wanted to see what she would do."

"The fuckin' wing could have come off."

They were on the port side of the Stirling, just below the fist. Unmoved, Ernie glanced up at the root of the wing. It was thick and massive.

"What are you worried about – the wing or your arse?"

"There aren't any fighters up over England in broad daylight." Words choked in Robin's throat.

"We don't know what's going to happen tonight, Robin. You can't take chances." Ernie's tone softened. "I feel safer now. That's good for all of us."

Robin, feeling a bit better, shrugged reluctantly and lapsed into silence. By the time the crew-bus arrived to take them back to the station building complex, the argument was history.

The target that night was Hamburg.

3

They piled out of the Bedford lorry at nine-twenty that evening. It had been over two weeks since their last, ill-fated op. They noticed how the nights were drawing in. At nine-fifty, they flashed their code letter to control and received the answering green light. A minute later the Stirling had passed over the hump and was banking to port to start its laden grind up to 14,000 feet.

The route to Hamburg took them due east to Southwold, 250 miles over the North Sea to a point in the Heligoland Bight, then east-south-east to the Elbe estuary. Navigation was straightforward and Elton took frequent fixes on the strobe of his Gee scope to check wind speeds. In some ways Hamburg was an easy target requiring relatively short penetration inside night fighter range. Ernie flew straight over the North Sea, only weaving intermittently to relieve monotony. Despite this alleviatory measure, the journey took on the tedium of a long drive down a darkened autobahn punctuated only by the occasional sickening drop as the aircraft encountered an air pocket.

A little under two hours after take-off, Arthur thought he saw an island through the gap in the low stratus cloud. Elton checked his charts and took a fix.

"That's Heligoland, if my calculations are correct. We've got the wind behind us and ground speed faster than air speed by twenty knots."

He gave Ernie a new course for the estuary, the Stirling banked again and ten minutes later Robin Huxtable sighted the German coast. They flew north of and parallel to the estuary. The pale waters of the Elbe shone below and to starboard. The Nord Ostsee canal, a silver thread, slid under them, then the broad band of water thinned and in the darkness ahead they saw signs of battle where the shining band finished in a blunt hammerhead. Ernie started weaving, the tips of the wings describing enormous arcs in the sky.

"We'll go in from the north-east, but I'll stooge around a bit first."

The Stirling banked steeply. The gunners quartered the night sky and looked earthwards. Arthur saw fires burning in an area he assumed was occupied by the docks. He swivelled his turret as he had done periodically since take-off. Ahead and above them several shafts met in a cone. A moth-like shape was fluttering ineffectually in its apex. Arthur watched in horror-struck fascination as the apex filled with orange flashes and ragged black puffs.

Ernie said, "We'll go in while they're shooting hell out of that poor bugger."

The Stirling banked again, steeply and the fires and muzzle flashes came nearer.

Flak was still pouring skywards into the cone. The flashes intensified and Arthur, unable to take his eyes from the spectacle, fancied he saw small pieces dropping through the light and into the void.

They were over the target now, flying straight; the vulnerable climax. Tony and Tom had left their stations for the astral dome joining the gunners in the search for enemy aircraft.

Ahead and to port, the dark shape in the cone was no more. An incandescent ball lit up the sky as small glowing particles fell from the glowing mass. On his couch, Elton saw fires crawl into the wires of his bomb-sight. Flak shells burst in a desultory fashion around the Stirling, a couple so near that they disturbed the trim of the aircraft.

"Hold her steady; steady. We'll put them on the fires."

Elton's hand reached for the bomb-release tit.

There was another crump and the Stirling rocked again. Ernie had seen the fires disappear an age ago. He shouted, "How much fucking longer?"

The glowing mass had disappeared. The searchlights wavered ominously around Arthur's turret. The aircraft rocked again, this time as the five 2,000 lb bombs left the bomb-bay in sequence. Seconds later came the photo flash as the bombs exploded, pounding a path of orange flashes near the fires below.

"Let's get the hell outa here."

Ernie put the huge aircraft into a turn and the port wing cut across the dazzling web of lights, flak and fires to darkness and relative safety.

It took Ernie several minutes to jink through the tripods of searchlight beams. When later the void closed in on them, Arthur screwed up his eyes and squinted. The darkness, after the flashes and lights over the city, seemed more opaque than ever; even the estuary was difficult to make out through the patches of cloud below. Arthur felt tired and stiff; as if a walk somewhere would be beneficial. Aft of the navigator's compartment the situation was similar. Tony was draining the auxiliary tanks. Tom Campbell had taken up his coffee thermos. In the front turret, Robin had done the same. Elton, oblivious of all else, was checking his charts ready to give his captain a new course once out over the sea.

It was then it happened, as things like that always happen; when one is least prepared. The words over the intercom came like cold water over half-dozing men. They took a second to register but by that time the bomber was already falling like a slate from a roof-top.

"Fighter, port go!"

Ernie's foot hit the rudder bar and his arms wrenched at the aileron controls as if his body had received a jolt from a high-tension cable. In the mid-upper turret, Arthur thought that his last moment on earth had arrived. The echoes of Billy's voice were still in his earphones when he saw flashes and sparks in the sky aft of Billy's turret. Arthur's body froze; there was an empty hollow in the region of his abdomen and he found himself pressing his triggers, at the same time elevating his guns. Above the whine of the tortured engines the staccato chatter of the brownings penetrated the confines of his helmet. As the aircraft fell, Arthur thought of Eve, asked God to forgive his sins and thanked him for everything life had given him. It was then he heard a familiar voice. It appeared to come from inside his head.

"Down port changing."

Arthur's brain cleared. He made out a smear below and to port. He depressed his guns. The smear filled the sight graticule, then burst beyond it. As if in confirmation of the observation, sparks and flashes lashed out again and Arthur replied with his own stream of flimsy tracer. It laced the night sky falling away gracefully to port.

"Up port."

The engines changed pitch as the Stirling climbed, its speed slowing from 200mph to 100. Arthur swung his turret firing continuously as the fighter swept away to port in a broad arc. The cloying smell of cordite filled the cupola.

"Rolling up starboard."

Ernie was using all his strength as he threw the aircraft across the sky. The engines screamed in protest, rivets on the fuselage popped, the cupola and farings shuddered. The thin ribbon of the Elbe estuary seemed to cartwheel; the instrument panel went haywire, the horizon level had a will of its own. Robin Huxtable, trapped in his perspex bubble, saw the estuary see-saw wildly. He realised now that Ernie had been right earlier that day. The NFT had been a mere curtain-raiser.

"Changing down starboard."

The altimeter varied, losing and regaining 1,000 feet as the Stirling dived and climbed to evade its predator. After the initial fall, Arthur's aiming platform became steady and Ernie's litany, coming as it did, a fraction before the execution of the manoeuvre, gave Arthur time to change his aim. Minutes had passed since the fighter had curled away to port. It would certainly make another sally, but where was it? He called up Billy on the intercom but without success.

During the whole course of the action, muzzle flashes had been conspicuously absent from the rear turret. Suddenly the speck appeared again. Arthur judged its distance to be 800 yards as it hovered aft waiting to pounce. For a fleeting moment, Arthur felt as a mouse feels when a cat won't quite kill it. The fighter closed. The mouse roared. Arthur had fired two bursts and was wondering how long the action would last when without warning a white blanket was thrown over the top of the turret. The corkscrew evened out. Shrouded in fluffy stratus cloud, they had found temporary refuge.

In the relative calm of level flying, the men on board made Herculean efforts to bring some sort of order into their lives. Tony had pitched forward on to the floor, suddenly and painlessly vomiting into his mask. He regained his feet at the same time as Elton. He plugged in his intercom as Elton scurried back and forth picking up his charts. His hands were still shaking.

"Ern, Tony. I'm going aft to see if Billy's all right."

"Arthur's already gone. You can go, but close the cow gills. I don't want any icing."

Tony hurriedly turned each of the knobs which closed the cow gills and cast an eye over the other gauges – if anything was wrong, it hadn't registered – then tore his stinking mask from its studs. He unplugged his leads and weak-kneed, with the rank taste of bile in his mouth, groped his way ponderously aft. When he had climbed the tail turret access ladder, the sliding doors to the rear turret were already open and a shadowy shape was leaning into it. Arthur turned, put a hand to his mouth and screamed, "Wounded; right shoulder. I've aligned the turret. We'll get him out."

Gasping and grunting, they prised Billy's body from the turret. He was as heavy as a pig. Tom Campbell appeared with a portable oxygen bottle and together he and Tony lifted the stricken, bootless Billy through the tail plane double frames and down the access ladder to the rear fuselage walkway. Tony held Billy's upper body in his arms, the damaged shoulder close to his own body. The journey was long and arduous without oxygen. They were forced to go slowly, circumventing obstacles, treading carefully so as to counter any sudden disturbance in the trim of the aircraft. Each breath they took pained them, like swallowing hot coals. They arrived at the sick-bed just aft of the wireless operator's chair groaning and wheezing, their windpipes stinging from the very act of breathing.

They placed Billy on the bed. Tony lifted off his comrade's goggles and unbuttoned the studs of his mask. His face was grey and shiny; almost unrecognisable. Glazed eyes stared into infinity. Then, in the dimness of the fuselage Tony thought he noticed a flicker of recognition. He put his lips close to Billy's ear.

"How're you feeling, Bill?"

"Fucking rough." Billy gasped for a lungful of air.

His eyes rolled. He was barely conscious. "What a fucking mess!"

"Don't talk to him. Put the mask back on."

Tony looked up. It was Elton. He was holding a morphine ampoule with a needle.

"Any head wound?" he screamed above the confusion of the engines.

Tony shook his head and pointed to Billy's shoulder.

"Wound-dressing, left-hand leg pocket."

Tony took out the large wound-dressing from the pocket on the left leg of Billy's battle dress.

"Up with his trouser leg."

Tony tore Billy's left trouser leg along the seam and pushed up the leg of his combinations. "His leg's as cold as ice."

"He's been in the rear turret, hasn't he?"

Both men screamed and gesticulated violently. Elton injected the morphine into Billy's leg after which he unbuttoned Billy's jacket, holed and stained, to reveal a dark, sticky mess of blood, viscera and bone splinters. Elton slipped the antiseptic dressing under the jacket and buttoned it again. He turned to Tony and pulled him nearer.

"I'm going fore. I'll tell Ernie the position." He gestured fore and starboard. "Don't forget your gauges." He looked briefly back at Billy whose eyes had closed. "I'll work out the quickest course to England."

Arthur had torn Billy's boots from the turret and was now ensconced there himself, his leads plugged in. He pressed the triggers. Three of the guns fired. He called up Ernie and told him the position: rear gunner wounded, one gun damaged, starred perspex. Ernie, who was still sweating like a bull, sent Tom up to Arthur's turret and asked Elton for the quickest course home.

Tony didn't hear the gabbling on the intercom but felt the nose of the aircraft rise as Ernie pulled the control column towards him. He crossed his fingers and prayed.

A minute later the Stirling had levelled out and was flying over a white continent, alone except for the twinkling stars. Presently, the cloud thinned and became patchy. Robin made out a chain of dark patches below and to port. Elton took a fix and gave Ernie the quickest course home.

"250 degrees, Ern. Straight in. We cross the English coast between Great Yarmouth and Lowestoft."

The return journey took an eternity flying into the wind and with a wounded man on board. Tony divided his attentions between the sick-bed, his station and his oxygen mask. Kneeling on the vibrating, intermittently rocking floor, he suffered anguish for his crippled, drugged comrade and the torments of impotence. He prayed for survival, for deliverance, for a tomorrow. He willed the kite homewards, through the airstream, across the wastes of the North Sea. From time to time his eyes fell on Billy's and he wondered if they would ever open again. Only the faint consolatory hiss of Billy's oxygen told him there was still hope. He thanked God when they crossed the English coast at 10,000 feet and at 200 mph.

He gave a sigh of relief when they got clearance to land and didn't uncross his fingers until the massive aircraft had bumped down on the main runway. He rose stiffly, his entrails taut and twisted, a dull band of pain over his forehead. He staggered down to the entry door and threw it open. Ambulance personnel were already on the pan. Within minutes, the rear doors of the ambulance had closed on Billy's still, prostrate form and the vehicle was speeding towards the sick-bay where Billy would receive initial treatment before being sent to either RAF hospital Ely or an emergency military hospital in Cambridge.

Later, at debriefing, they sipped rum-laced coffee and told of their ordeal. Visions of hunted pallor and relief; they had been the quarry of malign and shadowy forces, but had won through to fight another day.

4

The next day when Arthur got off the crew-bus just after eleven, the elation and relief of the night before had gone; remaining was only a nagging sense of fear.

Seeing the Stirling, he had the unmistakable impression he was revisiting the scene of a near-fatal accident. He walked over to the huddle of airmen standing aft of the rear turret where an armourer and a fitter were already engaged in replacing the damaged perspex. They exchanged the usual greetings. The turret and the near do had been the subject of attention and comment. The consensus was that they had been very lucky.

At the first opportunity, Arthur took Ernie, Tony and Tom over to the edge of the pan. He spoke in a low voice.

"Billy had a torch in his hand when I got to the turret. He was groaning something like – I nearly had the bastard, I nearly had him. The torch was on. I didn't mention it at debriefing, for obvious reasons."

A pregnant silence descended. The looks on the faces of the three men betrayed a whole gamut of emotions as their powers of deduction led them to draw the only possible conclusion. Arthur, who didn't need to recover, broke the silence.

"Are you thinking what I'm thinking, Ern?"

Ernie had one of those deep, perplexed looks on his face he normally had when he was worried about something.

He nodded. "I've flown twenty-three trips with an imbecile in the rear turret."

Tom said, "He's been using a torch to lure in enemy fighters. My Christ!" He pursed his lips in a long soundless whistle. "Damned good job we didn't know about it before; we'd've all shat ourselves."

The argument between Tony and Ernie started unobtrusively, Ernie saying that if Billy ever came back on the squadron, he would bust his arse and Tony defending his comrade in a tone of voice which suggested that Ernie was being unfair. All gunners carried torches and other kites got attacked. Ernie controlled his rage at first. Speaking with the measured exasperation of the long-suffering parent, he told Tony that he was well aware that other kites got attacked and explained to him the inherent dangers in the job they were doing; but his control disintegrated before Tony's insistence on what he termed Billy's commitment to the war. Ernie's pallor vanished. His pinhead flushed to the roots of his short sandy hair.

"Commitment my arse!" he said.

Tony was oblivious to danger signals. He whined on about cramped conditions, the cold, getting fighters and winning the war. It looked for a moment as if Ernie was going to plant his sixteen-stone behind a right cross on Tony's jaw.

"Listen, sonny. I'm not interested in winning a war; I'd just like to survive one. At the beginning of my tour I thought I was for the chop. After fifteen ops I thought I maybe had a chance, but I didn't dare think about it. Now, I've got one left, and no thanks to your buddy – just one." Ernie wagged an index finger under Tony's nose. "And I've started to think of fuck all else. I might be able to get back to Canada. I might be able to do all sorts of things. I might still get the chop too."

The message still hadn't got through.

"He only wanted a shoot-out."

Arthur broke in. It was the first time anyone had seen him irritated.

"For Christ's sake, Tony! Ern's right. What Billy did was bloody risky. Look what happened last night. If you want to do something to help Billy, go in and see how he is this afternoon."

The message had got through. Silence fell. Ernie looked exhausted after his tirade. Tony hung his head.

Arthur reckoned they should keep mum about the whole business. They all agreed and repaired to their stations in silence.

5

Tony went into Cambridge in the afternoon. Sitting on the bus, he felt the aches and pains from the tremendous effort he had been forced to make the previous night. He had borne most of his comrade's not inconsiderable weight and towards the end, only the adrenaline pumping in his veins and fear lest he drop his precious charge had kept him going.

At the hospital he was fortunate enough to talk to the doctor who had operated on Billy. He was a large, portly man with a thick mop of tangled hair who spoke in a loud, authoritative voice, as if addressing a group of medical students round a sick-bed. His tone was optimistic and he had dismissed Tony's apprehensions with a wave of the hand. They had operated. The patient was still under the effects of the anaesthetic. His right shoulder was in a mess, but he'd been lucky: no vital organs had been touched. Apart from the wound from the canon shell, he had extensive damage to his back from shrapnel. It was too early to say whether or not Flight Sergeant Hamilton would be incapacitated, but the doctor could almost promise that he would not fly again. If the Sergeant came back tomorrow, he would be able to see his comrade when the effects of the anaesthetic had worn off.

The next day being a stand-down day, Tony went into Cambridge with Arthur and Eve. The nurse who came in response to the call from reception had the crisp erectness of a cut-out figure. She was reluctant to let the patient receive visitors but Tony insisted, rather as he had done with Ernie the day before. Arthur and Eve stayed in a waiting-room just opposite reception while Tony followed the starchy straight-backed nurse along an endless maze of corridors lit by lamps behind white glass covers in the ceiling, up a flight of stairs, along more corridors – same lamps, same covers – until they came to a cream-coloured door with a frosted glass panel in it. With a swish and a starchy rustle they were on the other side of the door.

Tony's heart almost stopped. Less than two yards away lay Billy, his blond hair almost white and his face small and grey against the pillow. Tony noticed rubber tubes running from the blanket to somewhere under the bed, and a bottle of some colourless liquid hanging over Billy's head. Tony opened his mouth to speak but no words were forthcoming. He turned to the nurse.

"He doesn't look too good," he whispered doubtfully.

"Well, he's been through a lot, hasn't he?" The nurse stood at the door like a prison guard.

Tony edged timidly forward. As he did so, Billy's eyes opened as if his comrade's mere presence had communicated itself to him. The faint suggestion of a smile crossed Billy's features. His lips moved. Tony froze in his tracks and said, "How's it going. matey?"

Billy didn't answer the question, he just started talking.

"Don't tell me I'm still alive. Christ Almighty! Fucking mess. That doctor said to me, you're lucky not to lose that arm." Billy spoke in a whisper, but still managed a tolerable imitation of the doctor's modulated tone. "I'd give both fucking arms to get out of this bed."

He stopped and breathed heavily as if collecting himself for one last effort. His head lay on one side. He hadn't moved it since Tony had come in.

"I'm sorry," he said in a voice hardly audible. "I missed the bastard. I had him and I missed him. Fuckin' luck."

Tony bent over and wrung his forage cap in his hands. He was about to formulate a question when there was a creak of starch and the nurse suddenly stepped forward.

"I'm afraid that'll have to be all today; he's very weak."

Turning to leave, Tony raised a hand but Billy seemed not to notice. On the way out, Tony expressed his doubts and fears to the nurse.

"I don't think he looks at all well."

"Well, you can't expect anything else, can you? – not after all he's been through."

The nurse had a way of addressing Tony which the latter found annoying; as if he were old enough not to make such naïve statements. Outside, in the irregular sunlight of early afternoon, Tony shared his fears with Arthur and Eve.

"You'd think a guy like Billy was indestructible, wouldn't you? – Well, he bloody well isn't. I've just seen him. He doesn't look too good at all. Although," he added bitterly, "nobody in there seems to be unduly worried. You'd never think he got wounded fighting for his country. Makes you bloody sick."

Eve tried to reassure him. "People who work in hospitals are hardened to suffering. I suppose they have to be. Billy's been under an anaesthetic too. Normally you feel worse after an operation than you did before."

Tony was not convinced. "You'd still think they'd show some compassion. I couldn't say anything in there without that nurse snapping my head off. I dread to think how Billy's going to react when he gets better; he gets shirty with the personnel on the station sometimes and they're wonderful compared with that nurse."

"Well," Arthur said, "There's not much we can do about it, Tony, old son. I expect he'll be moved to Ely as soon as he's well enough. We'll have to keep our fingers crossed. He must be in good hands. Eve and I thought we could go somewhere for a meal. We'll have missed lunch at camp. Fancy a ham salad?"

"Spam more like." Tony was already cheering up.

"What does your nurse look like, Tony?" Eve asked.

Tony looked up at the uneven sunlight streaming through the row of limes just beyond the hospital wall. He tried to recall her features. "Short, dark, frizzy hair, pointed nose, a bit turned up, small mouth. Why do you ask?"

"There's someone like that coming towards us now."

Tony turned. The moment he caught sight of her he knew something was wrong. The nurse came up to them. She had lost most, if not all, of her self-assurance. As she opened her mouth to speak, Tony's head started to swim. He knew what was coming.

"It's your friend, Sergeant; I'm afraid... I'm afraid he's just died. If you'd like to come inside, the doctor would like to speak to you."

Tony heard nothing after the word died. Drums hammered in his head. "Died! Died!" he shouted. "He bloody well can't have. I was talking to him five minutes ago."

"I'm afraid there's no mistake."

Tony walked some way with the nurse, then his pace quickened and suddenly he found himself bounding towards the entrance. He entered the building swishing through the partition doors. He tore off his forage cap and, holding it like a baton, plunged, arms pumping, into the intricacies of the building. He had to get to Billy. Hadn't he carried him from the turret all that way to the rest bed, nursed him, prayed, hoped? Billy was as much his patient as theirs – and what had they done?

He ran in panic, his steps echoing against the plaster walls, through doors, around corners, up stairs – the bloody place was like a maze – eventually slithering to a halt on the grey linoleum beside a door not unlike the one he had gone through barely fifteen minutes before. It opened and a man in green trousers and a green smock wheeled out a bed. Tony glanced inside and glimpsed knives, spatulas and scalpels lying on a metal tray on a trolley just inside the door. He looked up and down the corridor. Confused, he started to retrace his steps. The nurse, gasping, came running starchily up to him.

"You've come the wrong way. The doctor wants to talk to you."

"Bugger him; I want to see Billy."

"Well, all right, follow me; but I can't walk as fast as you can."

As they walked down the corridor, Tony, still panting, clutched at straws. "Look, Billy's a joker. He might be kidding. He's got this incredible sense of humour, really quirky. He's definitely not normal."

Suddenly they stopped in front of a door with a frosted glass panel which Tony thought he recognised. The nurse pushed it open. Tony, clutching his cap in both hands, entered.

Although Tony Reeves had lived in the forecourt of death since mid-April, he had never seen a corpse. Instinct told him to run for his life but an undefined, irresistible urge made him advance towards Billy's lifeless form. Tony's eyes were fixed on Billy's face. But for its waxy, bloodless pallor Billy might have been sleeping.

There was a swish and a rush of air. The doctor entered. He looked mildly harassed; something which shouldn't have happened had happened. He brushed back a grey forelock as a defensive measure and started talking like a defence counsel in court.

Tony didn't look back as they left that small room with its recently deceased occupant. The doctor talked loudly and dispassionately, but Tony was stunned. He stared glassily at the doctor, hearing words, registering nothing. When they had shaken hands, Tony stood motionless for several minutes before his numbed brain started to function. The doctor's bass drum voice boomed inside his head. At last, words and then phrases became recognisable. Cause of death difficult to ascertain - blood clot - heart - everyone a heart patient - most unfortunate - tragic loss - never more than an even chance - suffering from shock - been through a lot - operations always fraught with the unexpected. Tony walked mechanically through two sets of double doors and found himself bathed in the sunlight and fresh air of an English summer's afternoon.

They ate spam salads in an upstairs restaurant near Market Hill. The restaurant was divided into three parts by a white-painted trelliswork around which some plant with white flowers had twisted itself. The conversation at table was in accordance with their low spirits. Tony spent his time, fork in hand, pushing a piece of cucumber round the rim of his plate.

"He said one thing before I left."

Arthur and Eve pricked up their ears. Anything was better than this silence.

"He said he was sorry that he'd missed the bastard."

"He meant that he'd put up a black with that fighter, perhaps," Arthur suggested.

"Or the torch," Tony countered.

"Well, Tony, whatever he meant, it's too late now. There's no point in dwelling on the past. It's the future that counts. One more trip and we lose Ernie; and we've already lost Billy, so that's fore and aft going or gone."

Tony looked thoughtfully at the sodden piece of cucumber. "Guess you're right, Arthur. We don't know who we're going to get as a replacement either: panic merchant, splitarse type or even an officer."

"Whether Billy was using that torch or not, his warning came just in time. If that fighter had got in a good burst, we'd all have bought it. I reckon that's what's getting most aircraft now, fighters not flack."

Tony nodded. He looked over the stained table cloth at the empty plates opposite. Eve's hand had snaked up from under the table and had gripped Arthur's. It must have happened while Arthur was talking.

Arthur raised a finger and beckoned. The waitress came over and they paid the bill.

"Lovely, dear," Eve said.

The waitress smiled at Eve then her expression changed to one of reproof when she saw Tony's plate. Eve left some coppers under a saucer, they rose and picked their way through a sea of white-topped tables and white wicker chairs to the top of the stairs. The two men waited while Eve went to the ladies' room.

Tony looked at Arthur out of the corner of his eye.

He had seen Arthur the flight sergeant and Arthur, Eve's husband. The former had a very tough exterior. He wondered which of the two he was looking at now. Suddenly he blurted out with the abrupt innocence of the child and the sudden perception of one come of age, "You and Eve really love each other, don't you?"

The exterior cracked. Arthur coloured slightly and smiled. "Well, yes, we do."

"Why don't you pack it in, Arthur?"

The mild surprise and amusement on Arthur's face disappeared to be replaced by puzzlement. "I don't follow, Tony."

"I mean, walk into the Wingco's office, tear your brevet off and tell him you've had enough. There's nothing they can do to you that's worse than going up in one of those bombers, anyway. Who cares if they send you to Uxbridge and stamp LMF over your papers. You survive. Well, that's what counts."

For a moment Arthur looked taken aback, as if the thought were an unnatural one. Then the softness vanished from his features; the crack sealed itself.

"It's not as simple as that, Tony. If I did what you suggest, I wouldn't be the person Eve loves, would I? And then I'd be leaving you and the others to face the music. Domestic commitments don't enter into it. My life isn't worth any more than anybody else's. Make no mistake, Tony, I hate this war, but someone's got to go out there and do it; although God knows where it's all going to end. That's the way it is."

Tony flushed deeply and looked down at his shoes. He should have expected that answer. He had been a fool to put the question. At that moment Eve emerged from the ladies' room, skipped happily towards them, and put her arm through Arthur's. She kissed him on the cheek. They went down the stairs, Arthur and Eve hand in hand, Tony bringing up the rear, his forehead creased in thought.

6

The next night ops were on and they flew back to Hamburg. The opposition - wavering searchlight beams and sporadic flak - was minimal, the raid routine. The journey from the target to the coast was, however, a nerve-tingling affair, each shadow in the black void taking on a sinister significance. Afterwards, Ernie, who had had the shits all day, said the op was a piece of cake, but it had enabled him to survive a tour and his crew come a step nearer thirty. Ernie even survived his farewell party in the Still and Sugar Loaf on Market Hill. He was posted up north on instructional duties.

The trip to Hamburg was also notable, because that night they had had a new gunner and a co-pilot. The latter was another Canuck: William Robson Kransky RCAF. Bill Kransky had arrived at Oakington in early July and had flown second dickey with Benny Goodman before Benny's transfer. He was nineteen years old, buoyant and confident. His qualities of leadership would have made him anybody's choice for head boy at school. To the perceptive, his frank, fearless attitude and unbiased amicability seemed to be in open defiance of traditional Anglo-Saxon concepts of class thinking.

The other newcomer was a gunner; Oliver, 'you can call me Ollie,' Howlands. Ollie had come to England from East Africa with £200 in his pockets, had sampled the delights of the Prince of Wales and the Windmill, spent two nights at the Savoy – the foyer had a certain ambience, and a week later had found himself washed up, penniless and destitute, outside an RAF recruiting office in Marylebone. He had been on the station ten days. His manner was quiet to the point of diffidence, but the glint in his eye and his motley past suggested that still waters ran deep. He was rated by the few acquaintances he had as a good chap.

The next day, Arthur and Tony were detailed to go through Billy's locker and the billet he had shared with Tony and to make an inventory of his personal effects. The task was a simple one. In Billy's wallet they found a pound note, a ten-shilling note and some loose change; a summons to appear in court and the citation he had received with his DFM. In a small cardboard box on top of the wardrobe they found some photos. One, of a pretty blonde woman, who they thought must be Billy's mother, attracted most attention and speculation. There was also the school football team – Billy back row far left; a boxer with a mop of dark hair and a rugged, scowling face who Arthur recognised at once as Jack Dempsey and a pornographic photo. At the bottom of the box was a letter written in bold feminine handwriting, the gist of which was that the writer – the letter was signed Annabel – was pregnant and wanted her and Billy to get married. Arthur perused the content. He passed the letter to Tony who, after reading it, shook his head.

The mystery deepened. Billy left behind debris of one kind or another wherever he went. Trying to know and understand Billy Hamilton was like walking out in a swirling mist. Sometimes you thought you recognised a tree, the contour of a rock or a bend in the road; then the mist would move and the tree was no more than a shadow, the rock a gap between two trees and the bend in the road a fork. Tony looked up from the letter.

"Billy was a funny chap. Secretive, a real puzzle. He was very emotional, but you never ever got close to him. Know what I mean?"

Arthur nodded.

"This letter, the summons," Tony held up the creased piece of paper, "Breaking and entering. Do you think Billy was a criminal?"

"That's only the charge. We don't know the verdict. He might have got off."

"And this photo." Tony looked distastefully at the couple about to embark on the sexual act.

"He was a man, Tony; it's not so unusual. If you want to keep it, hide it somewhere; otherwise tear it up. I can't imagine his next-of-kin wanting it." Arthur put his hand into his breast pocket and drew out a slip of paper. "I got this from the orderly room. It's the address Billy gave on coming here; his next-of-kin I suppose. We could go down and pay our respects; take the DFM - that's something to be proud of - and the photos; the Effects Officer won't miss them. It's East London. I've got almost a tank of petrol, which isn't worth saving; should get us there and back easily. We'll be down there in an hour and a half, the way I drive," he added with a grin. "Next stand-down day."

Tony smiled. "Next stand-down day it is."

The opportunity came the following day when ops were scrubbed early and Arthur, Eve and Tony drove down to London under a slate-grey sky which threatened rain. Tony sat in the back of the 8 HP Ford with the DFM and the photos in a buff envelope.

They found the street where Billy presumably had lived with surprising ease. It looked like something out of a surrealist painting: a solitary, scarred monument in a blasted landscape spared by a quirk of fate. They drove down the deserted street between grey sash-windowed tenements. Black drainpipes marked the limits of each house. Many of the windows had no glass. At the end of the street they saw a ramshackle building of boards, bricks and corrugated iron. There were one or two sandbags around the entrance and the words air-raid shelter were written on the door. The place didn't look strong enough to shelter a flock of chickens from a thunderstorm. Arthur stopped the car. They got out and looked around.

"Looks bloody depressing," Tony said.

Arthur said, "I heard the East caught a packet, but this has to be seen to be believed."

Eve gripped Arthur's arm and said, "Which house do you think it is?"

"None of them I hope," Arthur replied. He took up the address. "18, Devere Street, E5. Well, this is Devere Street. Wonder where 18 is?"

Tony located a house with an eight on it, walked a little way down the street, found a number four and retraced his steps counting the doors. "It must be this one, although there's no number on it. Wonder how the postman gets on around here?"

"There's no handle on the door either," Arthur observed, "And as for the postman, if he's got any sense, he'll have cleared off out of it. Pity Jerry didn't blast this street too while he was at it. Come on, let's get this over with. Got the envelope?"

Tony waved the envelope and Arthur pushed in the front door. They walked along a dark passage. At the foot of a flight of stairs they stopped and looked at one another hesitantly. Tony said, "This place stinks."

They went up the first flight of stairs. The smell, which was indeterminable, became more pungent. On the landing, a baggy shape appeared in a doorway. Tony, clearly feeling his responsibility, stepped forward with the zeal of a door-to-door salesman.

"We're friends of Billy Hamilton. You wouldn't happen to know him by any chance?" For some reason Tony used the present tense.

The shape beckoned them on and a second later they found themselves in what functioned as living-room, bedroom, kitchen and attic. The smell was unbearable.

They looked around. The place hadn't been tidied up in months. On a sideboard, dirty cups, plates and saucers lay in piles. In one cup, green mould had begun to form on the surface of some black substance and an enormous fly was making its way gingerly around the rim. Between the sideboard and the floor there were more flies darting and winging about over scraps of food and a saucer of milk. On either side of the fireplace stood an armchair, a pile of newspapers in one, a potted fern in the other. The threadbare sofa was covered in animal hair. There was a table and two chairs by the door. The old woman, who had straggly, matted hair, glazed eyes and a look of being perpetually hunted, stood by one of the chairs with a hand on the table for support. Her knees were slightly bent as if she were unable to make up her mind whether to sit or to stand. They were about to apologise and leave when Tony saw the photo on the mantelpiece. Clutching the envelope, he strode over to the fireplace kicking over a glass as he went. He picked up the photo and examined it.

It was of a young boy, ten or eleven years old. He had blond, wavy hair and was sitting at a table. The background of blobby, water-colour paintings and the pose told Tony the photo had been taken at school. The smile on the face was radiant. It belonged to another world, a world of hope, innocence and faith where good was good and bad was bad and where good was always victorious. It was the smile they had all seen in the briefing room the morning of the fateful Hamburg raid: hope and innocence briefly rekindled; the smile that lit up the world. Tony sighed and replaced the photo. There could be no doubt. The Orderly-Room Corporal was seldom wrong about anything.

A glimmer of comprehension lit up the woman's glazed eyes. "Billy's friends?"

The three of them nodded simultaneously. The breakthrough was encouraging. She pointed to herself. "Billy's Grandma," she said, then straightened her body. She picked her way over to the mantelpiece, took up a buff envelope and announced, "Billy dead!" She shook her head, with her last threads of reason trying to understand a world gone mad. She shuffled back to the table and sat down. "War terrible," she said, her eyes seemingly fixed on some invisible point on the floor somewhere near the saucer of milk. The three of them nodded again with affirmative grunts and looked uncomfortably at one another. This was hardly what they had been expecting. There was a painful silence. "Terrible, terrible," she muttered. The old woman spoke with single words as though the trauma of life had robbed her of all syntactical ability. Suddenly, she looked up. "Cup of tea?"

With a simultaneous movement three heads turned to the pile of discoloured crockery on the sideboard. Tony had been about to say, 'not bloody likely' but showed restraint and presence of mind. He smiled. "No thank you, dear. Just had one." He looked at Grandma and thought he detected some facial resemblance to Billy under the cross thatching of wrinkles.

After another silence Tony waved the envelope with the medal and photos. Arthur took it and said, "Medal, Billy." The loss of syntax was clearly contagious.

Grandma took the envelope and opened it with the involvement of the small child on Christmas morning. She took out the medal and held it up for inspection. Looking at Arthur she said, "Pretty!" More nods.

Arthur wondered if anyone else lived in the house. The distant sound of a flushing toilet furnished an immediate answer.

After another helpless silence, Billy's Grandma rose with the medal and citation and hobbled past Tony, who stood untidily in the middle of the room, over to a wardrobe which stood to the right of the mantelpiece. She opened it and from its dark recesses took out a cardboard box. Her three visitors watched in fascination as she removed the lid and put the envelope in the box with God only knew what other treasures. She was about to replace the lid but had second thoughts, rummaged for several seconds and produced a photo. It was the photo Tony and Arthur had unearthed in Billy's box: the pretty blonde woman. The young boy, the buff envelope and now the duplicate of the pretty blonde. Overwhelming evidence.

The old woman put back the photo, replaced the lid and thrust the box back into the darkness of the wardrobe. When she had got back to the table, she sat down and took no further interest in her guests. They left in silent resignation, tiptoeing down the stairs as though leaving a child's bedroom.

They drove off quickly, leaving the depressing rows of blackened houses, slate roofs, chimney stacks and wireless aerials behind them. By the time they had reached Enfield, a watery sun penetrating the thinning cloud cover went some way to dispelling their own clouds of depression. Arthur turned to Eve. "I'm sorry about that, darling."

"That's all right, dear."

"Tony, the next time I make a suggestion like that, kick me up the arse, will you?"

"It was all my fault, Arthur; you drove down for my sake; I'm the one who deserves kicking. I'm sorry about the petrol you've wasted. Let's forget it. I owe you one, that's all."

They sat in still silence, only the occasional movement of Arthur's left hand and foot breaking their collective immobility. As the undulating fields of Hertfordshire sped by, Tony brooded. Wherever you looked there were gaps in the records, and the more you looked, the more gaps you found. Billy's mother was dead; that was fairly certain; but where, when and how had she died? How long had Billy been living with his grandmother? How long had she been out of her wits? Had she brought up Billy? Where were the men in Billy's life? There couldn't have been any. The grandma was next-of-kin; the Orderly-Room Corporal's infallibility was proof enough.

They reached Royston. Beyond lay the flat Cambridgeshire countryside: Bomber Command's backyard, scattered with systems of tarmac airstrips, littered with the wrecks of burnt-out aircraft. They neared camp. The skyline became familiar and thoughts of Billy receded. Here was the future; the day-to-day struggle for survival and sanity. No records: only gaps. The unknown.

7

Flight Sergeant Billy Hamilton's last journey, from the camp entrance down the road to Longstanton churchyard, took place two days later. Six members of his section carried his coffin which was draped with the Union Jack. The Station Commander, the Squadron Commander, Billy's crew and ground crew followed the coffin. The Padre, Billy's erstwhile adversary, led the procession. Before the coffin was lowered into the ground, the Padre said a few well-chosen words. Tony listened intently as the Padre spoke in dulcet tones of Flight Sergeant Hamilton's unswerving loyalty to his comrades and his commitment to the cause of freedom. Tony could agree, to a certain extent, about the loyalty, but to what exactly Billy was committed, Tony was unsure, as he was about much. On the way back to camp, Ollie suggested naming their Stirling Billy's Revenge. The suggestion was the only glimmer in an otherwise cheerless day. It received immediate acclamation.

PART THREE

CHAPTER ONE

1

At Oakington life had an unrelenting quality: it pursued its inexorable path regardless of day to day trauma. It was now August. Ernie Watson belonged to the dim past and the crew of Billy's Revenge were now captained by Bill Kransky who, in that first week of August, was promoted to flight sergeant. Ollie Howlands was their new rear gunner. They flew a couple of cross country navigation exercises but no ops. Rob and Tom took Ollie under their wing. Arthur spent his spare time with Eve, Kransky spent his with sixteen-year-old Ann-Charlotte, a popsie who he had met at the local post office.

Arthur introduced Eve to Kransky and Ann-Charlotte at the monthly dance in the Sergeants' mess. Ann-Charlotte was clearly very smitten with her Canadian boy friend, which wasn't surprising. Kransky was popular. He oozed confidence as if he had already survived two world wars and was well on his way to surviving a third. He was going to take Ann-Charlotte back with him to Canada. He lived near the Great Lakes which, he assured everyone, was the nicest place to be. The two airmen and their girls made an attractive foursome. After tripping the light fantastic to Jack Doyle's orchestra - both Eve and Ann-Charlotte loved dancing - they chatted happily in the billiard room, which had been converted into a buffet for the evening, until Tony loomed in, picked up a sausage roll and loomed out again followed by at least two pairs of anxious eyes.

Tony, for whom life up to that time had been a sailing trip along a friendly shoreline in fine weather – even the transitory nature of life at Oakington in the context of the war made some ghastly sort of sense - had lapsed into a state of semi-oblivion, a fact not unnoticed by his crew and ground crew. To the latter, it seemed that the flight engineer was going to great pains over small things. They could understand him pottering about on the lips of the wings unscrewing the dripsticks, checking and rechecking the content of each tank; but his preoccupation with the exactor throttles – the Stirling's engine control system utilised hydraulic pressure – was, in their opinion, carrying caution to the extremes. Finding an old can in a hangar, he had attacked it with plate shears and soldering iron, filled it with oil and gone to work to check possible leakage. His prone position between the co-pilot's seat and the control pedestal suited him as much as did the attitude of genuflection when, the control boxes filled and the filler caps replaced, he pulled each throttle in turn with infinite care to see if there was any evidence of sloppiness which would indicate that there was still air in the system.

Away from the therapy of the daily round, things were worse. Even the mess dance wasn't up to much until the buses taking the land girls back to their hostels had departed and Kransky had winged away with Ann-Charlotte on Corporal Worral's motorbike. Beds were pulled out of the billets and sofas and armchairs arranged in the ante room for the Grand National. Tony found himself drawn inexorably into the fray. Being less inebriated than the others, he was one of the best stayers as bods vaulted, jumped and fell over the obstacles, pounding around the ante room and along the corridors. In the end only Tony and a Canuck gunner stayed the course. On each completed lap, the gunner 'refuelled' in the ante room, gulping down mouthfuls of ale. Tony refuelled too. On what proved to be the last lap, Tony, running woodenly, but gaining with every stride, came into the ante room to refuel when the Canuck screamed, "Bale out!" To Tony's astonishment the Canuck pitched himself out of the nearest window. Tony went over to the window and peered into the darkness. A spread-eagled figure lay motionless in a flower bed. That he was unhurt was in no small way thanks to one of his crew who had managed to open the window before his comrade had flown through.

Tony went up to his bed with heavy steps and a feeling of nausea in his stomach. Ollie, his new room mate, wasn't there. He had gone off with Rob, Tom and three land girls who had missed their bus on what they termed 'an exercise in the art of cross-country navigation'. Ollie said the five miles to the hostel would be a cinch even in the dark. He had used to walk up the slopes of Kilimanjaro every morning before breakfast. One of the land girls told him to stop telling whoppers, and that she didn't believe there was any such place as that Kiliman-whatever it was.

Tony's billet was worst, but in fact, the whole camp was haunted by a swearing, rumbling spectre with blond hair and a rolling gait.

He had to get out. One dull evening, under a covered, rolling sky, Tony left camp and started walking.

He followed a winding road, blindly passing farms, barns, cottages, all alive with the sounds of early evening. After half an hour, he came to a village street. Ahead of him was a church. He took a right turn down River Street and followed the road out of the village. The countryside was flat; everywhere smelt of cabbage and the road he was following was higher than the surrounding fields. After a quarter of an hour he walked up a slight incline and stood on a raised bank. The Ouse was on the other side, dark and sombre in the evening light.

On the other side of the river a launch was moored to a jetty. Beyond, on the far bank, groups of stately willows dominated a collection of low buildings which could have been a farm or even a hotel. Tony walked upstream a short way to another willow and leant against it, heavily, like a man at the end of his tether. Billy was everywhere. In his dreams at night Tony heard the creaking of the springs and mattress opposite and he felt the pain in his back and lungs as he struggled down the fuselage with his precious burden; he saw the pale glistening face through the murk around the sick bed and the head of his dead comrade on the white hospital pillow, shrivelled like a gargoyle. On the station, everywhere he looked, wounds opened. At dispersals it was worst. Billy's name was immaculately stencilled on the side of the kite, and there was the fist, challenging, defiant, powerful. Yet he was gone. His body with the shattered shoulder and the insidious clot of blood – it had touched Billy's brain not his heart – was in the cemetery, but his ghost was omnipresent. Tony looked downstream at the river, dark and secretive like Billy himself. There was no knowing how deep it was or what lay on its bed. His gaze swept the countryside to the south-east. It ended in a foreboding horizon: a backcloth of dark cloud. It was then he broke the silence with a strident, piercing cry. "Billy! B-i-l-l-y! B - i - l - l - y!" It was a cry of desperation, despair, misery. Silence came back at him; silence and the rustle of leaves in the branches above his head. He fell to his knees and beat the grass. Tears came to his eyes as he gave himself up to his grief. "Billy! For Christ's sake! Billy!"

Tony remained motionless, on all fours, his head hanging limply, for several minutes. Then, like a child who has worked off a tantrum, he rose sullenly, picked up his forage cap and placing it on his head, started walking back the way he had come. When he got back to the village street, he went directly inside the pub; for no particular reason as he hadn't finished a pint of beer since Billy's death. He entered the lounge bar. He saw a row of bus seats along one wall which should have told him something, then the barmaid came through from the other side. It was Paula Gilder. Bells started ringing in Tony's head. He was about to leave, but her disarming smile of recognition stopped him in his tracks. Two destinies were about to entwine.

"Hello! Long time no see!"

Tony flushed. "H-hello."

"What is your pleasure?" She smiled warmly and disarmingly. She was wearing a white sleeveless blouse done up to the neck with buttons of white pearl. On her left arm were four enormous vaccination marks.

"A pint please."

"On your own tonight I see. Where's your friend, the blond one?"

Tony's heart missed a beat. "That's Billy. He's dead now." Tony's voice trailed off. His head fell. A wound had been reopened.

"Oh I am sorry." She put the pint on the bar and Tony paid.

Tony related the barest details of Billy's death and the tall woman listened attentively.

When he had finished, she said, "That's terrible," adding with almost philosophical calm, "I suppose it happens a lot. It's best to try and forget. Life has to go on."

A bell rang on the other side and the barmaid excused herself. Tony brushed off his uniform, straightened his tie and took a large gulp of beer. The barmaid returned with a high stool.

"You get tired standing all evening."

Tony looked round. "You aren't so busy tonight."

"No. Sometimes the place is packed; other times it's like this. We don't get many RAF boys. Couples come in for a quiet drink sometimes. I should imagine they prefer Cambridge."

"That's true, actually. I used to go into Cambridge a lot with Billy. There's more action. Although sometimes it's nice to come to a place like this."

The woman smiled at the oblique compliment. She was leaning on the bar, her arms folded under her large breasts. Tony could smell the scent from her body and hair. He took out a silver cigarette-case.

"Like a cigarette? They're Canadian. Our pilot's Canadian, but he doesn't smoke so we get the cigarettes he gets in the forces' parcels from Canada."

"Not now, while I'm working. I'll have one later."

There was a faint tinkling from the other side of the bar. When the barmaid had gone, Tony wondered what she had meant by later. He looked at his watch: nine-thirty. Through the small lattice windows, darkness was falling and the dull orange light from the bulbs in the lounge was becoming more pronounced. Tony sipped at his bitter and puffed on his cigarette. The barmaid returned.

"Aren't the nights drawing in?"

"Yes, I was just looking out of the window. Just the ticket; means we'll be starting earlier. Fancy a drink?"

"No thanks, not when I'm on duty." She gave Tony another disarming smile and he felt his knees weaken. "What's your name?"

"Tony. What's yours?"

"Paula."

"Pleased to meet you."

Paula smiled again, coyly this time and flushed slightly. There was a clatter from the other bar followed by a muffled cheer. Paula looked uneasily over her shoulder.

"I'd better get back. I've the locals to look after. They'll think I'm giving you too much attention. Do you like coffee, by the way?"

Tony shrugged. "Well, yes. Why do you ask?"

"I've some at home. It's chicory, actually," she confessed. "You could come round afterwards for a coffee."

Tony looked down at her hands. They were small and fine for such a big woman. She was wearing wedding and engagement rings. He hesitated.

"I'm completely alone. You've nothing to worry about. Just a minute." Paula disappeared round to the other side to return a moment later with a key. She let it glide surreptitiously over the bar counter under her hand. "Take this. You can let yourself in. Go out of here, turn left, cross the street then right. It's a hundred yards further down on the left; detached house. I'm the lady of the manor," she added with a wink. "It's best you go on ahead. I've got some glasses to wash and tables to wipe."

Tony nodded and took the key with a trembling hand.

2

The house where Paula lived was a half-timbered, rustic building situated some way back from the road.

Tony thrust the key into the lock, his hand still shaking. Opening the door he found himself in a passageway flanked by wood-panelled walls. It reminded him of stories he had read as a child of big houses with secret passages. At the end of the passage a door was ajar. He walked forward, treading carefully as if the floor were hot, and entered the semi-darkness of a low-ceilinged room which appeared to have dark wainscoting harmonising with the furniture: dining-table, chairs, a rocking chair and a wooden sofa pushed up against a wall. Even the beams, running transversally across the white ceiling seemed to match. The fireplace, of red brick, was opposite the carved wooden sofa. Standing in the centre of the room, Tony turned full circle. A double bed filled a large alcove. As far as he could make out, the bedspread, the cushions on the sofa, even the carpet between the sofa and the fireplace were the same colour. Tony stood for several minutes as the last light of evening falling through the small windows faded. A knock at the door made him jump.

"I'm sorry," he said as Paula entered. "I forgot to put the door on the latch."

"That's all right," she answered breathlessly. She swished past him down the passage into the living room, kicked off her shoes and put on a pair of pink mules. "Make yourself at home," she said, made a careless gesture of the hand indicating the sofa and pulled a cord under the shade of a standard lamp by the fireplace. The reds of the cushions, bedspread and carpet were bathed in yellow light. Paula pulled the curtains with business-like efficiency and disappeared through a doorway to the right of the fireplace.

Tony sat down on the sofa and looked idly around him like a man who has strayed absent-mindedly into a home-furnishing store. Kitchen sounds came from behind the door and a few minutes later Paula reappeared with two steaming cups on a tray and a round tin with a tartan pattern on the outside. She went over to the bedside table, threw the two photos on it on to the bed and with the tray carefully balanced in one hand pulled the table over the carpet to the sofa. Tony had never seen her full length before. She was wearing a dark blue skirt which stretched tight over her thighs, buttocks and belly. She sat down beside him.

"Take as much sugar as you want. I don't use it when I'm on my own." She laid a self-conscious arm over the bulge between her thighs. "It isn't good for me, but tonight I'll make an exception." She popped three lumps into her coffee. "Help yourself to biscuits; I'm a bad hostess." She gave Tony a smile that brought blood to his face. "What do you do in your spare time?" The question was put with some trepidation as if much depended on the answer.

Tony shrugged. "Go out drinking mostly, while the money lasts. Not much else to do. We natter, play cards, snooker, read, try to get some rest. Doesn't seem worth starting anything constructive. When Billy was alive, we took out girls."

Tony suddenly became silent as the image of the tart, pale and tubercular, passed before his mind's eye. He shot a sideways glance at Paula. She had crossed her legs. Her dark skirt was drawn tight over the curve of a plump thigh.

"There was always something happening when Billy was around." Tony chuckled. "You know, I shared the same billet with Billy and some nights," he took a sip of coffee, "some nights he'd toss and turn, swearing and cursing. Billy fought the Germans in his sleep. He believed did Billy."

Tony turned his head and gave Paula a wan smile. She sat with cup and saucer in hand. She twisted her body, slightly lengthening her thigh. Her breasts were almost resting on her belly.

"Oh I'm sorry, I forgot." He stuck his hand inside his tunic. "Cigarette, Canadian." He took out the silver case. "Twenty-first birthday present from my parents."

Paula took a cigarette and Tony lit it. She exhaled blue smoke. "Tell me about yourself," she said.

Tony shrugged again. "There's not so much to tell. I'm a flight engineer. I wanted to be a pilot, but I joined the RAF at fifteen and then you're too young; you have to be eighteen to become a pilot. I was told to enlist, then re-enlist when I was eighteen. Well, I did my training as a fitter/rigger for three years, then at eighteen I tried to re-enlist to train as a pilot. I applied five times and each time they threw the application back at me. Five times!" Tony held up five fingers and blew out a cloud of smoke in mock exasperation. "They said it only took nine months to train a pilot but three years to train a fitter/rigger; in reality six years, because I'd been trained to do both jobs. I think they were trying to save money, or something. Still are for all I know."

Paula rose and went over to the mantelpiece after an ashtray.

"Anyway, that's why I'm not a pilot. When these new four-engined jobs came along, I saw my chance to get into the air so I volunteered as flight engineer and was accepted. Did a training course at Longbridge at the Austin factory before going to gunnery school; that's how I got my stripes." Tony pointed to his sleeve. "And here I am," he finished with a grin. He took another sip of coffee.

Paula smiled. She looked mildly bored. "Do you have to be in by any special time?"

"Sergeants and officers, eight tomorrow morning. Other ranks, midnight." He stifled a yawn and looked at his watch. "Crikey, it's about that now."

He drank the last of his coffee and stubbed out his cigarette. They rose together and Paula followed Tony over to the door keeping close to his side. At the door Tony stopped and Paula, who was nearly as tall as Tony, put a hand around his neck and kissed him on the lips.

"It's been nice talking to you this evening. I'm so glad you came," she added in a breathless whisper.

Tony's body tensed. His breathing quickened. He wrenched at the door and a coat rail and shelf loomed at him out of a dark recess. As he rolled backwards like a boxer avoiding a blow, a cardboard box and a clothes-brush came down on his head.

Paula smiled. "Silly, isn't it? – the cupboard being next to the door."

They both knelt down. Paula, giggling girlishly, retrieved the box and almost overbalanced. Tony took the brush and helped Paula to her feet. She took the things from him and tossed them on to the bed. Moving nearer to him, she took his hands and held them up to her breasts. He felt their weight through the mesh of her brassiere. Her face came closer. Tony's head started to swim. She was in his arms. She seemed taller and stronger than any girl he had been near before. Her face neared his and his hands dropped, sliding down to the material of her skirt, caressing then gripping her buttocks. Their lips met and their tongues touched.

"If you want to come over, you know where I live and where I work. Just be discreet."

Tony mumbled an unintelligible reply and groped for the latch. He found himself clawing at the wood of the door.

"The latch's on the left; silly, isn't it?"

Everything was silly: the handle, the cupboard, perhaps he was too. He opened the door with a shaking hand.

"Thank you; it's been a nice evening," he blurted.

Going out he lurched into the door-frame. Paula had followed him along the passage. She gave an umpteenth disarming smile and raised a coquettish hand. Tony turned and waved before pounding away into the darkness.

3

The next day it rained and the depression and accompanying fronts spread eastwards over the Continent. Ops were scrubbed at five, all possible targets being covered in ten tenths cloud. On the pans, armourers began the thankless task of debombing. Later that evening a light wind and a watery sun were already drying the roads as Tony retraced the path he had taken twenty-four hours before. He opened the door in the stone wall and slipped into the lounge bar. He might have been on his way to his own execution. In the corner, two officers with pilot's wings were sitting in the far corner with two WAAFs. Tony raised his right hand in an informal salute. The officers acknowledged him with a smile. On the other side the public bar seemed full. For a moment he wondered if he'd done the right thing in coming. Then Paula appeared. She was wearing a pink blouse with leg of mutton sleeves. It didn't fit as tightly as the one she had been wearing the evening before. He smiled weakly at her and ordered a pint of bitter. She slid the beer towards him and through the amber liquid Tony saw a Yale key. They exchanged looks of coy complicity. Tony understood.

Sitting on the sofa waiting, Tony Reeves was beset with the doubts and apprehensions of someone going into the unknown. After half an hour he got to his feet and went out into the passage. The panelling seemed solid. He might have been in a densely-wooded forest; only latches betrayed the existence of doors. He lifted one and pushed in the wall. He found himself in a spacious bathroom. He urinated copiously, pulled the chain and went over to the wash basin. Minute globules of sweat lay in the palms of his engineer's hands. He found a brush of wood and black bristle, scrubbed and washed until his hands stung. Then, strongly suspecting that his breath stank of stale beer, he extracted a flat tin of Gibb's tooth powder from the cabinet over the sink. Ten minutes later, when he had regained his seat opposite the brick fireplace, Tony was breathing hot coals and his hands were sweating as profusely as they had done a quarter of an hour before.

When Paula breezed in half an hour later, Tony leapt smartly to his feet like the obedient pupil. She wasted no time with formalities; only a coy smile and a kiss before leading him towards the bed. "Get undressed," she said in an unnerving dulcet whisper. She lifted the counterpane and sheets to reveal sparkling linen, kissed him again, reassuringly, and skipped out of the room.

Tony undressed and got into the bed as if it might have been booby-trapped. Paula returned, undressed behind a screen covered by bottle-green canvas and came to him with an eiderdown draped over her shoulders. Lying in bed, seized by fears of inadequacy, Tony discerned the dark patch between her legs and the folds of her belly before darkness obscured his vision and Paula was on top of him drowning his face in kisses.

He ran his trembling hand over the soft curves of her buttocks, the length of her smooth warm body. For some reason she was still wearing her brassiere. He broke off his exploration to fumble with the hooks and Paula raised herself whispering in his ear, "Slowly, darling, gently, we've all the time in the world." She continued to kiss him, her tongue flickering, searching, pushing between his teeth, touching his tongue. With an effort he controlled himself and his hands steadied. He unhooked the offending garment, removed it and her breasts, warm, soft and heavy tumbled free on to his chest. They rolled over, a tangle of limbs and kissed again deeply. Tony felt Paula's breasts and belly against his thin body. She lifted a leg and wound it around his lower half. Desire rose in Tony like an intoxicating gas coupled with some strange feeling of desperation. Their lips parted and Tony's breathing quickened. The lower part of her body seemed to melt and he entered, enjoyed a brief orgiastic spasm before withdrawing, quickly and stealthily. He rolled over on to his back gasping for breath.

When Tony awoke with a start the next morning, the sun, filtering through the cracks in the thick curtains, was already dispersing the shadowy warmth of intimacy and the intoxication of coition. The naked woman at his side, the tangled bedclothes, the screen, the blue serge uniform on the sofa, filled in the gaps as his mind started to focus. He rolled out of bed, tottered over to his clothes and started to dress quickly and furtively like someone leaving the scene of a crime.

He had tied his shoes and was looking towards the door when the sound of Paula's voice made him freeze.

"Tony."

He turned towards the bed. Paula was awake, half sitting, half lying. The enormous curves of her breasts pushed out the sheet which she had prudishly pulled up under her chin.

"Take the key, Tony, I've got another one."

Tony went over to the bedside table and took the key. Paula reached out with an arm, pulled him towards her and kissed him. They wrestled for a few moments, Tony laughing, Paula giggling. Even in his uniform he could still feel the curves of her body. He kissed her again, with more skill this time; he even managed to nibble the lobe of her left ear. He could have taken her there and then; he glanced at his watch. Christ! Was that the time? This war was a bloody nuisance.

"Will I see you again?"

"I don't know." There was a trace of desperation in his voice. "They're pushing on in earnest now. It's building up all the time. We're in a state of perpetual readiness. Only the weather stopped us last night. The armourers were debombing when I left camp to come to you. You'll have to expect me when you see me."

It was then that the terrible thought struck him: he might get the chop and never see her again. Perhaps he had made love for the first and last time. He felt a lump in his throat.

"I might not come again, i-it's possible. In that case thanks for everything. You've been very kind."

Paula grabbed his lapels and kissed him again.

"Take the key; hang it around your neck on a string, like a talisman." She spoke in a hoarse, melodramatic whisper. "It might bring you luck; and you won't lose it either." Tony nodded obediently. "One more thing, darling." Her voice regained its normal pitch, became more authoritative. "Don't come to the pub again, come straight here. I'm home soon after ten. It's best; walls have ears. You know what I mean. I don't come from this village but I have to live here and rumours spread quickly, even with so much else to talk about."

Tony nodded gravely like a man possessing infinite wisdom.

"I'll keep my fingers crossed."

They kissed one last time and Tony left.

4

Tony Reeves began the homeward journey on unsteady legs but when elation struck him at the far end of the village street, he broke into a trot slowly increasing speed until he was running, exaltation in each stride. He didn't slow down until he came to Longstanton church, where Billy was buried. He stopped, straightened his tie and cap and proceeded with dignity up the road to the counter-balance barrier pull and sentry-box that marked the entrance to camp.

Tony was already aware that something was wrong when he passed the camp entrance. He forked right in front of the large building housing the administrative sections. Outwardly nothing was amiss. The brick buildings, the flower beds, the well-kept lawns were as they had always been. Ahead the water tower rose on black girders, a sombre sentinel against the limpid blue sky of early morning. He entered the mess. The entrance hall looked the same too: coin box telephone, mail-rack, coat hooks; even the green felt of the regulations board and the notice board appeared to be cluttered with the same white patches. He disappeared along the corridor and upstairs to the billet he shared with Ollie. His comrade was sitting on the edge of the bed scratching himself, ostensibly collecting his strength for the walk to the ablutions. He showed no particular surprise at Tony's hour of return – why should he? – he was, himself, a man of the world. Tony followed Ollie down to the wash-rooms, shaving tackle in hand. There, he saw Arthur's face appear in the mirror by the side of his own and the truth dawned.

"Wotcha, matey!"

"Hija, Arthur!"

He took up his safety razor, soap and brush. That was it! He was in the same boat as Arthur; no longer screened off from the outer world by the peri-fence. Paula was going to keep her fingers crossed – and, he suddenly remembered, she'd given him a key. That morning he had experienced what Arthur had been going through all summer: home – front line – home again with intermittent interruptions in the routine to be sent into battle over Germany at the most ungodly hours imaginable. It was bad enough for anybody, what with all the tension and the waiting and the not knowing if you were going to be alive the next day. For Arthur it must be worse. Saying goodbye to Eve each time and not knowing whether he'd see her again. How could he stand it? It was cruel, that's what it was, bloody cruel. This must be the most hellish way of waging war ever devised by man.

Tony rinsed his face in cold water, straightened up and wiped the remains of shaving lather from his lobes. A shy, newly-shaven face stared back at him from the mirror. Its brow below the hairline was puckered in thought. Where would it all end, he wondered? Where would it all end?

CHAPTER TWO

1

For the boys at Oakington time passed, but such was the intensity of activity and so fatal the consequences of error or misfortune that its passage was counted in hours rather than days, in days rather than weeks and in weeks rather than months. For men whose lives could be snuffed out like candle flames, the years to come didn't exist. If they did, they would inevitably be occupied by the war because nothing else existed. It would go on pitilessly, inexorably; maiming, killing, misshaping, deforming, destroying. They pressed on, the Stirlings bombing notionally less well-defended targets in Germany on a wide front. On the ninth, six machines flew to Osnabrück, an industrial town in Lower Saxony. Billy's Revenge didn't fly that night; instead, on the following night, they flew to the Baltic to lay mines to stop the Prins Eugen slipping out into the Atlantic. The weather was vile. They were cloudborne even before the two-stage undercarriage had disappeared into the wings; a foretaste of things to come. The aircraft rocked, bucketed, dropped suddenly as it went through air pockets and reared like a frightened horse as it translated each barometric deviation into sickening reality. Tony stayed at his station for the whole trip, staring, sometimes blindly, at the dull glow from the luminous dials on his panel. They were out the whole night. Dawn was breaking as they crossed the East Anglian coast, squat and grey in the half-light of morning. They climbed down the access-ladder on legs stiff with fatigue. Tony staggered over to the edge of the pan where he retched up his misery. When he rejoined the others, they were chatting to the ground crew. The trip had been a success and although tired to the point of exhaustion after seven hours without moving, they looked pleased with their night's work. Descending to six hundred feet with bomb doors open they had successfully laid the mines. They had seen Grosenbrode and pinpointed the islands of Fenmaara and Laaland. There could be no doubt that the mines had landed in the right place. Debriefing would be no problem.

Tony spent the rest of that day recovering from the dreadful battering he had taken during the gardening trip. The next day he resumed his duties and his tall, stooping profile could be seen moving ponderously along the wings checking the tanks, peering at the calibrations on each dripstick.

Towards evening he had recovered sufficiently to entertain carnal thoughts. Since his first guilt-laden excursion into the world of coition, he had been over to Paula's on three occasions. In her arms he had learnt fast, although hardly an intelligible utterance had passed between them. Now, in the ante room early that evening he found himself wondering about the woman between whose sheets he had found this sensual haven. He knew nothing about her, she nothing about him, yet their relationship had almost from the very beginning reached a stage of intimacy which, before the war anyway, he would have associated with marriage. Had life become so transitory that accepted standards of decency had been waived for the duration? If the conduct of the blokes on the station was anything to go by, they had. Their language was atrocious; they'd never speak like that at home; and judging by the amount they drank, you would have thought that their lives depended on filling up with as much beer as possible. They beat up the mess and then, for no apparent reason, turned on some poor bugger and debagged him. Tony looked up at the clock over the door. That hadn't been there long. Its predecessor had been smashed to smithereens the last time they'd had a stag-party. A sergeant gunner had picked up one of the pork pies on the cold buffet and hurled it defiantly at the clock. Tony knew him vaguely; a spare bod flying with any crew who needed a gunner, his own crew having been killed at the beginning of May. Since then he had defied the law of averages with the same success as he had defied the discips on the station. The boys must have hated that clock, Tony concluded. He didn't like it much himself. Billy had reckoned that some sadistic bugger in authority had put it there for the express purpose of reminding aircrew that time was running out, although what they were supposed to do about it beat him. All hell had broken out when the clock had crashed to the floor under the pork-pie bombardment – those bloody pies were like hand-grenades – and he had cheered loudest. They had finished the evening with a game of mess rugby, sergeants against officers, during which the place had practically been wrecked and several chaps had got crocked.

And what about him? – knocking off a married woman; and the worst of it all was that he was enjoying every minute of it. The situation, however, gave Tony cause for unease. There'd be the devil to pay if her husband came home and caught them at it. He might kill them both in a fit of rage. Tony shuddered at the thought. He'd have to be careful there; the Sunday papers were full of that sort of thing; not that they'd ever had those papers at home; his guv'nor always had the Sunday Express: King and Empire; but on occasions, while waiting his turn at the hairdresser's, he had picked up the News of the World and perused several piquant stories never dreaming that one day he, himself, would be featuring in the shabby drama of marital deception. Dying in his mistress's bed was not how he had seen life ending when he had volunteered for aircrew. This couldn't go on. He'd have to have it out with her; there was no other way. He swallowed and put a hand up to his chest. It was then he felt something hard through his uniform and suddenly realised it was Wednesday, Paula's evening off. He'd go down there right away. There was no time like the present his guv'nor always said, but, as he made to rise from his upholstered chair, a voice interrupted his thoughts.

"Fancy going into Cambridge for a drink, Tony?"

It was Robin. He had come into the ante room with Tom and Ollie. Tony sank back into the chair feigning tiredness. It wasn't difficult.

"No thanks, Rob. I'll think I'll get an early night. I still feel buggered after that gardening trip," he lied.

The three of them peered at Tony like interns assessing a patient's state of health. Robin said, "Yeah, you look a bit buggered. Well, we'll be seeing you, Tony. Don't want to waste valuable drinking time."

When they had gone, Tony prized himself up from the armchair and lumbered over to the door. Apart from seeing Paula, he thought, the walk would do him good.

2

Tony had determined to have it out with Paula the moment he arrived, but when he opened the door to her sitting room, she had just finished drying her hair and came to him, a matronly figure in a dark dressing-gown covered with cascades of red stars. She threw her arms about his neck and kissed him deeply and passionately. He squeezed her tightly, felt her heavy breasts and ran his fingers down the smooth silk of her dressing-gown, gripping her buttocks. Paula was wearing nothing underneath. They wrestled for a few moments.

Paula's fingers worked quickly with no little skill. In no time it seemed, Tony was standing in a pile of his own clothing. He untied the sash of her dressing-gown and the cascade of stars fell to the floor. He covered Paula's plump white shoulders with kisses, working down to her breasts. His tongue touched a huge nipple and it swelled like an enormous fruit. Paula's hands moved into Tony's hair pushing him down over her deep navel, and her soft round belly and down to between her legs.

His tongue flickered and probed. She took two steps backwards and Tony's hands tore into her buttocks, lifting her and causing her to fall backwards on to the bed. Paula tried to push back Tony's head, but she only succeeded in toppling over completely, her legs flailing. Suddenly her giggling and laughing stopped and languorously, half sitting, half lying, she lifted one of her legs placing a plump thigh on Tony's shoulder. Her breathing quickened as her vulva opened before the persistence of Tony's tongue. Once, briefly, Tony looked up. Paula's breasts rested heavily on the curve of her belly, her eyes were closed, her mouth fractionally open. Her hair, long and silky, framed a face which had lost its tautness. Tony hardly recognised her. It was only later, much later when Tony's resolution stiffened again that he broached the subject of Paula's marital status.

He raised himself on an elbow and looked down at her tranquil face and the sweep of newly washed hair on the pillow. "Paula?"

"Yes, my lover?"

"What are we going to do about you being married?"

"Nothing as far as I know." Paula's voice had a matter of fact tone which might have been a defensive measure.

"I mean, what if he comes home one night and catches us at it? What if I come down here one night and find him here with you? What do I say – sorry, wrong house – I just found the key in the street?"

"Don't worry, Tony, it's safe. My husband's just been home on leave. He won't be back for a while. He's in North Africa."

"What's he doing there?"

"Fighting, I suppose. There's a war on, isn't there?"

"I meant, what outfit is he in?"

"I've no idea. I'm not particularly interested."

Tony rolled over on to his back, seemingly satisfied as to the distance between himself and the man whose conjugal rights he was usurping. He was still in a talkative mood, however.

"How did you come to be in this village? Bit out of the way. You haven't always lived here?"

"I used to be on the stage; a dancer," she said.

Tony let out a coarse, ill-mannered laugh and rose abruptly. "Really!" He looked down at the generous curves of Paula's body. She gave him a hard dig. "Ouch!"

"That's enough of your cheek, young man. I haven't always looked like this; anyway, dancers are often quite big, and I've always been big."

"What sort of dancing did you do?"

Paula, realising that prevarication would only fire Tony's curiosity, told her young lover of her life as a dancer. Dingy, provincial theatres, the clatter of feet on the stage boards at soul-destroying rehearsals in front of rows of empty stalls; cramped dressing-rooms, the make up, the grease paint, the sweat; digs: cold, cheerless rooms lurking behind lace curtains and potted palms; revue, pantomime, cabaret.

All the girls were tall and big, but Paula was the one who usually caught the backers' eyes. She got plenty of dates; which meant lunches and dinners in enormous rococo dining-rooms in large provincial hotels with flabby, middle-aged businessmen with paunches, puffy faces and thick gold rings on podgy fingers which kept touching her legs under the table, pawing at her nylons and suspenders. They had bought a share of the show, they thought they had bought a share of her as well. When she had been lean, hungry and seventeen, she had been tempted, but the romantic shimmer of this world was to prove as thin as the sequins on the costumes.

Years later, the lustre of promise had faded as had the giggles and laughs of the teenager. Exercise, a slim waistline and her height protected Paula from corpulence; but like a flower she had to be picked whilst in bloom.

Her chance came at a party in London two years before the outbreak of war. He was upper-class, fairly wealthy, good-looking and had an ease with words which passed for charm. Their courtship was brief; the period of marital bliss which follows all weddings even briefer. There was more to Paula than the curves of her body. Her character had a depth in which her husband showed no interest. For them both, but for different reasons, the conjugal hearth proved to be a wasteland. War broke out. Paula's husband joined up, got a commission – that was all Paula knew about his career. Upheaval and separation completed the work which infertility and barrenness had begun. The security which she had sought had become a sterile prison. Mind and body lay fallow. What she had to offer remained unwanted, accumulating like the layers of flesh on her body.

"Ollie, our rear gunner, has been to the Windmill. He says the women there prance around with next-to-nothing on. Did you ever have next-to-nothing on?"

"Pretty close at times."

Tony let out his breath slowly but gave no comment. It seemed a rum do, but the whole thing was beyond him anyway. His own problems, as he saw them, were connected with the basics of existence: life and death, survival and destruction. Anything as banal as marital tiffs, or whatever they were, hardly merited a thought.

Paula crept up against him. Tony lay on his back caressing the soft skin of her arm, running his fingers over the rough of her vaccination marks.

As his head rolled over, his glance took in the shapes and forms he saw in the darkness. Good training for night vision, he thought; chairs, the sofa, the screen which she invariably undressed behind, a huge opaque mass to the left, the foot of the bed and the mound under the bedclothes made by Paula's hip. She was breathing heavily now; at peace with the world in spite of life's deceptions. Who cared if she was married? War was war; that was the way it was. He couldn't change anything.

His lids too began to weigh with the heaviness of sleep. The last lingering remains of consciousness he spared for his comrades, the men whose fate he would surely share, and especially for Arthur and little Eve. Even Billy ghosted back to the edge of his consciousness. How long had he been gone? Tony calculated swiftly: two weeks. My Christ! It made you think. It felt like two years, or twenty-two. Life was being speeded up. It was flashing by: blurred images seen from the proximity of a speeding railway carriage. Life was being reduced to a series of brief sensations: your ears popping, your stomach turning over, intoxication, nausea, vomiting. Even sleep, when you could get any, was brief. Friendships were brief too.

Perhaps too, when the moment came for you to die, even that would be over before you had time to become aware of impending danger; no last prayer, no mental readiness, no last wish. He shuddered and squeezed Paula's shoulder.

As sleep gradually overcame him, the perennial question posed itself, rearing its ugly head like a venomous serpent – where would it all end? Where would it all end?

CHAPTER THREE

1

They were on the following evening; another gardening trip to the Baltic. Tony sat beside Arthur in the lorry, comrades in misery, and stood beside him by the massive silhouette of Billy's Revenge watching the barely perceptible descent of a fiery orange sun. Its passage as it abandoned the world to the shadows of night might have been marking the remaining seconds of a deadline. Clouds tinged with reds and blues scudded across the sky. The wind was ominously strong. They went up at nine thirty.

The North Sea was stormy again that night. The Stirling buffeted its way eastwards, the black swell visible at times through the patchy cloud. They reached the Heligoland Bight and pinpointed Sylt, one of the North Frisian Islands, before rocking and lurching further east. Elton gave Kransky a course which took them over Southern Denmark to avoid the flak concentrations at Flensburg. Through the clouds ghosting by Robin made out the Flensburg Fjord, a crooked silvery finger. To starboard, searchlight beams pierced the night and anti-aircraft batteries began hosing flak skywards.

"Some poor devil's buying it." Robin's voice was terse and unsympathetic.

"I don't know what he's doing there; we were routed north to avoid that flak." There was a note of callous reprimand in Kransky's voice.

They all watched with bated breath as the aircraft made the usual feeble attempts to avoid the inevitable.

The customary orange flashes and the ragged residue of back puffs were the prelude to the soundless whoomph as the aircraft and its luckless occupants perished. Arthur wondered briefly who the hell they were.

A belt of cloud appeared below them which later disappeared as swiftly as it had come, as if by some cosmic sleight-of-hand. Elton's Gee fix put their position east of Jutland over the area of the Baltic where they were to drop their mines. They started their descent to six-hundred feet.

It was Robin who saw the long black shape surge at them out of the darkness and disappear under the fuselage. He fancied he saw others spaced out like a chain of cigars, some to port, some to starboard, fringed at their extremities by white foam. His brain was still wrestling with the equation when his earphones came alive. It was Arthur.

"Bill, convoy, starboard and port. Don't climb, try to weave."

Within seconds the leading ship had opened fire. The others followed suit. The flak had an uncommonly low trajectory. Shells exploded with a flash and a crack around the dim shape winging its way over the water.

"We'll have to jettison the mines," Kransky's voice had a panicky edge to it.

Tony hadn't been feeling any better this trip than the previous one, but he rose from his seat, his nausea disappearing before a rising tide of cold fear. He moved fore to the co-pilot's seat.

"Open the bomb-doors, Bill! I'll pull the toggle."

While the bomb-doors were opening, Tony plugged in his intercom. He pulled the jettison toggle, Billy's Revenge lurched then was rocked by a gigantic explosion.

Kransky said, "Christ, we've been hit!"

Tony said, "Weave, Bill, don't climb."

Billy's Revenge yawed and rolled, twisting like a tormented animal, riding the storm of exploding shells. Once the sea came right up at the nose before Kransky corrected the swing and the line between sea and sky became horizontal again. An age of hoping and praying passed before the long chain of muzzle-flashes decreased in intensity and the keel of the aircraft became even once more. At last only darkness remained and Billy's Revenge began a laboured climb up to 14,000 feet.

The homeward journey proved uneventful and they arrived back by four thirty. Kransky, tired and shaken after his efforts over the Danish islands, cut the throttles eighteen inches above the runway. They landed with an unnerving jolt. On the pan Tony and the ground crew inspected the aircraft, poring over the frames and rivets with slowly mounting incredulity. The ordeal they had survived was lacking in tangible evidence. The aircraft was undamaged.

The whole episode had temporarily shaken Bill Kransky. In the wake of the success of the previous trip to the Baltic, he had voiced his liking for gardening trips. Now, he had gone right off them.

Of the four other Stirlings operating that night, three had returned early with mechanical failures.

The fourth had fallen foul of a marauding Me 110 south of Flensburg. The rear gunner had been the Canuck who had baled out of the ante room window the night of the dance. Alas, he didn't get the chance of baling out when it really mattered. The kite blew up in mid-air. All on board perished immediately.

2

The offensive continued. It must have seemed to many aircrew that an enormous effort was being made to push over the defences of the Third Reich before the onset of autumn. After the long gardening trips, Billy's Revenge flew to Düsseldorf on the 15th with five 2,0001b high-capacity bombs. They went up at midnight in pitch darkness and arrived home just after four in the morning. Threading their way through flak and searchlights they bombed what they thought was the eastern side of the town. At debriefing Ollie reported seeing a built-up area on fire as they left the target area.

Tremendous efforts were being made behind the scenes, too, which were to have far-reaching consequences. Moves were afoot to remedy Bomber Command's target-finding shortcomings. The C-in-C had been given a direct order from the PM through the Chief of the Air Staff to form a pathfinder force. Harris had opposed the idea tooth and nail but had been given no choice in the matter. He had, however, insisted on appointing the leader of this special force. He chose Wing Commander DCT Bennett who had served under him on 210 Squadron at Pembroke Dock. There was no better navigator alive than Bennett and path-finding, Harris knew, was basically a question of navigation. Bennett came to Oakington on the 15th August 1942. Crews assembled in the briefing room saw the Base Commander enter followed by a group captain with a red DSO ribbon. He spoke with an Australian accent. He was brief and to the point.

"Good morning, gentlemen. My name is Bennett. I don't have to tell you that too many bombs are killing cows in Germany. We are going to rectify that. I have been selected to form a new force, composed of veteran crews who will find the targets and mark them so that the main bomber force can come in behind and really make a mess of them. This squadron has the best bombing record from August 1941 to the present so it has been selected to be the first squadron in this new force which will be called the Pathfinder Force. The tour of operations will be sixty ops."

A low whistle went up from among the ranks of serge.

Bennett was unmoved.

"This force will consist entirely of volunteers. If any crew does not want to volunteer, they must inform their flight commander within the next twenty-four hours. They will be posted out and replacements posted in. Good morning, gentlemen."

Bennett and the Base Commander made their exit. The Pathfinder Force had been born.

3

The new order was the subject of discussion in the different sections and in the messes. There were two main bodies of opinion: those who felt they could continue as before – we didn't have a pathfinder force at Cologne and that worked out; and those who felt the present situation called for new thinking – but there was an incendiary force which lit up the target and that's what this idea is all about. But what happens if the Pathfinders light up the wrong place? – then all the bombs fall in the wrong place. It'll be a waste of bloody time.

One sergeant gunner was particularly pessimistic.

"It all hangs on the boys going in first, doesn't it? If they do their job, all right, I agree the system's an improvement, but if they don't, everybody fails and the operation falls like a pack of cards. At the moment there is always somebody who finds the target and bombs it. This way, everybody might miss it and in that case there's no point in going to Germany at all."

To these two groups, the Cynics and the Progressives, there could be added a third: the Realists, who were mainly concerned with practical problems such as navigational difficulties. The principal navigational aid, 'Gee' was becoming increasingly subject to enemy jamming, the strobe time base and co-ordinates disappearing in a confusion of vertical green lines, rendering it virtually useless inside enemy territory. Without better equipment it didn't matter who went in first, the result would be the same.

One day when Tony and Arthur came into the ante room, a discussion was in full swing. The Progressives were in the majority, their chief spokesman being a young sergeant pilot who had joined the RAF straight from school. His fair skin was tainted with the marks of adolescence; he had the beginnings of a moustache and he smoked a pipe.

"Now the best crews will go in first, surely they have a better chance of finding the target. It stands to reason that in this way our forces are better organised and we have a better chance of succeeding. Experience counts, you know," he added precociously. He took his pipe out of his mouth and waved the brier knowingly at his audience. "I personally feel that this innovation is long overdue." He put the pipe back into his mouth. There was a note of finality in his statement.

The few Cynics sprinkled about the assembled company were not convinced. "There are snags. If they go in first, they might suffer heavier casualties. Soon Bomber Command won't have any experienced crews left."

"Yea, they'll be like fish in a barrel."

"And even if they don't get hacked down, their reception will be so damned hot that it'll be impossible for them to do the job."

"But the defences might not be fully awake," retorted the Sergeant Pilot who was trying to re-light his pipe. "We also, if we stream well, have a good chance of saturating their defences. Besides, experienced crews must have a better chance of survival; I can't believe it's all just a matter of luck. I've volunteered for Pathfinder. I don't expect to survive, but I feel it's my duty. It'll be my own personal contribution to the overall increase in efficiency. There are always pitfalls, but personally I feel that we must go forward and hope that by trial and error we can develop a more effective system."

"Let's hope so," someone said mournfully.

The small group vacated their chairs and went in for lunch. The young sergeant's selflessness and commitment made Arthur feel a twinge of guilt in spite of himself, but he said nothing to Tony. Tony wondered vaguely how Billy would have reacted. Himself, he was no longer sure what to think.

4

The next day at morning prayers John Truex talked about Pathfinder. The principle was, in fact, similar to the Thousand Raids. Crews would volunteer but could give up and put in for transfer. Nobody would call it LMF. They would attack in waves:

first wave, incendiaries, no flares. These had to fall accurately on to the target. The next wave would be carrying flares. These would be called the Finders. They would drop a flare every thirty seconds in order to illuminate the area in which the target was situated. The third wave would consist of the best crews; they would be carrying bundles of flares which they would drop on the aiming point to illuminate it just like daytime for the main force. Timing was of the essence. They would all be on strict schedules. Navigation must be exact.

"If you arrive at the wrong place or arrive too early, the flares will either be in the wrong place or gutter and die. In either case the raid will be a botch-up."

There were knowing nods from some of the Cynics as if to say they had thought of that all along.

"As far as navigation is concerned, dead reckoning is our motto. We'll need a good wind and we'll use our nav boxes to check our winds before jamming puts them out of use. There'll be no time allotted for training, which is unreasonable, I agree, but in complete accordance with the press on spirit and in accordance with the general principle of never wasting war effort or ceasing to strike at the Enemy. We'll be learning as we go along."

Truex looked down at a slip of paper he had in his hand. When he spoke again, it was with a kind of detachment. The new order would mean new men. Truex's days on the squadron, even if one disregarded quirks of fate in the air, were numbered. By September, October at the latest, he would be transferred.

"We need to improve our bombing accuracy. It simply isn't good enough. Things won't be easy, I can promise you that; don't expect remarkable improvements immediately; but Pathfinder is here to stay. It's the shape of things to come."

This time it was the Progressives turn to nod.

Truex sat down. The Medical Officer took over. He talked about night vision, mentioned vitamin tablets and advised them to eat carrots.

5

The squadron operated on the 17th August; again the target was Osnabrück. It was to be their last raid before Pathfinder. They were routed due east over the Ijseelmeer, which slid under them like a silver plate, and across the flat wastes of Northern Germany. The target area was well-defended with much flak and searchlights. The crew of Billy's Revenge saw their five high-capacity bombs cut a swathe across the target and they turned for home. The trip was uneventful. Just before three, Bill Kransky cut engines six inches above the runway thus executing a perfect landing.

After debriefing, Tony felt a desire rise within him stronger than his need for sleep. As he followed the road down to Paula's, each bend, each sequestered house, each chimney-stack loomed out of the darkness like an old acquaintance. Even the small stunted profiles of the fruit trees had a vague familiarity. The ringing of a bicycle bell startled him. He looked around and saw Arthur pull up beside him.

"Hop on the parcel-rack, I know where you're going."

Docilely, Tony obeyed and they sped together at an alarming speed along the flat winding road entering Stowe ten minutes later. Arthur let Tony dismount opposite where Paula lived. For a moment he stood dumbly on the pavement.

Arthur said, "Don't pretend you don't know where you are."

"How did you know?" Tony said in the hurt voice of the child whose secret is no longer his own.

"Walls have ears," Arthur said with a laugh. "Happy hunting, you wolf. Can't stop, got someone waiting for me too." Arthur cycled briskly back up the street to put Eve out of her nocturnal agony.

Tony entered the darkened house with a certain unease. He had never come this late before. He tiptoed down the passage to the door at the far end. The dull click of the latch echoed in the silence. As the door opened, the sound of Paula's breathing became audible. He walked over to the bed with slow, timorous steps and stood there watching with close interest as the mane of her hair on the pillow, the contours of her plump neck and shoulders and the features of her face slowly detached themselves from the darkness. He was standing there, undecided, tiredness returning to his limbs when a languid groan broke the train of regular breathing. Paula stirred. Her lips parted in a vague smile.

"I heard you open the door. I've been counting aeroplanes all night. I wondered if you'd come."

Her welcome renewed Tony's confidence. "Sorry I'm late. I had to fly to Germany," he said with an attempt at humour which was entirely wasted.

Paula showed no interest in conversation. She threw back the sheets to reveal her plump, well-rounded body. Her legs were unashamedly apart.

"I want you," she said.

Tony's heart pounded, his head swam. He tore off his clothes with his last, desperate reserves of strength, falling on top of her, giddily giving himself up to her, to warmth and temporary safety.

Tony was first to wake later that morning. He felt dreadful after only two hours sleep. His limbs and back ached, and a band of lead lay tightly across his forehead. He hauled himself up into a sitting position on the edge of the bed. Paula opened her eyes.

"I got a lift here last night. Bloke who lives in the village. He knew all about us. Aren't you surprised?"

"A little. I didn't think anybody knew."

"Walls have ears. It's our mid-upper gunner. He lives unofficially off the station; just opposite, actually."

A glimmer of comprehension registered in Paula eyes. "I know who he is. I know his wife too. They come into The Happy Angler sometimes. She's called Eve. We walked home together the other day from the shops. Pretty woman. Small too; wish I was."

Paula made to rise. Tony made a clumsy attempt at rolling her over which she avoided. She rose. Tony grabbed at her.

"You're pretty too, and beautiful."

Paula freed herself. Her face was prim and hard. Warmth and intimacy had, once again, disappeared with the light of a new day. She tripped over to the screen. The dressing-gown with the cascade of red stars disappeared from view. When Paula emerged, she was wearing it.

"Tony, there can never be anything between us. I'm twenty-nine years old. Would you like a cup of tea?"

"No thanks," Tony replied sullenly.

"Suit yourself."

Paula went into the kitchenette. Tony let his head drop into his hands. Faced with the prospect of a day on the station and perhaps ops that night, he felt the reluctance that he had sometimes felt as a small child before a day at school. He was beset by a nagging fear of impending disaster. Why did life have to consist of such terrible extremes - love, passion, warmth and the perennial threat of sudden violent death? He had been a fool even to start this affair. What had possessed him? He must have been mad.

"I've changed my mind about the tea," he shouted.

A voice called back from the other room, "Coming right up."

Tony got dressed and wandered over to the table. He collapsed on to a chair in front of the tea which Paula had placed there. He started babbling, a disjointed, breathless spate of words, to no one in particular.

"What the hell's going on? How many battles are we supposed to fight? I've done twenty-four; been at it since the end of March. We were nearly all killed the other night when flak ships opened up at us. Every time you go out, you wonder if you'll ever see daylight again. What do people expect from us? I'm only twenty-one. Our pilot's nineteen. Nineteen! His girlfriend's sixteen. I accused him of cradle-snatching the other day. It's not him who's cradle-snatching; it's the bloody Air Force."

Tony gasped for air. Two eyes stared wildly from a ravaged face. Paula was taken aback. Not even her experience stretched to unsuitability for combat duties, or what the Brass were pleased to call L.M.F.: 'lacking moral fibre'.

"Now they've started this pathfinder business. If it's not one thing, it's another. It's just press on, press on, press on. You wouldn't think we were flesh and blood, any of us. How much are we supposed to take? And who the hell cares, anyway? We'll never see the end of this war, none of us will."

Tony consumed most of the tea in the cup in two frenzied gulps and rose. He looked as if he had lost his bearings. It was then that Paula relented. She came over and embraced him as a mother might embrace a child.

"I'm sorry, darling. Be careful. I don't want anything to happen to you. I think of you all the time. Don't forget, you've got the key."

Tony disengaged himself. From somewhere he had collected a last residue of fortitude. He straightened his body, kissed Paula gently and left.

6

The Stirlings of 7 Squadron were dispatched to Flensburg that evening, the 18th August, forming part of the Pathfinder Force together with the Halifaxes of 35 Squadron. They took off in near daylight at 20:30. Flying out over Cromer, Robin, Arthur and Ollie saw the sun set and the sea turn from red to dark blue to inky black as they pressed on north-east. Owing to deterioration in the weather, the operation was not a success. Billy's Revenge was carrying high-capacity bombs and attacked the centre of the submarine yards. Ollie and Arthur claimed they saw the four bombs burst and fires burning in the centre of the town. They touched down again at Oakington at 01:30 hours.

In the mess dining-room the following day Tony sat opposite Arthur. Lunch that day was meat pie, boiled potatoes and carrots. Arthur took up a piece of carrot on his fork and held it up for inspection. "Good for night vision."

"Should be raw, really," Tony countered.

They ate in silence for some moments before Tony broke the silence. "So you're on to me?"

"Oh that. Don't look so serious. You aren't the first, you won't be the last."

"Do you think I'm wise?"

"You're all right as long as you don't get caught. If her old man comes home suddenly and catches you at it, you're in shit street."

That wasn't really what Tony meant, but before he could explain further Robin came and sat down next to Tony. He was clearly upset about something.

"I'm bloody annoyed," he said.

Arthur was in one of his frivolous moods. "What's up, Rob? We haven't surrendered, have we?"

"No. I've just read the paper; the Americans have started bombing."

"What did they bomb – the Isle of Wight?"

"No, Rou-en."

"That's all right, Rob; that's in France."

"Well, I know it is." Robin's voice squeaked with indignation. several heads turned. He continued in a more subdued tone. "That's not the point. You should have seen the spread they got; it was as much as we got when we bombed Cologne."

A white-coated mess orderly winged down on them from nowhere, picked up an empty water jug and in the same deft movement deposited a full one. Arthur filled his glass. A plate with meat pie, potatoes and carrots appeared in front of Robin. Robin went on regardless.

"Well, it makes me sick. It was a daylight raid too. I'd just like to see them bomb Happy Valley in daylight. And I mean France; well, Christ Almighty! We send sprogs to targets like that. Well, don't just sit there, say something."

Arthur and Tony looked at one another helplessly. It was Arthur who spoke. "What do you want us to say, Rob? The Yanks are in the war; be thankful; we need the fire power. They're the biggest, they think they're the best. They'll want to do things their way. They'll just have to learn the hard way. Anyway, I can't see us winning the war without them, so you'll just have to get used to them hogging the headlines." Arthur drank the remains of his water and wiped his mouth with his napkin. "Well, chaps, as we aren't on the battle order tonight, I'm clearing out before someone sends me as stand-in to Berlin... or Rou-en," he added with an outburst of jocularity.

Arthur left at the gallop. Robin suddenly discovered his meat pie. He attacked it as though it was the last meal he was ever likely to get. Tony sat and watched his comrade. He didn't care about the Americans. They were one more feature in a war which he didn't want to know anything about. At that moment he cared naught for newspaper coverage, daylight bombing, fire power, winning or losing. He was simply wondering how he was going to stay the course.

CHAPTER FOUR

1

It was Wednesday evening. Paula was in a skittish mood which didn't suit Tony at all. He wanted to talk, she wanted to play and whenever Tony opened his mouth, Paula silenced him, either with her lips and flickering tongue or with one of her huge, suffocating breasts. Twice Tony managed to roll Paula over on to her back, but her thighs were powerful. Swiftly, and with no little skill, she turned the tables on him and each time he ended up under the heavy smothering warmth of her body.

"What do you think of me?" Paula straddled Tony's body. Her back was erect, her hands behind her head.

"Paula, you're wonderful, but..."

"You don't think I'm too fat?" She brought down her hands and laid them on her belly. "I can pull it in but then my top half's so enormous."

"Paula, you're the personification of complete perfection, but..."

The flow of Tony's words were reduced to a muffled jumble as Paula pushed his head into her breasts.

"Do you think so, my darling? That's lovely."

Tony freed himself, gasped for breath and garbled, "Your husband, Paula; I fail to see how you can be so carefree. Haven't you any idea when he'll be coming home? We get leave every six weeks – if we survive."

"My darling, you're so serious." She hung over him on all fours her pendulous breasts sweeping the contours of his face.

"Paula, for God's sake – you be serious instead."

"I am serious, my darling."

"You aren't at all – I'm the one who's serious."

"I know you are, my pet. That's what attracts me to you so madly," she cooed.

"Oh for Christ's sake! Your husband." Tony made an effort born of desperation and managed to roll Paula over on to her side, but it didn't get him very far.

"You have a lovely head of hair, my darling."

"Can't we forget my hair?"

"Your hair attracts me too."

"What'll happen if he comes in the door?"

"My darling, you've got a grey hair!"

"That doesn't surprise me in the least."

"Keep still, I'll pull it out. There it is. Look!"

Paula thrust a forefinger and thumb under Tony's nose.

"I'm not interested," Tony said peevishly. "I asked what would happen if he walked in the door."

"I don't know; I honestly don't know," Paula answered.

She rolled over on to her back. Her eyes were fixed on the ceiling. A cloud had covered the sun. Suddenly, without warning, the air was chill. A note of vexation had crept into Paula's voice.

"I would have thought that you had enough on your mind without thinking about him."

Tony was taken aback. Uncertainty replaced exasperation.

"Well, I-I'm sorry, Paula. It's this situation. Look, I agree I should mind my own business, but try to see things from my point of view."

"You've nothing to worry about."

"But what about him?" Tony persisted.

"I said you had nothing to worry about."

"You haven't told him, have you?"

"Don't be ridiculous," Paula sounded more than mildly irritated.

"Where does he come into it?"

"He doesn't. Trust me, Tony."

"But what if he comes home?"

"He won't."

Tony was not to be denied. He had a nagging persistence, oblivious of rising temperature.

"How can you be so sure? I thought you might have asked for a divorce."

Tony had a momentary vision of himself in a divorce court. A man in a wig was cross-examining him in a terse voice from the bench.

"There's no need," she said with a sigh of annoyance.

"No need?" Tony was perplexed.

"Don't ask so many questions, Tony. You share the same bed with me; try and trust me. He can't possibly come home."

Paula made a clumsy attempt at embracing him again, but Tony sat bolt upright in bed scenting danger.

"Can't possibly? No need?"

"There's a buff envelope on the table." Paula's voice was tired and resigned.

"A buff envelope? Can't possibly? No need? A buff envelope?" The penny teetered then dropped. "He's dead, isn't he?" Tony's voice was hardly more than a whisper. The news was too horrible to be true.

"You can read the War Office telegram if you want."

Tony climbed over Paula's prostrate form and walked over to the table in a trance. The telegram was short and to the point. They didn't waste words. Reading it, Tony Reeves had the unnerving feeling that he was looking into his own coffin. His hand started to shake. Suddenly, he hurled the offending document down on to the carpet and began to circle it making jerky, agitated movements.

"Do you have to make such a fuss?"

"Fuss! Fuss!" Tony was verging on hysteria. He stopped walking, his arm hanging out like a piece of washing, a reproving finger pointing at the white patch on the floor. "Don't talk to me about fuss. My guv'nor's going to get a telegram like that, me, his only son, gone and I won't even be cold and stiff; I'll be burnt to a fucking frazzle."

"Don't swear! I don't like it. I won't have that sort of language in here!"

"It's too bad about you, dear. What are you going to do when I'm gone? – Find someone else? Shouldn't be too difficult; it's like a bloody fairground where I come from: five ops and then the chop. I've been on that station since the end of March and there are about five blokes left from that time." Tony thrust out the digits of a hand. "Five!"

Paula rose. Her naked body trembled; her eyes were already moist. She slipped into the dressing-gown as if taking refuge from a storm. "You don't have to shout; I'm not deaf. And put some clothes on, you look ridiculous."

Tony slipped into his underpants, one eye on the War Office telegram as if it weren't to be trusted where it lay on the carpet.

"I suppose you're clearing out now; well, go. See if I care."

Tony tucked his shirt into his trousers. "You know, I really loved you. I was going to ask you to get a divorce and marry me."

"Well, considering you say you're doomed to die, that's not much of an offer." Paula was standing between the bedside table and the fireplace. The dressing-gown was drawn tightly about her. Her arms were folded under her bosom. She was visibly shaken.

Tony slipped into his shoes. "You're right there; I must have been stupid. What a mess! What a bloody mess! There's just no hope; no damned hope. I didn't join up for a war. I was interested in aviation, that's all, and look where it's got me." He knelt down and tied up a shoe-lace. "When did you get it?"

"The beginning of last week."

"Oh Christ!" Tony sank down on to the sofa his head in his trembling hands. "So you've known all the time. I wish I'd never started this. I wish I'd never set eyes on you."

It was then that Paula started to cry. Suddenly, without warning, her face just cracked open and her noble features were raddled to ugliness.

"I didn't ask him to go," she wailed. "He volunteered. He couldn't get away fast enough. He came home once with his friends, laughing and joking. You'd have thought it was some sort of adventure. Now he's gone and left me all alone. Do you think it's always so much fun living?"

Tony looked up, a beaten man. "Well, I should imagine that most of the blokes at camp would prefer that to the chop." Suffering was bringing out the philosopher in him. "Forty years of life is no mean consolation."

"What do you do with forty years of life when nobody wants you, you're all alone, getting older and have no children and live in a dump like this?"

"I wouldn't know. I'm not in that enviable situation. There might well be a crew on the station who haven't even forty hours left, let alone forty years. It might be my crew, who knows."

Tony's tone became more mollified. The tide of righteous indignation which had born him up subsided. Doubt crept into his voice.

"Why haven't you had any children?"

Paula shrugged, went over to the bed, pulled out a handkerchief from under the pillow and blew her nose loudly. The dressing-gown fell open and a huge breast hung free, down to her belly. Tony noticed for the first time a blue vein which crossed her breast near the nipple. Her belly was enormous too, and her raddled face rendered even uglier by the lips which turned up, exposing red gums and uneven teeth. Thus, on looking at a work of art the discovery of one defect brings others to the attention, so the beauty Tony thought he had perceived crumbled before his very eyes.

Tony rose stiffly, put on his jacket and picked up his cap. They looked at one another: two pictures of abject misery.

"I'd better go," he said weakly.

Paula waved a hand which could have been a goodbye or a good riddance. On the other side of the door he hesitated, his hand resting on the latch. Paula's sobs were just audible through the thick wood of the door. Her crying had confused the whole issue. He was the one who should have cried. Bloody civilians! They didn't realise how lucky they were. He placed his forehead against the door embrasure. As he did so, Billy's death mask replaced Paula's crumpled, tear-stained face. That mask kept on popping up like one of those figures in a shooting gallery. How long had Billy been dead? Today was the nineteenth. Three weeks it was. Three weeks! What should he do now? What would his guv'nor have done? Well, his guv'nor wouldn't have got into a mess like this in the first place; that was the simple answer to that question. He ought to go back in there – he had some vague notion that she needed him – but he just didn't have the strength. His hand released the latch. As he took his head away from the door embrasure, Paula's sobbing faded. Tony lurched down the passage and let himself out of the house with a trembling hand. He walked back to camp on unsteady legs, sick with the feeling of his own cowardice and inadequacy.

Paula crept back into bed and lay in a quaking bundle, sobbing pitifully so that her pillow became sodden with tears. The War Office telegram was still on the floor where Tony had thrown it.

2

Arthur's nightmares had begun the previous week after the second gardening trip, for no apparent reason. On the two stand-down nights he had fallen asleep fairly quickly only to wake up again two hours later. On both occasions the nightmares followed the same pattern. Their kite had been hit, he didn't know by what, and was plummeting from the sky. Arthur struggled to escape from his turret, but his body was welded to his canvas strip. His efforts at smashing the perspex of the cupola proved as fruitless. The aircraft fell with ever increasing speed. Arthur had the impression that the air was being squeezed out of his body, but, just as his lungs were about to burst, he woke up, breathing heavily, sweating profusely. The bedclothes weighed a ton.

That night he half stood, half sat at the window. He had risen a couple of minutes earlier and had seen a tall, stooping figure walk by with laboured steps. He had tried sleeping with bedclothes and the window open, without and the window closed, but his disturbed metabolism defeated every attempt at finding an equable temperature. Outside, the church spire and clusters of surrounding buildings were black and cavernous against the night sky. Inside, the bedstead and wardrobe were dark shapes against the pale distemper of the bedroom walls. On the bedside table, Arthur could discern the alarm clock. The halting progress made by the luminous second-hand reminded him of time and its peculiar, inexorable passage. Sometimes he had the impression that their lives were being speeded up: youth, maturity, middle-age, condensed into two or three months. As a boy, he had spent hours looking into the viewers of the hand-operated film machines at the amusement arcade in Luton. The Dempsey-Willard fight had been his particular favourite. It was possible, by varying the speed at which one turned the handle, to vary the speed of the film. It was like that on the station. Perhaps the hand of Providence was turning a cosmic handle, varying the speed at which their lives slipped away, changing the pace of growth, development and decay.

He went over to the bed and looked down at Eve. After five ops in ten days including the two gardening trips when they had been away all night, she was sleeping the sleep of exhaustion. He slid under the bedclothes. Eve groaned and turned over. Falling asleep was never easy. Fixing one's eyes on a point somewhere did help and after an hour or so sleep would come. Arthur never worried much about insomnia. After all, they were all in the same boat. Most Bomber Command aircrew must have suffered from it at one time or another.

3

For the next five nights the weather precluded operations. Time was spent on Gee training – a must as this was the only navigational aid – cross-country navigation flights, air checks and intake of new crews.

In the absence of special radar equipment, efforts were made to improve night vision. The gunners were equipped with anti-searchlight goggles. Tablets were consumed in varying quantities, either to improve night vision or to keep awake. One lunchtime Arthur and Tony came into the ante room to hear some poor devil complaining bitterly that he hadn't slept for thirty-six hours after taking 'wakey-wakey' tablets. Physical fitness was important. Truex detailed Gunnery Leader Mike Smith to lay on a cross-country run.

"It's twice round the camp perimeter," the Flight Lieutenant bellowed to assembled airmen. "Nine miles."

"Nine miles! Christ, Mike, you said five to six."

"No, that's the time some of you lot'll be finishing - Ha! Ha! Ha!"

One day the squadron received a visit from an ophthalmologist, a senior WAAF officer, ostensibly to check and talk about night vision. The boys played her up something cruel. No formal lectures as such were held, although discussions continued unabated in the messes and the different sections.

For the crew of Billy's Revenge, after five ops in ten days, it was a time when warm rays of hope penetrated and dispersed the damp mists of despair. They had two main grounds for optimism. Firstly, fears about changing pilots hadn't materialised. Bill Kransky had come through his first trips as captain with flying colours. Secondly, all of them, except Kransky and Ollie, had completed more than half a tour. Tony, Elton and Tom were well over twenty. There was a faint light at the end of the tunnel. That week the prevailing mood was one of quiet optimism.

Originally, it had been Tom and Robin who had suggested a quiet evening out in the country. Arthur suggested The Happy Angler. The others, especially Elton, had readily agreed, except Tony, whose reluctance had the same source as Elton's enthusiasm, and Bill Kransky, whose popsie wasn't of age.

That Sunday - it was the 23rd August - the crew of Billy's Revenge met Arthur and Eve on the village green at Stowe. The green was being used as a collection point for salvage. It looked as if it had been visited and ravaged by a hoard of day-trippers. It was a balmy evening, warm and windless. Low stratus cloud obscured the sun. Eve was radiant in a polka dot cotton frock. She had tied up her hair with a large white ribbon. It looked as if an enormous white butterfly had settled on her head. She was sitting on a bench with Arthur.

Elton and Tony arrived first. Arthur said waggishly, "We're admiring all the rubbish!"

Eve rebuked him sternly. "You mustn't let Mr Jarvis hear you saying that. That's our salvage campaign. It's important. It's going to help us win the war."

Robin, Tom and Ollie brought up the rear. On arrival, Robin lost no time in commenting on the state of the village green. It was as distressing as news-coverage of the American air war.

"Look at this! I mean, I know there's a war on, but you'd think they could keep the country tidy. What are we fighting for? Makes you wonder."

Eve rose. "Don't you start too. This is the Cambridgeshire salvage campaign. It's part of the war effort. Come on, let's go to the pub."

Eve pulled a jocular Arthur to his feet and they proceeded up the main street, a white butterfly bobbing amongst a cluster of blue forage caps. A short way from the pub Robin said, "Last one there pays!" The cluster of blue exploded to become a straggling line. Eve moved forward in a series of playful leaps, frisking like a young calf. Arthur took her by the waist, lifting her so she took seven-league strides. They arrived at the entrance panting, laughing, Eve whooping, within seconds of one another and burst into the lounge with a clatter. Elton brought up the rear. He walked straight up to the bar with the air of a man who had planned the move carefully. Paula was serving an elderly couple in tweeds. The man had long grey hair and a drooping grey moustache. The woman, also grey-haired, wore brogues. Her socks were rolled down to her ankles. They both looked as if they'd been for a long walk.

Tony seemed to catch Paula's eye at once. They exchanged the looks of those who have seen one another's souls. The half-naked, sobbing, broken woman with the raddled face and the huge pendulous breast was unrecognisable. Her complexion was smooth and untarnished; her eyes sparkled. She was wearing a low-cut orange blouse of some sort of taffeta material which exposed the creamy white of her bosom. Her whole being seemed to have possessed a capacity for self-healing which Tony found astonishing. As he sat down next to Ollie, he felt relieved. Elton bought the drinks.

They talked shop at first. The talking point in the Flight Offices during the past week had been an Air Ministry Training Staff decision not to carry second pilots. The arguments were that it was impossible to train sufficient pilots to carry two per aircraft and that for the new four-engined heavies, a pilot and a flight engineer were sufficient. Many were dismayed by this decision as it meant that newly-trained pilots had no chance of experiencing battle conditions before taking complete responsibility for an aircraft and crew. Crews whose captains would be completing a tour before they would felt a threat to their chances of survival. Criticism, consequently, was severest from them. The fact that Bill Kransky had eleven ops under his belt including invaluable experience as second dickey with Benny Goodman gave the crew of Billy's Revenge more fuel to fire their optimism.

Then Ollie took over. To the others in the crew, apart from Tom and Robin, he was an unknown quantity. That evening he proved to be quite a card.

He had been born and brought up in the White Highlands of Kenya where his parents farmed fifteen acres of coffee. In the clipped accent of the White African he told of a world of which the others knew, if they knew at all, only from the tales of Buchan and Ryder Haggard: a world of grandeur, vastness, rugged peaks, sweeping horizons, a world of purples and greens, of blue skies, of glorious mornings, afternoon thermals and sudden evening darkness. His stammer - he had a problem with initial plosives - only served to add piquancy to his story-telling.

One day he had gone to visit a pal on a neighbouring farm. His knocks remained unanswered and he was about to leave when he fancied he heard a "p-p-peculiar rasping sound" as if someone were attacking an iron bar with a fret-saw. It grew louder. His curiosity got the better of him. He felt the handle of the door. The door opened. On the other side was a rather large lion. "The b-b-beast was p-p-purring; that was the rasping sound."

There were nods of comprehension as the logicality of lions purring - after all, they were cats - dawned. Ollie told them about the blacks too and of a 'chicken game' which they played by standing with their toes on the railway line when a train was approaching. Their preoccupation with honour and courage explained the large number of toeless Africans in villages near the railway.

"We have some working on the farm. They aren't b-b-bad chaps, b-b-but you've got to keep an eye on them. They don't associate oil with machinery."

"Good job we haven't got any on the station," Tony said.

Arthur said, "They'd probably all be over by the railway line testing one another's courage."

Tony tested his own courage by buying the next round. Paula came round from the public bar.

"What's it to be?" she said. Her manner was guarded, her tone neutral.

"Six pints and a shandy, please."

Paula started to pull the first pint and Tony said, "I owe you an apology, for last time. I made a complete fool of myself. I had no business carrying on like that, none at all. I shouldn't have behaved as I did."

Tony ground on in the same vein, more excuses, then excusing his excuses.

"Put it down to strain, the war. Well, that's no excuse really. I mean, it's the same for everybody, isn't it? I'm sorry about your husband. I should have said that instead of carrying on as I did. It was wrong of me. I'm sorry."

From the corner came a raucous laugh from Tom and a squeal from Eve. Paula placed the third pint on the counter.

"Stop being sorry, it's too late," she said cryptically.

She took down a fourth glass. They spoke instinctively in low voices. Tony was leaning over the bar top, hands clasped. He might have been praying or confessing some mortal sin.

"I haven't told anyone about us, been bragging or anything."

Paula's features relaxed in a smile. "I know. You aren't like that. I've known that all the time. That's one of the reasons I asked you home."

"One of the reasons?"

"I liked you, of course."

"I like you too." Tony found his gaze drawn towards the creamy divide between her breasts. Paula flushed.

There was more laughter from the corner. Elton was telling a story which everyone seemed to be enjoying. Paula started on the fifth pint.

"I found out my husband was being unfaithful. A 'friend' told me. There wasn't any point in having it out with him. He'd probably have begged for forgiveness and then at the first opportunity have gone out and done the same thing again. In a sense the war's solved a problem. I've never been unfaithful before."

Tony leant further over the bar. He told Paula she was the first woman he'd ever slept with. For a moment it looked as though she was going to laugh, but she restrained herself and said she was flattered.

"We're out as a crew tonight. We're in a confident mood. We're well up; near the end of a tour. We've got through the summer, just about. Couple more weeks and we're home and dry. Be due for a spot of leave too."

Tony paused, licked his lips, visibly collecting himself. Paula was filling the sixth glass. "Look, Paula, couldn't we go out sometime? Into Cambridge? We could see a show, or go to the cinema. Live it up a bit."

Paula flushed and smiled. "I'd love that, Tony. There's an arts' theatre in Cambridge; they put on plays, quite good ones, with actors and actresses from London. They have concerts at the Guildhall too. We could hear the Cambridge Philharmonic, if you like."

Tony nodded with the eagerness of a child who has been promised a treat. "I don't know anything about music, but it'll be fun learning with you." As they put the glasses on a tray, Tony saw vistas of culture unroll before his mind's eye: vast orchestras, conductors in immaculate black, footlights, scenery, actors and actresses tripping between props throwing their voices out over rows of spellbound theatre-goers. He picked up the tray and a bell rang on the other side. "I'll come over tomorrow whether we're on or not; but it might be late."

"I'll look forward to that, Tony." Paula waved discreetly and disappeared into the public bar.

When Tony returned to his crew, they had just started playing a game: seeing who could smoke a cigarette down to the shortest stub. Eve won amidst roars of laughter. Arthur gave up first, Ollie was a surprising second, Elton burnt his lips and offered to buy his second round of the evening.

They left The Happy Angler just before ten. It had been a wonderful evening. The war had become peripheral. The fear, tension and discomfort which accompanied their waking hours; the nightmares which racked their few hours of sleep were banished. Of the war, only comradeship remained. As they walked back to camp in the warm evening under a tinted sky, languor was their companion. It followed them into camp, up to the billets. As they crept lethargically between their sheets, it was a soporific. That night they slept a dreamless sleep.

The languor of that evening became the sluggishness of the following day. They woke after a heavy sleep, ate breakfast and assembled in the briefing room at nine. Ops were on. Billy's Revenge was on the battle order. After morning prayers, they made their way out to dispersals. The aircraft was in perfect trim so they dispensed with the NFT. They stood in the morning sunshine and chatted to the mechanics. At ten, when the NAAFI wagon jerked to a halt on the pan, they drank weak tea and ate Chelsea buns. Tony climbed up on to the port wing and took a photo. As he looked down into the viewfinder, the men on the ground stared up at him with blank indifference. Two of the mechanics didn't even bother to turn round.

After lunch in the mess, they repaired to their billets to rest. Arthur cycled home to Eve. Briefing was at four. He wouldn't have time to go home again.

4

Up to the time at Oakington and the long nights of fear and uncertainty when Arthur was on ops, the most traumatic experience in Eve Johnson's life had occurred at the age of eight; a fall from her bicycle into a patch of stinging nettles. It hadn't been the first time she had ridden down that steep, uneven path near her home which had the bend at the bottom where the path levelled out, on a bicycle which, in order to sit on the saddle, she had to stand on the pedals. The whole episode seemed so silly afterwards. It really shouldn't have happened. A bird flying out of a thicket of hazel had distracted her and swiftly and inevitably she had toppled, finding herself in the nettles the bicycle on top of her. Rescue, in the form of her sister, Olive, had been almost immediate, but had seemed to little Eve to take an age and she had cried all the way home. The incident was indelibly engraved on her memory and had consciously steered her behaviour in difficult situations ever since. Avoiding accidents was a question of concentration and circumspection. Distraction was a luxury one couldn't afford. While Arthur was away over Germany she never let herself be distracted. Vigilance, hope, and prayer were the stuff that gave telepathic armour its protective properties. He would survive if he was in her thoughts. This was Eve Johnson's belief. This was her hold on sanity through those dark nights of loneliness and fear, nights without end, of heavy, unnerving silence broken only by a ticking clock and the beating of a small heart.

But that Monday morning in late August, as Eve came back from the village with her shopping, there was an air of insouciance in her bearing. It was as though the pleasantness and warmth of the previous evening had blunted the finely honed edge of her vigilance. She reached Mrs Badesby's house and opened the gate with the casualness of the village housewife. No one would have guessed she was a woman perpetually teetering on the edge of the abyss of widowhood.

This insidious process had, in fact, begun nine days earlier when the Cambridgeshire Salvage Campaign had got under way. This campaign differed from its predecessors in that it had both short and long-term aims. The short-term aims were voiced abroad on hoardings, notice-boards and in newspapers: "Turn your waste into weapons", "Salvage saves shipping", "Your iron makes mighty tanks", and a target was set for the two-week campaign. In the long term it was hoped that people would become more salvage-conscious. The campaign, which put the whole county on a salvage footing, brought the best out of Mrs Badesby who, like a good general, saw to it that she was in the thick of the fighting. She quickly established contact with the two local salvage stewards: the ironmonger, who was responsible for the main street and the butcher, who looked after the side streets. Eve received a visit from Mr Jarvis, the butcher, while Mrs Badesby was away on an errand. He was a short, portly gentleman with healthy, chubby cheeks rather like a baby's. He had been furnished with a certificate of authority which he produced and flourished in the manner of a jovial bailiff. It was his job to educate the householder in the ways of salvage. For example, did she know what types were needed? She didn't? – Well, all types really: paper, metal, rubber, rags. Did she realise that each scrap of salvage collected hastened the dawn of victory? Had she thought about bones? – She hadn't? Well, he was a butcher, he knew about bones all right; they were of the utmost value. It was simply amazing what could be done with bones. Yes, indeed. They could be used to produce fats for explosives, lubricant greases, camouflage paint, feedstuffs for pigs and poultry, all sorts of things you could never dream of. He told Eve where to look for salvage, how to sort it, and indicated the whereabouts of central dumps for collections. Eve tried to tell him that Mrs Badesby was in charge, but her words only bobbed on the tide of the butcher's voluble chatter.

Later, when Mrs Badesby returned, Eve had given her the gist of Mr Jarvis' information. That night Arthur had been on ops – the target was Düsseldorf – and the two women had spent the evening and night going through drawers in the more obscure reaches of the house. It had been a difficult night for Eve. She broke off continually to go into the parlour and smoke, fixing her gaze on the mantelpiece clock. Mrs Badesby, indefatigable, popped out and in waving threadbare cardies and holding up yellowed bed-linen for inspection and advice on what to keep and what to part with. Mrs Badesby hadn't been oblivious to Eve's plight, however. She held up her fingers; they were crossed. Mrs Badesby said that two hearts were better than one and that she was hoping too. Eve smiled with gratitude. The two women then worked into the small hours as if sunrise would bring with it the dawn of victory. It hadn't done, but it had brought with it Arthur and the sun had risen on a new day of hope reborn.

The following days had seen the battle intensify. Mrs Badesby was mounting her own offensive. Having gone through the house like a dose of salts, she turned her attention to the garden shed. The morning of the Flensburg raid, Eve had helped her dismantle an old bicycle – the rubber tyres would come in useful, Mrs Badesby removed them with kitchen spoons – and collected metal, sacking and paper. During the afternoon they had filled an empty paint tin with old nails – every little counted – which they pulled out of pieces of an old plank.

The campaign gained momentum. In Stowe, piles of newspapers stood at the entrance to houses and shops. One half of the village green looked like a gigantic junk-yard. In Cambridge the campaign was no less in evidence but there was a carnival atmosphere. The day after the Flensburg raid, Arthur and Eve had been on Market Hill where an ARP messenger's band paraded in a specially built salvage lorry from which the inevitable Union Jack hung limply.

The passage of the days had seemed to gain momentum too, so that Eve had been hardly aware of them flying by. Suddenly it was Monday, the 24th August.

5

Eve felt the washing on the line. It was bone dry. She went into the house where she unpacked her shopping: a loaf of bread, a small pot of marmalade, sugar wrapped in stiff blue paper and two ounces of cheese, a week's ration, in greaseproof paper. The sugar, she was saving little by little to make jam for the winter. She was already looking forward to Arthur's next leave which would be due in just under two weeks. The evenings would soon be drawing in. Images of cosy stand-down nights in front of a crackling fire – there was a supply of firewood in the shed – suffused her brain.

"Monday wash-day!"

Eve jumped and turned quickly. She squealed with delight and scurried to the slight, dapper figure standing in the doorway to the scullery. She hurled herself into his arms and kissed him. "Hello, darling. I didn't hear you coming."

"You're slipping." Arthur squeezed her, lifting her off her feet. He carried her into the parlour. "We're on tonight. Briefing at four. We'll be going up fairly early so I won't be home in between."

That was Arthur's news. He would be forsaking rural England and his own domestic hearth for the searing hell of a battlefield. Eve said, "We'll have the afternoon. I'll just pop out and get in the washing."

Arthur slumped down on to the settee and stifled a yawn. The pain-killer of the previous evening and the night's untroubled sleep hadn't worn off. Somehow the prospect of searing hell wasn't producing the usual effects on his system. Eve returned from the garden, barely visible behind a bale of washing.

"I can iron these while you're away." She spoke in a matter of fact tone. Arthur might have been spending the evening playing darts at the local pub.

The young couple spent the afternoon looking at a Kodak wallet of eight prints, six being from the last time they were home together on leave. They studied them carefully, one by one, as if in silent appreciation of works of art. There were two which merited comment. The one was of Eve and Arthur standing against the great oak at the entrance to Bankside. The camera shutter had caught Arthur, cigarette in hand, exhaling. The other was of Arthur, alone, sitting on a gate, the collar of his tunic turned up. Eve always felt an urge to turn down that collar, but that was impossible; the faces, the wisps of smoke, the upturned collar had been caught and frozen for all eternity on Velox paper. The last print was of Pa. Arthur said, "I like Pa."

"Everyone likes Dad. He's that sort."

Pa was sitting in the field at the back of the house with outstretched legs which reached almost into the camera lens. The soles of his shoes looked enormous. He was wearing the clothes he had worn that Sunday they had gone to church and he and Arthur had rummaged in the hedge for bottles of beer. He was smoking his pipe and looked the picture of contentment.

Arthur took out a wallet and removed a small photo of Eve. It had been taken when they had lived in Northern Ireland. She was standing on a grass landing-strip near Limavady. The wind had swept her hair to one side and had filled her wide slacks. She wore a thick jacket tied at the waist with a belt of the same material. He held up the photo.

He said, "My favourite."

"Why do you like that one?"

Arthur shrugged. "Don't know." He twisted his neck and kissed Eve. She responded. "It's important to me. I have to have it with me, all the time. Lucky charm."

After they had looked through the prints again with a slow reverence, Eve went into the kitchen to make a cup of tea. When she came back, she caught Arthur stifling another yawn.

Eve said, "You should be resting." She gave Arthur his tea.

"Ta, love. Just what the doctor ordered. I'll be all right. Slept too well, that's all. When will Mrs Badesby be back?"

"Tomorrow."

"I don't know how she does it. You'd think she was fighting the war all on her own. When's that salvage do over?"

"Another week." Eve sat down beside him and sipped her tea.

"Well, there can't be anything more to take here. I half-expected to come home one day and see you two chopping up the furniture."

"Wood's not salvage," Eve riposted with the eloquence of a salvage steward.

"You see how much I know." Arthur sipped at his tea. "Pity she's away just tonight. I don't like you being here alone."

Eve responded like a soldier; as brave as any in the front line.

"It doesn't matter, darling. I'm used to it now. I just want to be with you, that's all. It's not so bad. Besides, the evenings are drawing in. You'll be going up earlier, I'll have the wireless for company and we'll get to bed at a normal hour."

They sat in silence and drank their tea. The mantelpiece clock registered the inexorable passage of time. Arthur glanced at his watch. Some of the colour drained from his cheeks and his face tautened perceptibly. He rose and put his cup on the table.

"I'll have to go, Eve. It's best not to leave it too late; might get a puncture."

Eve's little heart fluttered as she collected herself for her eighteenth act of bravery that summer. Things got no easier. Each time might well be the last. Each time was like the first time, worse, in fact, because the first time she really didn't know what hell lay in store during those long, dark, endless nights. Things would be better for Arthur when he got back to camp. For Eve there would be no relief, just an empty house peopled by her thoughts, her fears, her doubts, her dreads. She rose, put down her cup. She threw her arms about Arthur's neck in a hug of desperation.

"Don't forget to pray for me."

Arthur's voice was steady. He had nerves of steel. The strain and fear he must have been feeling he hid well.

"I always pray, darling, you know that." She squeezed him with all the strength in her small frame.

She released him and Arthur, as if obeying a sudden, mysterious impulse, thrust his hand into his pocket and took out a stub of pencil. The wallet lay on the settee. He picked it up, put it on the table and with the stub started to write in block capitals on the inside of the wallet. "EVE, MY DARLING, I LOVE YOU DEARLY, FOR EVER AND EVER UNTIL THE END OF THE WORLD." It wasn't strictly grammatical, but that didn't matter.

They went out into the warmth of mid-afternoon. Arthur took the bicycle and they walked together down the garden path. The sun shone from a near cloudless sky. It was an afternoon made for relaxing in the garden not for embarking on the first stage of a journey to a battlefield. A rustling sound caught the attention of the young couple. A bird flew out of the undergrowth.

"Garden looks a bit of a mess," Arthur remarked. "If I get time, we'll have to do something about it." He placed his forage cap on his head.

"You're hopeless at gardening."

"I know that, but I thought you could do it. I could just act in a supervisory capacity."

"Naughty boy!" Eve slapped him playfully. Arthur stumbled slightly. The bicycle fell into a tangled flower-bed.

"Now look what you've done. Now I might be late for the war."

Their banter concealed nerves as taut as violin strings. Arthur wanted to stand at the gate forever, but he had to be going, he really had to. He took her in his arms again as if for the last time on this earth.

"I'll love you for ever and ever, ever and ever."

"I'll love you too, my dearest, for ever and ever. I'll pray too, all the time."

"I hope this'll soon be over, I really do."

"Everything'll be all right, you'll see. I'll pray."

Then Arthur went, quickly, resolutely. He mounted and waved; with determined pushes on the pedals he was up the street and away. He waved once more, wobbled and rounded the corner. Eve looked for some moments at the deserted street before turning to go inside the house. Her heart beat rapidly and there was a small tear at the corner of her eye.

Entering, the first thing she saw was the open wallet with the last message at the end of the known world.

CHAPTER FIVE

1

At four o'clock exactly, the Station Commander, a large, straight-backed man in his early fifties, entered the briefing room moving up the centre aisle like a ship of the line. The Squadron Commander and other senior officers responsible for the briefing followed in his wake. When he reached the dais, he turned and surveyed the assembly with an aggressive sang-froid. His eyes swept the room. His attitude provoked some cynicism from the ranks of the battle-hardened twenty-year-old veterans, but not a lot. Their CO was on the battle order that night, flying with a young sergeant pilot who smoked a pipe and had the beginnings of a moustache. The CO removed his hat to reveal a bald pate bounded by glossy dark brown hair brushed back. He motioned to the seventy-odd airmen to sit down. There was a noise of scraping chairs and shuffling feet and a general rummaging after cigarettes and matches. As the first column of smoke started to rise, a high-pitched squeak sounded from a roller. The blind covering the wall behind the dais snapped up violently revealing a map of Europe.

A red ribbon extended from Oakington to Orford Ness on the East Anglian coast, south-east to a point in Belgium just inside the Franco-Belgian border. It threaded its way through red patches along the same border to the foothills of the Ardennes before turning almost due east to a point where there was a bend in the Rhine.

"Gentlemen, the target tonight is Frankfurt."

The Station Commander's announcement was greeted with sighs of relief from those to whom the target was news; at least it wasn't Happy Valley and the red blotches were correspondingly sparser. No one had ever been to Frankfurt before and with the exception of four crews who had bombed Mainz on the 11th and the handful of survivors who had flown to Mannheim the day Arthur arrived at Oakington, no one had ever been near the Lower Rhineland. The Group Captain gave Frankfurt a short introduction.

"Frankfurt is a commercial centre," he boomed in a voice like a loudhailer, "a large inland port, a railway nodal point with extensive marshalling yards. By striking a blow against this city we strike a blow against his communications. Communications," the Station Commander paused and swept the room with a steely glance before booming on as if his audience consisted of stone-deaf geriatrics, "are the arteries of the Enemy's war-machine. Without good communications the Enemy can't fight the war, or will at least find its war effort impeded. So, Gentlemen," another pause, a lull in the reverberations, another steely glance, "we're going to hit those marshalling yards hard and," he paused once more, "while we're there, we're going to kill as many of the bastards as we can." He sat down, visibly relieved at having let off steam.

The different officers responsible for the briefing made their contributions. The night's scenario unfolded. It was to be an incendiary raid; the squadron's first real effort in its role as pathfinders. The first take-off would be just after eight, a fact welcomed by many as the lucky ones would be home earlier. Zero hour would be at 23:30 when twenty aircraft of the Pathfinder Force would mark the target by releasing either 30 lb or 250 lb incendiary loads in a salvo in order to produce blobs of fire at the aiming point. At 23:38, and no earlier, aircraft of the second section were to attack with incendiaries. In this section were included the remaining aircraft of the PFF, Stirlings (including the eleven machines from Oakington), and Wellingtons loaded with 4 lb incendiaries, Halifaxes and Lancasters with loads of 1000 lb or 4000 lb high-explosive bombs made up with incendiaries. The attack by this section was to be completed by 23:59 hours. The third section was to attack with high explosive between 23:55 and 00:10 hours.

The Navigation Officer had the most information to give and although he had already briefed captains and navigators very thoroughly, he went over the route in some detail for the benefit of the others, dragging his pencil over the red ribbon, pausing to give times and positions in degrees and minutes. Aircraft of the PFF were to follow the route: Base – Reading – Le Crotoy – Target, and return to eight miles due west of Le Crotoy to Clacton and Base. Sections two and three were routed: Base – Orford Ness – Furnes – Mons – Target returning to base via Courtrai and Furnes. It was expected that Gee would be effective at least as far as Mons on the outward journey and navigators were advised to obtain as accurate fixes as possible in order to check wind velocity before that point.

At the back of the room, the serious Tony and the impish Arthur puffed at their cigarettes and listened as the Navigation Leader pattered on in his irksome way. He impressed on the assembled company the esoteric nature of the discipline of the men for whom he was leader. Elton, in the front row, nodded knowingly as his master spoke. From time to time he glanced down at his chart. Other navigators did the same. They would prepare the spell that would take them to the target and home again. They could make sense of the apparent mumbo jumbo.

By the time the Navigation Leader had finished, the room was thick with cigarette smoke. Through an open window, a gentle breeze disturbed the fug. In the distance, a lawn-mower clattered and a winch clanked faintly. Somewhere a lorry backfired.

Other officers continued the briefing. They each had their own personal styles. Some went over the top in their enthusiasm. Others, like the Intelligence Officer, were more unobtrusive. He read out facts about Frankfurt: nodal point, inland port, important industrial town, chemicals and engineering, with basic demographic and geographical data as though he were delivering a report to the board of a firm of merchant bankers who were considering opening a branch in the city. The dissonant note came at the end when, in a matter of fact way, he gave the aiming point as the city centre and the marshalling yards.

It was ten to five when John Truex stood up for the final word. He spoke at some length and with gravity. Arthur lit another cigarette. He felt some strange detachment as if the whole business of pathfinding didn't really concern him. As the Wing Commander spoke there were nods from some. Arthur noticed Elton and the young Sergeant Pilot. Truex said that the raid marked a turning point in the war. Hundreds of bombers straggling all over Northern Europe, getting picked off by enemy fighters, some finding the target some not, was out, as was bombing on fixes and ETAs.

"The future will be the concentration and saturation that marking and illumination can give us. To win this war we need more Colognes. We can only do that by improved accuracy and to get that we need good marking."

Truex went on to emphasise the importance of marking and good navigation.

"Keep to your schedules," he said in a voice only marginally less loud than his base commander's. Elton stopped nodding and stared transfixed, struck perhaps by the weight of his responsibility. "And there's one more thing." Truex gave everyone his own version of the Base Commander's steely glance, "Creepback. You can count on the markers bombing short. If in doubt, overshoot. Put your incendiaries on the far side of the target, then, with a bit of luck the main force should be spot on even allowing for optical foreshortening. We've an important job to do tonight, boys. Overall success depends on each crew doing their bit. Let's get out there and do our job well, for the people of Britain, for those in Occupied Europe, for the RAF and for the honour of the squadron." Truex's serious features parted in a smile. "Have a good trip, boys; and let's see you back here tomorrow morning."

Crews smiled back as the spell of silence was broken. They rose and shuffled out into another world of fresh air, late afternoon sunshine and the scent of newly-mown grass.

2

Crews repaired to their respective messes. High tea that evening was shepherd's pie and baked beans. The crew of Billy's Revenge minus their navigator, sat together. They were all thinking about Frankfurt and the possible reception going in first would mean. But pathfinding was as yet an unwritten page in the history of aerial warfare. The ifs and buts were many. The pros and cons weighed evenly. Nobody seemed unduly worried about what the future might hold.

Arthur's crew were last to leave the dining-room. They wandered their different ways. Arthur went up to his billet. He opened the door and went over to the window. In the west, the sun hung precariously in the sky like a golden saucer standing on its rim. From the mass of foliage forming the horizon rose the spire of Longstanton church. Beyond, there were groups of stone houses, orchards, flat fields and the village of Stowe. He thought of Eve, not that he ever stopped thinking of her, but just then in the silence of that room nothing else troubled his thoughts. He hoped she was looking at the sun too; it would be something they could share. In another hour it would have gone down behind the trees and he would be rolling out to dispersals, but at that moment it emblazoned the early evening sky, colouring the few wispy clouds with the reds, blues and purples of a day which it was laying to rest. As he watched, its rim visibly neared the darkening line of the tops of the trees.

Arthur turned away from the window, went over to his bed and slid his hand under the pillow. He took out a photo wallet and removed a photo which he turned slightly towards the window. It was a portrait of Eve. It really did her justice and before it Arthur sat as transfixed as he had been before the beauty of the golden evening. Eve's lovely face was framed by short, lustrous auburn curls. He picked out each feature: the kind eyes, the immaculate profile of the nose, the lips, the chin, her complexion, the lobe of her ear just visible below the curls. Eve's beauty was as ethereal as any film star's. An enlargement could easily grace the foyer of any cinema alongside the likes of Carole Lombard or Veronica Lake. He slipped the photo back into the wallet and the wallet back under the pillow. He lay back on the bed, yawned and closed his eyes.

The scenes of a long summer stretched before him like an immense, awesome fresco. Cologne, a vision of the apocalypse, a raging, pulsating inferno of fire, smoke and explosions was succeeded by other scenes: the horror of Essen, the web of searchlights and the unnerving beauty of the night sky festooned with flak; the mid-air collision and the sickening plunge into nothingness; the flashes from the nose canon of the night fighter as Billy Hamilton lay dying in his turret; the gardening trips, the convoy and the flak hanging after them like a paper chain as they strove to allude their predator; and now pathfinding, the shape of things to come. A glorious summer was almost gone. Three months. Seventeen trips. Two more weeks and they'd be due for a spot of leave. Then Autumn would be nigh. Perhaps he could finish a tour before the onset of winter. At the beginning of June he thought he was for the chop for sure. The Upper Rhineland had been hell on earth. Frankfurt didn't sound too bad. Going in first might have its compensations. He heard doors slamming and footsteps in the passage outside. He looked at his watch: seven thirty-five. It was time to get moving.

They kitted up quickly. That warm evening, only the gunners had jackets, the others were in battledress, their harnesses worn with varying degrees of slackness. Robin Huxtable was wearing Tony's jacket having mislaid his own. They piled into the Bedford lorries less clumsily than usual and within minutes of boarding, Arthur and company were clambering down from the tailboard on to their dispersal pan where the haughty silhouette of Billy's Revenge waited stoically in the fading light. The ground crew were standing around the battery-cart.

While his crew smoked a last minute cigarette, Bill Kransky walked a little way from the Stirling, turned and stopped. He craned his neck as he looked up at the bomb-aimer's perspex fifteen feet above his head. The majesty and grandeur of the aircraft were almost too much to take in. He thought back a year to the time just before he had started to train as a pilot. He had just got his driving-licence and was to borrow his father's car. What a fuss there had been! – over a mere car! His father had handed over the keys with great ceremony accompanied by a lecture: – do this – don't do that – don't drive too fast – never take your eyes off the road – take extreme care when reversing – don't forget the rear-view mirror. Terminating, his father had informed him that he was still very vulnerable and would be for the next six months.

Kransky peered up at the Stirling's lantern jaw. Here, no questions were asked. You just signed a form and the biggest aircraft in the world was yours. His popsie was equally impressed. He'd never forget the day he'd gone to meet Ann-Charlotte outside school before she broke up for the summer vacation. She had run up to him and kissed him. Everybody had looked. She'd already told her friends that her boyfriend was a pilot at RAF Oakington flying one of those gigantic bombers which could be seen from the road on the other side of the fence. They had both been in uniform. Ann-Charlotte wore a white shirt, blue tie, blue pleated skirt and a straw hat with a blue band round it. They had walked off hand in hand. He had never been so proud, in fact, his pride in Ann-Charlotte could only be matched by his pride in Billy's Revenge. They both had to be seen to be believed.

He looked along the fuselage, all eighty-seven feet of it, tapering at the end, standing on twin tail wheels and then let his gaze run over the aircraft; the gigantic wheels, the wheel housing panels flaring out just above the tyres, the undercarriage with its knee joint, the massive Hercules engines; everything was impressive. You simply had to give it to the British; there was style with their aircraft and their chicks. He had written home describing his situation, but could as little convey the grandeur of the Stirling bomber as he could the beauty of Ann-Charlotte. The obvious conclusion was a photo, like the one he had of Ann-Charlotte. He was wrestling with the problems of photo angles and distances when Arthur's voice broke into his thoughts.

"We'd better get moving, Bill."

Kransky signed for the aircraft and they boarded. Ollie, the last man to board, pulled in the ladder and banged shut the door. They went to their stations and plugged in their intercoms. The captain signalled to the battery-cart and pressed the ignition firing the starboard outer motor. When all four engines had spluttered into life, Kransky put his fists together and pulled them apart. Outside, a figure left the battery-cart and scuttled over to the fuselage. Seconds later their last link with the ground was severed. At his station Tony peered at his gauges in the light cast by his angle poise lamp. He crackled, "Oil pressure and temperature okay, Bill. Cylinder head temperatures okay too."

Kransky opened the throttles slightly and released the brake. As the Stirling lurched forward, he closed them a fraction and Billy's Revenge trundled forward more evenly. They were on their way.

3

Eve had just started ironing the sheets when she heard the laboured drone of the first Stirling at a little after ten past eight. She noted the time with satisfaction. She was unsure as to what time Arthur would be back, but unless it was a gardening trip, and she was fairly sure it wasn't, he should be back by two. She switched off the iron and sat and waited. She heard the second aircraft three minutes after the first followed by three more take-offs in quick succession. By twenty-two minutes past she had counted six. Then there was silence. She sat for some moments looking out of the window at the red glow in the evening sky.

Eve rose and went out into the garden. In spite of the warmth of the evening she shivered slightly, but didn't know why. She walked round the house, past the apple tree, now laden with fruit, down to the garden gate where she had touched Arthur for the last time. She looked up and down the empty street. Down the road the greens of the bushes and trees had merged into a dark uniform mass. She shuddered again and moved back the way she had come into the house. As she entered the kitchen, she heard another aircraft. The clock on the mantelpiece showed twenty to nine. It was Billy's Revenge starting its laboured climb, the first stage of a journey into the unknown.

By nine, Eve had noted eleven aircraft. By quarter past she knew there would be no more. Moving the ironing board over to the window to make full use of what little light there was she resumed her task. She ironed each sheet with a business-like dexterity, folded it, ironed it again, folded it twice more and applied the iron again for good measure. By the time she had finished the underwear, she was working in almost total obscurity, the fruits of her labour stacked in a neat pile on a chair by the dining-room table. She drew the blackout curtains and switched on the standard lamp. It was a quarter to ten. Sitting back in the armchair, she lit a cigarette, inhaled, then watched as the exhaled smoke formed transient, ponderous patterns in the harsh yellow light cast by the twenty-five watt bulb. She inhaled again, deeply.

An hour later she heard the noise of a returning aircraft. Half an hour later, another. Two early returns. The first time she had heard the noise of ailing engines, nearly three months ago, she had been frightened: now, she was a veteran. It was unusual for there not to be at least one aircraft returning early when ops were on. Eve felt nervous, a trifle exasperated. Time was hanging heavily. She wished Arthur home as she'd never done before. She wished she were somewhere else, somewhere with Arthur, away from this loneliness and terrible, unnerving silence. At length, she did something she had never done before: she took a library book and settled herself to read. She usually read during the day. This particular story intrigued her for some reason.

4

Billy's Revenge droned on over the Ardennes. Elton made frequent use of the Gee set, twiddling the knobs, watching the cathode ray tube as signals from the transmitting stations in England appeared on the screen. After centralising them on the strobe time base, he read off the co-ordinates, plotted his fix on the Gee lattice chart on his table and checked the fix with his own course. They crossed the German border at eleven and Elton calculated that they had forty-five minutes to the target which would put them well within the allotted time span for the second wave.

The gunners quartered the night sky. It was hardly noticeable that they were in Germany. Beneath and all around was blackness. They had seen nothing since leaving the English coast except their own bands of tracer curling away over the North Sea. Flying as they were, seemingly alone in the vast expanse of night sky with only the full moon for company, they needed to make an immense effort to convince themselves that briefing, the CO's sang froid, the PFF and the raid itself hadn't been a dream and that in less than half an hour the flak would be exploding around them and that they weren't the only human beings in existence.

In fact, their CO was no longer in existence. He and the young Sergeant Pilot had been dead for nearly an hour. It had happened just outside Mons. A night fighter had fired a salvo of canon shell into the belly of the Stirling. The methane-petrol mix in the 30lb incendiaries exploded into flame with gratitude. The four-pounders ignited too. The mid-upper gunner, the flight engineer and the wireless operator were burnt to death first. The pilot and the CO had a dim awareness of blinding light and heat a fraction before the end. The Stirling dripped from the sky in blazing pieces. It would have been difficult to imagine a more terrible death.

Elton took another fix. "Bill, we should be there in another fifteen minutes. Keep your eyes open for visuals, everybody."

The gunners redoubled their vigilance. Over the North Sea visibility had been good, but since crossing the enemy coast cloud cover had gradually increased. In places it was at least five tenths. At his untroubled Gee set, Elton took fixes in rapid succession as the target area came nearer.

A few minutes later Robin saw the silvery thread of the Rhine appear through the patches of strato-cumulus cloud. Presently, Arthur caught glimpses of the Rhine to starboard. Wiesbaden was silent. The cloud was functioning as an excellent cover. They continued westwards.

A gap appeared to starboard. Through it Arthur discerned a thin line of tracery glinting in what moonlight there was penetrating the blanket of cloud.

Elton took another fix. It was amazing; no jamming. Lately, on the runs into Northern Germany and the Upper Rhineland, the nav boxes were useless once you got into Holland. Tonight, thanks to the modified set, they appeared to be creeping in through the back door. He shone his pen-torch at the dial of his watch: 23:40. They were where they should have been and ought to be able to drop their load before 23:55. A minute later he unplugged his oxygen and moved down the steps to the bomb-aimer's station.

The cloud seemed to be thinning and the river could be clearly seen, a twisting bar spanned by frets running through the dark urban sprawl. Through the clouds ghosting by 5,000 feet below, the irregular fretwork pattern of streets was clearly visible. Kransky's voice came over the intercom.

"Elton, we'll fly on over the river and drop our load on the far side, like the Wingco said; don't forget creepback."

Kransky fidgeted nervously in his seat. He was beginning to enjoy himself. The opposition was virtually nil. To port, a few searchlights probed aimlessly, their beams lengthening and shortening as they bounced from cloud to cloud. There were flashes here and there. The defences were stirring, but they would be out and long gone before things hotted up. If this was going in first, he was all for it. They'd complete a tour in no time at all. Through the clouds just ahead a fire burned, throbbing like a hungry glow-worm.

Elton said, "Looks like a stick of 250 pounders burning. We'll put them down there, should be far enough, then get out of here and home; I'm hungry."

The others smiled constricted smiles. Elton never ate before an op. He always said he had too much to do.

"Bomb doors open."

"Steady now, keep straight."

The Stirling flew straight and level and the fires, contracting and expanding like a threadbare magic carpet, crept into the wires of the bombsight. As the flak started to intensify, Elton pressed the button and the incendiaries fell in their pre-arranged sequence. The incandescent explosion immediately afterwards under the aircraft told them that the photoflash had ignited. Elton climbed back to the flight deck.

The incendiaries, 1,700 small canisters of solid thermite, fell in blocks of 90, bursting in sticks on the ground, burning with blinding white light where they had landed. Kransky applied full rudder and turned the wheel to port for the long haul home. Ollie, in the rear turret, saw fires blazing in what he thought was the north-east part of the city. Their own incendiaries, a carpet of twinkling diamonds, burned nearby. Across the city, in the south-west, where the cloud cover was more dense, the shadows of two other bombers loomed out of the darkness.

5

Eve concentrated on her reading.

Raven, a hired gunman, had killed a war minister in a foreign country, but had been paid for the job in forged notes. The assassin, wanted by the police because he had passed one of the notes in a shop, had managed to find Cholmondley, the man who had paid him, follow him to Euston Station and from there to a town called Nottwich which was situated in the Midlands. The plot was tangled and full of suspense, but that wasn't the only reason that the book was intriguing. In spite of the fact that he had killed a man in cold blood, Eve couldn't help feeling sorry for Raven. Secretly, she hoped he would catch up with this Cholmondley so that the latter would get his just deserts.

At Nottwich, Raven couldn't leave the platform for fear of being picked up at the barrier. (He had, in fact, boarded the train at Euston by rushing the barrier just before the train left, saying he'd pay on the train. He was sure the ticket-collector on the train wouldn't know about the forged notes.) Eve wondered what she would have done on that platform in Raven's place and could see no way out, but a young woman was one of the few people left on the platform after the other passengers had gone. Raven went up to her, offered to buy her a ham sandwich and a cup of coffee and then told her that he wanted her ticket in exchange for his own, a first-class ticket issued on the train. The young woman was the girlfriend of the inspector who was still in London waiting for Raven to cash another note.

The girl's name was Anne and she had come to Nottwich to dance in a pantomime. Even though Raven had an automatic in his pocket, Anne wasn't frightened. They left the station together and walked away from the centre of the town to a new housing estate where they entered an empty house and went up to the bathroom. Raven was going to shoot poor Anne, but the girl was saved from almost certain death when the front door opened and a house agent entered with a prospective customer. Anne seized her chance. She took two £5 notes from Raven and, leaving him and his automatic in the bathroom, went out and actually made a deposit on the house under the nose of the other customer and then walked out the front door to freedom. That took nerve. Eve had never had many girlfriends, but if she had had, she felt Anne would have been one of them. Anne was Eve's type of person.

There were other twists. One of the backers for the panto that Anne was to be dancing in was called Davis. This Davis was the man who had paid off Raven in the forged notes. Cholmondley or Davis had tried to smother dear Anne with a pillow in a dingy bedroom. It was a little later that Raven, still on the run and looking for Cholmondley, saw an old woman pick up Anne's bag from a stall at a jumble sale in a church hall. Raven followed the woman to a house where, in one of the upstairs rooms, Anne's body lay. Eve had breathed a sigh of relief when Raven found Anne, bound and gagged, inside the large fireplace. Even though he was a murderer, Eve was beginning to feel something akin to affection for Raven. Several pages later, in a shoot-out in a marshalling yard, Raven made an escape wounding a police officer. The inspector feared for the man's life, but after Anne's miraculous escape, Eve was sure the man would recover. It was that sort of book.

One thing, however, gripped Eve and made her angry: the duplicity of this man Davis. In the beginning of the book, Eve had shuddered when Raven had shot the Minister three times, the last shot splitting open his skull – "like a broken egg shell." Raven struck Eve as a thoroughly nasty type; typical of the criminal class! Riff-raff. But when you thought about it, this man Davis was equally guilty, it was just that he couldn't do his own dirty work: he had to hire somebody else. Besides, he had double-crossed the man he had hired. Raven wasn't really so bad when you considered the facts and, as the plot unfolded, there were many: he had a harelip; his father had been hanged; his mother had committed suicide with a bread knife. The more Eve thought about it the more she was becoming convinced that the real criminals were men with position, money and power. They were seldom seen. They manipulated others. Surely, Davis and his employer, Sir Marcus, Chairman of Midland Steel, were the villains of the piece. If the murder of the War Minister in the first chapter had made Eve shudder with repulsion, then the cowardly deceitfulness of this man Davis – he had tried to kill dear Anne too – enraged her and the callous cynicism of Sir Marcus made her blood boil. Raven, a seedy outlaw, was a mere tool in the hands of mightier, more powerful men.

Fate, which was never very far away in this book – this was one of the reasons why Eve was enjoying it so much; Eve had a blind faith in destiny and poetic justice – came to Raven's rescue in the form of a gas drill. (Eve was familiar with gas drills; they had had one in Luton just before war broke out.) Dressed in a tweed suit and a gas mask stolen from a medical student who was involved in a rag stunt, Raven had bumped into Davis outside Midland Steel where

Davis worked. Davis had promised to give £10 to charity. He took Raven with him into the Midland Steel complex. This was where Eve's bookmark lay. Now she was hoping that justice would be done and that this Davis and Sir Marcus would get their just deserts.

CHAPTER SIX

1

Billy's Revenge had crossed the German border and was flying at 14,000 feet over the Ardennes. A heavy tiredness had descended over the crew. That particular night thwarting death in the form of German anti-aircraft defences had been easy, the raid had been routine. Now, the journey home, far from presenting them with danger in a more insidious form, was a long grind, a chore, irksome but necessary if they were once again to tread the soil of England and breathe the scented air of the English countryside.

Arthur swivelled his turret, elevated and depressed his guns. His sight graticule glowed a dull red. In the darkness aft the tailplane stuck up like the fin of a gigantic fish. It had been a strange op. On the trips to the Upper Rhineland the darkness was always pierced by sudden impromptu pyrotechnic displays: from the flak ships off the Dutch coast and the batteries around Tilbury, Breda and Eindhoven. Tonight these had been absent. Below was only inky blackness; above, the stars and the moon around which the faintest of faint lines could be discerned. Tomorrow night it would be full.

At his station Elton fancied he could smell bacon and egg. There was less for him to do now. They were nearly halfway home and by working the Gee set – it could be used as a homing device – he could check that they were on track. Soon they would reach Mons and change course for Furnes and the coast. Allowing for the wind vector the change would be a mere deviation. For the last part of the trip he had worked out a new course over Clacton which would take them straight to Base instead of flying the dog-leg over Orford Ness. Elton dreamt of crisp, salty bacon dipped in egg yolk, of the bump of the wheels on the tarmac, of the early morning silence at Oakington. He willed himself home. It couldn't come fast enough.

Bill Kransky sat solidly at the controls. From time to time he allowed himself the luxury of a glance at the empty co-pilot's seat where he had used to sit. Then he had been Crown prince, now he was King, enthroned under a cockpit canopy which was like a small sky. His gaze moved from the dull glow of the instruments out into space beyond the perspex and back, never still. A King had to be alert, had responsibilities, had enemies too. The Stirling bomber was worthy of a King, worthy too of the night sky which seemed without dimensions. He held a straight course at even speed. The control panel seemed still and frozen. They would soon be halfway home. This was the way he had reckoned on it going tonight. No trouble.

Tony Reeves had just finished jiggering with the fuel tank cock levers. The auxiliary tanks were now empty and they could finish as they had started, on main tanks. He eyed his gauges for the umpteenth time. Everything was in order. He peered at the electrical control panel by his head, let his gaze wander idly over the jungle of cocks, levers, wires and control wheels which lay across the width of the main spar, then stared into the blackness of the fuselage floor. His mind was miles away with Paula, in her bed, against her soft warm body. Theirs was a strange relationship, he thought at last. They had shared intimacy between the sheets, but had never been together outside the walls of bedroom. He wondered what it would be like taking her out, a smart attractive woman like that, and him in uniform and not even an officer; yet another step into the unknown. The Arts Theatre she had said. What sort of world was that exactly? His only recollection of the theatre was a hazy childhood one: panto, girls in shiny orange shorts tripping back and forth and a large woman – it must have been a man dressed up – bellowing at the top of his voice. The Arts Theatre conjured up in Tony's mind diffuse images of seedy gentility: a drawing-room, a pencil-slim woman in a long dress standing aloof by a standard lamp, a man in evening dress on his knees in front of her. Paula seemed to have intimate connections with the stage, which figured when you thought about it. She was refined in a way that he wasn't. The theatre was a world about which he knew nothing. This was his world. He looked at the main electric control panel as one might regard an old acquaintance or a faithful servant; with paternal fondness. It was a world of tapers, cocks and valves, hydraulics, fuel, oil and kerosene, spanners and wrenches. He knew little else outside of aviation. He'd probably make a fool of himself in front of her friends. Her cracked, raddled face loomed out of the darkness; the face of a lonely woman; if, indeed, she had any. On the other hand, had he any? There had been Billy – well, he'd been dead for ages, four weeks or so. There was of course Arthur; although Arthur was more of a father figure. As for his crew, well, they were all good pals, but that was due to the war. If it ceased tomorrow, they would all go their separate ways and that would be that.

Tony's thoughts were inevitably drawn back to Paula. To see her serving customers in that pub you would never have thought she could have been so uninhibited in bed with a complete stranger. He was going over to see her when he got back; which would be about two, half past at the latest. Four hours with Paula would be just the job. It was almost as nice seeing her slip out of bed and into that silky black dressing-gown with the red stars cascading all over it like a firework display. It was too small for her really, stretching tight over her bosom revealing the deep divide between her breasts.

Tony stared down at the milky white skin and the cascade of red stars shooting out like sparks from a grinding wheel. Her breasts rose and pushed hard against the constrictions of the silky garment and the sparks danced before his eyes, then vanished, suddenly, and he found himself back in the Stirling looking at the floor of the aircraft. The Hercules engines roared in his ears.

Tony blinked unbelievingly and stared at the darkness below him. Where the hell had those sparks come from? The floor seemed okay. He turned to his gauges and scrutinised each one in turn. They were using up fuel more slowly on the return journey, but that was normal. He looked down at the floor again. His first thought was a short circuit, but there was nothing under the floor except the bomb bay with the carriers and the drums which had held the incendiaries. Each carrier was plugged into a socket which was wired back to the interval selector and the bomb-release switch in the bomb-aimer's compartment. Then there were the bomb doors and the belly of the aircraft and the night sky underneath. Tony Reeves's stomach turned over sickeningly. The belly of the aircraft – the underside – the night sky – night – vulnerability – sparks – canon fire – night sky – night fighter. His head swam as the terrible truth dawned. He was about to scream into his mask when his earphones came alive. It was Ollie's voice. It had a ring of urgency and the stammer was gone.

"Hello, Bill. Enemy aircraft – port quarter below. 1000 yards, closing."

The crew of Billy's Revenge froze with fear. There was an executioner at their heels.

The speck grew larger, closing in for the kill. Peering through the graticule Ollie discerned the faint outline of the tailplane.

"Bill, it's a 110. Can you see it, Arthur?"

Arthur scanned the night sky to port. Within seconds he had seen it.

"Got it," he said. "600 yards, Bill."

Kransky engaged what was meant to be the Bomber Command standard corkscrew. Billy's Revenge started zooming all over the place as the young pilot fought to bring order and method into a world which had just broken into disorder. The others, rudely awakened, waited in horror for the sounds of battle. The seconds which elapsed were just enough to make them wonder if they hadn't been dreaming before the muted clatter of the brownings dispelled any lingering doubts. At four hundred yards the rear gunner had engaged the enemy.

Four streams of five-in-one tracer slashed through the night sky as Ollie Howlands pressed his firing buttons and twisted the grips to elevate his guns. The 110 surged at him, flashes coming from its forward nose canon, brighter and larger than those of the brownings. At 200 yards Arthur opened fire. Six streams of tracer poured at the marauder.

Just fore of the main spar, the sound of gunfire smacking in his ears, Tony had the peculiar sensation that the battle outside was taking place at the other end of a long distance telephone line. It was then that he felt a tug at his sleeve. He turned. In the gloom a hand beckoned. It was Elton. Tony followed him through to the navigator's compartment.

Through the enormous cockpit canopy the view was panoramic. Beyond the port-inner engine, the wing tapered away. Along its length there was a sheet of flame. Tony's lips parted. Later, as the shock left him, he saw that the two engines were still functioning. He moved quickly back to his station and plugged in his intercom.

"Where is it? Where is it?" It was Bill Kransky's voice.

"We thought we had him, Bill, but he just came on through our tracer. Now he's peeled away to starboard. Ollie! Ollie! Can you see anything? Ollie! Can you hear me? There's no answer, Bill. Something's happened to Ollie! Ollie, you okay?"

Tony Reeves thought quickly, in desperation. This was completely unexpected. Christ Almighty! They'd been jumped – surprised by a thief in the night. Now, he had to do something; that fire was his responsibility. Jettisoning was out of the question; they were on main tanks now. Damned nuisance! He called up his captain.

"Bill, Tony here. Can you feather the port engines?"

Flight Sergeant Bill Kransky, Royal Canadian Air Force was also thinking with the flustered desperation of a man caught off guard by the unexpected turn of events. He was still making ineffectual efforts at corkscrewing, flying in wide arcs and losing height slowly. The King was being dethroned. Kransky pressed the feathering buttons. outside, the port engines roared on oblivious to the sheet of flame trailing in their wake.

"Tony, there's no response from the buttons." The pilot's attention came back to the fighter. "Arthur, where is it?"

There was a short unnerving silence before Arthur spoke.

"I've lost him, Bill."

As Arthur peered out into the night sky, he was aware of the glow on the port side of the aircraft. The mottled fuselage and the tailplane were visible to the last rivet, but beyond, the night sky seemed infinite. Somewhere a marauder lurked waiting to pounce, but where was it?

Suddenly, as though in answer to a prayer, a burst of tracer laced the night sky aft. Arthur followed its trajectory. The shells exploded just short of a black speck.

"Bill, Ollie's all right. He's just fired a burst. I've got it." Arthur manoeuvred his guns and squinted through the gunsight. "Dead astern, 800 yards."

Kransky, sweat running down the small of his back, heaved a sigh of relief; the rear gunner was still alive and they had located the fighter. Their position was infinitely better than it had been a moment ago.

Tony didn't hear the conversation between his captain and the mid-upper gunner. He was working assiduously at his station. As he reset the supercharger controls, he cursed the feathering buttons; they were always unreliable. When he had finished, he looked up at the fuel cocks under the roof. It would be a waste of time touching those; the auxiliary tanks were empty. As he stood there pondering, the staccato rattle of machine-gun fire echoed in his ears and once again he had the uncanny impression that he was eavesdropping. It died abruptly as he pulled out his leads.

Back on the flight deck his heart sank. If anything the fire was worse now; a streamer of flame reached back almost to the tailplane and the engines roared on in undisturbed majesty. Tony glanced at Elton. He too was looking at the flames like a child peering in fascination into a shop window. It was a peculiar sight. The flame started some way from the trailing edge. To all appearances there was no contact between it and the surface of the wing. It didn't take Tony long to guess what had happened. The tanks had been holed by the 110 and the incendiaries had ignited the fuel when it had mixed with the oxygen in the air. He trailed back to his panel. He could plug in his intercom if he couldn't do anything else.

"Ollie's still firing, Bill. He seems to be okay. Enemy aircraft dead astern, 500 yards." Arthur had the 110 in his sight. The black speck touched the edge of the dull red ring. "He's closing and firing. Bill! Throttle back! Full flap! Use full flap! It's now or never! Now!"

As the last minutes of Bill Kransky's reign ticked away, he started to put together some of the things he had learnt at the Heavy Conversion Unit where he had done his Stirling training. The innovatory hydraulic system and the engines which drove them were, in this context, an irrelevance, but there was something which the instructor had shown them all: throttling back with full flap. The Stirling's stall was viceless. When the flaps were down, the wing area improved and the aircraft could be slowed down considerably without stalling. Kransky was no longer a helpless, harassed fugitive zooming around the skies in a tortured, blazing aircraft: he could fight back; he had a secret weapon. He stretched out his right hand covering the four throttles and throttled back. Then he put on full flap. As he pulled the control column towards him, the nose rose. The loss of speed was dramatic. To the gunners, the 110 seemed to explode beyond the confines of the glowing sight graticule. The wings, the engines, the cockpit surged at them out of the night. For a moment it looked as though the fighter would crash into them.

The pilot of the Messerschmitt saw in horror as the Stirling's tailplane, lit up by the tapering stream of flame to port, plunged at him filling his view from the cockpit. This was something he hadn't banked on; fighters are designed for speed, not for flying slowly. He did the only thing he could do: he pulled back the stick to overshoot. Suddenly and dramatically the tables were turned.

Ollie and Arthur opened up at 400 yards and continued firing as the 110 came at them. At 40 yards the belly of the fighter was completely exposed. Elevating their guns and firing simultaneously, the gunners raked its underside with fire. At such close range the brownings were deadly. Billy's Revenge, in its death throes, was living up to its name.

Arthur saw his shells, incendiary and armour-piercing, smash mercilessly into the fabric of the 110, ripping holes out of its belly. For the briefest of moments it seemed as if the enemy aircraft would explode directly above them as it hung in the air, buoyed up on a fountain of tracer. Then it turned steeply to starboard, breaking away trailing smoke. The gunners ceased firing.

Arthur noticed the smell of cordite for the first time. Rapturous, he spoke into his mask.

"We got him as he overshot, Bill. That was perfect. He peeled off to starboard trailing smoke. He won't be back."

There was triumph in Arthur's voice, relief too. The others on board, helpless captives, hissed sighs of relief through their masks. Their prayers had been answered. Thank God!

Billy's Revenge had won its greatest victory, but there were only minutes left. Just as the trickle of sand through an hour glass seems at first insignificant so the seconds and minutes of a man's life pass unnoticed until the end is nigh and the final seconds pass with a diabolical rapidity. As the 110 broke off, the remaining seconds of the lives of the men on board Billy's Revenge were as the final grains of sand in the constriction in the glass which divides life from death. Time was running out. Joy was to be short lived.

At his station, Tony was trimming the cowl flaps with the conscientious determination of a man who knows that come what may he must never give up. The images of his mistress were banished, never to return. Somewhere at the outer limits of his consciousness he heard voices. Elton's was first.

"Bill, I'm going back to see if Ollie's all right."

"No, prepare to bale out."

"Must we, Bill? Can't we make the English coast?" Elton sounded peeved. The prospect of barbed-wire and prison rations was not enticing to an empty stomach.

"No, bale out! We're still losing height."

"But we're over halfway home, Bill, and we're still flying."

"We'll never get home now, we're too low. You'll have to bale out."

Kransky looked at the altimeter. They were below 1,000 feet, under the altitude at which a parachute can be relied on to deploy. The air battle of two minutes ago belonged to a past age, like childhood innocence. Now he either had to belly-land the aircraft or perish with it. He glanced to port. Far away he thought he perceived trees, fields, a road, houses, a church spire. The countryside appeared to be wooded and undulating. He had the distinct impression that their speed was increasing. He glanced at the air speed indicator; the needle was stationary at 170 mph. The altimeter reading, though, bore out the fact that they were in a shallow dive. The remaining grains of sand were only a minute cone in the neck of the glass.

A voice called in the wilderness, "Has everybody gone?"

In the rear turret Ollie Howlands, the receiving side of his intercom still working despite the transmitting side having been unserviceable since the beginning of the action, heard the order. For the past minute he had been struggling with the port-side door to his turret. It was hopelessly jammed. His parachute was on the other side of the door.

Kransky's voice brought near panic to Tony Reeves. Gone! Gone! Christ, no! He hadn't. He was the last man and he hadn't even succeeded in limiting the fire. He tore himself free from his leads, took down his parachute from its stowage-rack with hands that trembled slightly and snapped the pack on to the securing clips of his harness. Even then, in near panic, he cast one last despairing look at the cocks and levers and wheels he was seeing for the last time in the manner of one loath to throw in the towel. He ducked under the main spar and made his way down the fuselage. Christ, what a mess! What the hell had happened? He passed the access ladder to the mid-upper turret. The canvas seat was hanging limply. To his right, the gigantic ammo box supplying the rear turret slid past him. Cold air gushed over his sweating face. Just beyond the flare chute he fancied he saw something move. He drew nearer. The shadow became a shape and took on form and substance. Details emerged: flying helmet, jacket, harness and parachute pack.

Tony saw Arthur's face, the face of a man marked by death. Arthur pointed downwards. They both peered down through the hatch and Tony saw what his comrade had already seen, trees and fields flashing past. He was gripped by shock. They weren't much above tree-top level. So this was it - the chop. This was what had happened to the other boys who'd come to Oakington only to fly a few ops and then disappear. What fools they had been to think they were any different! The hopes they had cherished were but the vain, fitful fancy of poor deluded fools. There was no chance of escape; there never had been. Then the shock gave way to calm as strange as it was serene; the calm of a man to whom, after months of terrible doubt, his fate has been revealed. Life would end through the ventral hatch of a Stirling bomber.

Tony pointed at Arthur then down through the hatch. Arthur nodded and took up position. As the last grains of sand trickled through the glass, he rolled out head first. Tony went round and took up position. He saw Elton standing by the flare chutes and over the navigator's left shoulder he caught a fleeting glimpse of Tom Campbell's disembodied face. Looking down through the hatch, he saw once again the ashen death-mask of Billy Hamilton. Down there, somewhere, far below, was Billy Boy. He'd be joining Billy.

"Billy Boy! I'm coming!" he screamed. Tony tumbled out through the hatch.

Bill Kransky remained at the helm throughout those final nightmare minutes holding Billy's Revenge in a shallow dive. He hoped his action would enable his crew to bale out. The silence in his earphones, strange and unreal after the sounds of battle, might mean they had, but he had no means of knowing. The possibility of belly-landing the aircraft looked remote. The countryside flashed past, surging out of the darkness at lightning speed before his eyes had time to focus. Suddenly, darkness closed in on him: walls of leaves and branches. Ahead, a gigantic shape with enormous outstretched arms loomed at him. When Kransky finally took his hands from the wheel to protect his face, nothing mattered any more. Now, he would never take that photo of Billy's Revenge. He wouldn't even be bringing it back. The kite was his now, all his. The catch was that he would die in it. He attempted to scream as the lantern jaw of the Stirling hit a gigantic oak tree smashing it to the ground, but eternal darkness descended first.

The hour-glass was empty.

2

Davis ushered his companion through the glass door at Midland Steel. He was met by a detective. The man Raven was not lying safely on an icy slab in the town mortuary: he had escaped. Davis was terrified; his buoyancy had disappeared. In his office he offered the student a glass of sweet port – typical for Davis; he was fat, cowardly and always stuffing himself with sweet things, which real men didn't do – which the student refused in a muffled voice. He wanted his money. Davis took out two £5 notes from a drawer and gave them to the white-coated figure. "Are these notes phoney too?"

The words struck terror into the heart of the weak, flabby Davis. In spite of her tiredness Eve's body tensed. This was poetic justice; this was what Eve believed in: just deserts. This was the way things should be; it gave life a meaning; it gave life sense.

Realisation of danger and death came to Davis as it had come an hour earlier to Tony Reeves. Davis collapsed on the floor and retched.

It was late now and there had been no more early returns. The next aircraft to land would have bombed the target. The circle of light thrown from the twenty-five watt bulb at the end of one of the three metal arms of the standard lamp gave the pages of the book a parchment-like pallor. Eve's eyes were heavy. She stifled a yawn. Sleep beckoned. Just a few more pages.

She read on following the terror-struck Davis on his last journey, the remorseless automatic in his back, through the intricacies of the Midland Steel complex.

The two men went up to Sir Marcus in a lift. They found him in an office eating a dry biscuit with some warm milk. His valet was with him.

Eve raised a tired finger to her lips. Sir Marcus, the hateful Sir Marcus; too old to be frightened; twisted with avarice and cynicism; behind the killing of the Minister to boost the armaments industry. The image of Sir Marcus paled briefly before the image of her own father: the good shepherd, loving every living thing. Even his faults – fault was just a word you used for want of a better expression – beer and baccy, just made you love him more.

Raven was irritated. He regretted killing the Minister, now that he had seen the real culprit. But death was too good for Sir Marcus. He had to suffer, like the Minister had suffered. Those were Eve's sentiments too. She yawned again and her head fell forward. The print on the yellow pages became blurred. Still the shot didn't come. Raven, aware perhaps that he had been cast in the roll of the hand of Providence, waited. He told Sir Marcus to pray. The old man inched his chair towards an alarm. Then gradually, the outlines of Sir Marcus, the bath chair, the cringing Davis, the valet, Raven and the automatic faded and disappeared and the voices grew fainter, dying to be replaced by nothingness. Only a bell remained, ringing pitilessly. Raven should have shot Sir Marcus when he had had the chance. Now it was five thirty; too late.

Eve rose and looked around her. The funnel of yellow light still bathed the chair, but through the narrowest of cracks in the black-out curtains a pencil of light fell. The ringing stopped and a hammering sound came from somewhere. It died and restarted, died again and restarted again. Eve struggled to collect her thoughts.

It was then that her little body was shaken by a visible spasm. A tide of fear rose within her; not the fear which wakes the instinct for self-preservation, or makes a man cringe and blubber, but the fear of all those who love. She did not retch, nor did her legs give way, but her heart jumped and started throbbing painfully against her small ribs. She was looking at the clock on the mantelpiece.

The persistent knocking from the hallway clubbed the truth further into her beleaguered brain. The person on the other side of the door didn't have a key: they had information. Rushing to the door, Eve fought to bring order to the nightmare world she had woken up to. Where were the planes? Something was terribly wrong; she hadn't heard any planes. She always heard planes. She opened the door.

The Gunnery Leader had arrived in Stowe in his little Austin to break the news that one of his boys was missing. He had opened an envelope which the missing man himself had given him a month previously. He had been on ops himself that night and was tired and unshaven. He stood on the doorstep searching for a verbal formula with which to alleviate the suffering of the distraught figure before him. The pale, devastated face, the wide staring eyes and the small hands holding the latch tightly caused him to falter. It would be as well to establish the identity of the woman in the doorway.

"Mrs Johnson?"

"Yes?"

The staring eyes mirrored helplessness, appeal and accusation. Even the tone in her voice suggested that he, Flight Lieutenant Mike Smith, was an accomplice in this terrible tragedy and held her fate and that of her husband in his hands. The poor woman stood there like a child waiting to receive a punishment.

"Your husband's aircraft was one of two that failed to return from a raid on Frankfurt last night. Nothing has been heard from them since take-off. They've been posted missing."

Eve opened her mouth to speak but the words choked in her throat. A voice in her brain kept repeating: Oh no! Oh no! Oh no!

Flight Lieutenant Smith wanted desperately to return to camp and bed but felt that fatherly consolation was needed, as far as that could go.

"I'm sorry. This must come as a great shock."

The poor woman stood there frozen to the spot. The Gunnery Leader decided to play his trump card; the one he always played when one of his young gunners had lost a mate.

"We don't know for sure, but there's every chance that the crew are safe, although it'll be sometime before we hear anything."

"Arthur said he'd be first out if they were hit. He was mid-upper gunner."

There was hope in the voice now. The formula had worked; a palliative. He still wanted to go back to the station but was loath to leave her alone.

"I suppose you'll be moving now. I'm not wanted back urgently. I could give you a lift to Oakington Station if you wish. I can wait if you want to pack a case."

The woman mumbled an incoherent thank you and the Gunnery Leader followed her through the hall into the parlour. He glanced around the room. A standard lamp with three curved metal arms and three shades stood in one corner like some peculiar plant. A yellow light shone from one of the flowers. A book lay on the floor and on a chair near the window there was a pile of ironing. The poor dear drew back the black-out curtains letting in the light of a dull day. Mike Smith sat down and started to chat therapeutically. The shattered being in front of him answered briefly and in monosyllables.

Eve had only fragmentary recollections of the next few minutes. The stairs, their bedroom, the bed, still immaculate which they would never share again, daylight streaming in through the small windows, the bedroom floor, her handbag, the stairs again, steep and vertiginous; the unshaven, middle-aged man in uniform waiting in the hall by the front door, stiff and erect like a sentry; her raincoat and scarf, the hook in the hall and the yellow Yale key. Eve had the presence of mind to check the back door and the downstairs windows. They left. Eve slammed shut the front door. Outside, the clouds were becoming darker. Rain was spreading from the west.

Eve sat in the front seat of the Austin. As the stone houses and shops of the main street slid past and gave way to mist-covered fields and small orchards of stunted fruit trees, a light drizzle started falling. It intensified and a hand stretched out to switch on the wipers. The languid efficiency with which the Flight Lieutenant drove: fingers resting lazily on the wheel, eyes quartering the road from side to side, stealing glances in the rear-view and side mirrors - he was, after all, a gunner, a natural watch-dog - was wasted on Eve whose mind was in turmoil. She willed Arthur still alive, willed him but at the same time wondered what had gone wrong. What could have happened? Eighteen ops, eighteen nights of tension, uncertainty, anxiety, anguish and now this. Why now, after so long? It wasn't fair. It wasn't fair. She had fallen asleep and now this had happened. She wanted to turn the clock back; start the evening again; take out the photos and look at them; weave a spell; hope and pray on her bended knees to the Almighty God who she had believed in since childhood, to protect her husband. But, she kept on hoping, he wasn't dead; she was sure of it. Hadn't Arthur said he would get out? Hadn't the RAF Officer said that there was every chance that the crew were safe? Arthur had to be alive. Anything else was too awful to contemplate.

Suddenly the car jerked to a halt and the engine and the windscreen wipers stopped. The driver's lips were moving. Confused, Eve looked out of her side window and recognised Oakington Station. She mumbled a thank you and struggled out.

After a brief stop at the ticket-office she found herself on the deserted platform where she waited in a trance as the hour grew later and the sky lightened. This was the time she normally went to bed. It was the best part of the day, Arthur safely packed off to camp, her vigil recompensed. She always stood at the bedroom window watching the colours of the countryside return with the new day. Relief, relaxation, then sleep, blessed sleep. Seventeen times she had done that. Now, she stood alone in the thickening drizzle.

The railway station at Oakington occupied a corner of the airfield. From where she stood, Eve could see across the field. The nine Stirlings which had returned stood on their pans; their turrets covered, they looked like huge blindfolded birds. The hangars were just visible half a mile away over a flat expanse of grass and tarmac. Eve looked across the two sets of rails at the words MARCH ST IVES written in bold white letters beneath the shiny brown flagstones bordering the platform opposite. Her gaze strayed absent-mindedly to the glistening rails which disappeared into a fine mist further up the line. She felt a lump in her throat, her eyes moistened and in spite of herself she started to sob; a small, pathetic figure all alone in the world.

Half an hour later the train from St Ives, pulling four coaches, clanked into the station and wheezed to a halt. As Eve struggled on board through wreathes of steam, the bureaucratic machine of Bomber Command was already in function. The crew of Billy's Revenge had been posted for the last time to No 1 Depot Non Effective. This was a paper transfer of missing airmen to save operational units from being involved in much administrative work: correspondence over dead men's wills, correspondence with next-of-kin etc. These depots also looked after the property of missing personnel until it could be handed over to next-of-kin or, in the case of POWs, stored until their return.

A cloud of white steam trailed past the carriage window where Eve sat. The Cambridge train lurched into motion and the level crossing slid past. At Oakington, the Effects Officer was already detailing men to collect and go through the personal effects of the fourteen missing aircrew. It was essential that their lockers and billets be vacated as quickly as possible. In the course of the next few days replacements would be arriving at Oakington, including a new batch of gunners.

THE CREW MISSING THE NIGHT OF 24-25 AUGUST 1942

STIRLING W7616 'G' 7 SQUADRON

R68751	F/S SHUMSKY W.N.	RCAF	PILOT
108247	P/O ANTOINE J.	RAF	NAV
1174036	SGT DEARLOVE G.C.E.	RAF	W/OP A/G
751249	F/S GRAHAM A.G.	RAF	A/G
570455	SGT KINSELLA P.D.	RAF	F/ENG
1365217	F/S WALKER E.A.	RAF	A/G
1059680	SGT SPARKS J.S.	RAF	A/G

If you enjoyed reading *The Great Illusion* and would like to learn of the fate of Eve and of the crew of Billy's Revenge, the sequel, *The Outsiders*, also published by Minerva Press, will be available from Autumn 1997.
Enter the Conscientious Objector. . .

Barry Graham